THE MESRINE CONCLUSION

THE MESRINE
CONCLUSION

☨

DAVID CULLEN

Culpro Books

The Mesrine Conclusion
First published 2005
Revised and updated International Edition 2009

A catalogue record of this book is available from the British
Library.

ISBN: 978-0-9559911-1-0

www.lulu.com/davidcullen

Published Culpro Books
an imprint of Cullen Productions

"If thou, O Lord, should mark our iniquities, Lord, who would survive?"

- from the Requiem Mass of
Jacques Mesrine in the church
of St Vincent de Paul, Clichy,
Paris, November 1979

‡

*"I have a story to tell you. A true story.
About a cop, about the most wanted man
in Europe and about a document
containing a secret."*

- Claude Gerard,
Tuesday 23 October 1979

For Jacqui and for Paul
- the best two ever

‡

Acknowledgements

For their invaluable help and assistance I would like to thank:

Veronique Lensens, who knows but will not tell;

and

Sylvie, who doesn't really know but wants to tell.

Finally, my respect and admiration – but not necessarily my approval – must go to Jacques Mesrine (you couldn't make it up).

‡

PRÉFACE

L'histoire de Mesrine

L'occupation, France, 1944

It was glorious. An azure sky, sun high but not overbearingly hot as befits an early summer's day.

It was quiet in the village of Château-Merle, near Poitiers in western France. A tranquillity which gave the lie to the circumstances. For people were joyful, but they could not show it. They wanted to cry in triumph, but they dare not. For the news had come through that the Allies had landed in Normandy. France was again, very soon, to be free. The German occupying forces were retreating. June 1944 was going to be a month to remember.

When the convoy of German vehicles left Poitiers that day for the last time, the people carried on their normal routine, only quietly, subdued. For one smile, one hint of the volcano of jubilation within, could bring untold reprisals from the departing forces. And no one wanted that at this stage, now that it was nearly over after four years.

The boy, Jacques, was seven years old. He had been staying in a farm outside the village with relatives after fleeing from

Paris with his mother, brother and sisters at the start of the occupation. Despite coming from a large family, Jacques was a lonesome child, never wanting to play with the local children, never becoming involved in any of their games or adventures, never speaking to them if he could avoid it, ignoring the encouragement of his aunt to "Join in, Jacques. Why do you not play with the others? It is not right, a boy of your age..." He preferred the company of just his one friend, Georges.

In fact Jacques was not lonely at all. He liked it that way. Why should he play with the stupid village children? He always had a nicer time on his own or just with Georges. But grown-ups never understood that, did they? They always thought children had to have 'friends'.

He was playing ball with Georges in the field opposite the farm when he first heard the rumble. He listened, letting the ball roll to a stop at his feet. Georges looked at him, a question in his eyes.

"Hear that, Georges? Hear that noise? What is it? Thunder? Is it going to rain?"

Georges shook his head.

"What can it be? It's getting louder. It's coming this way! *Allons-y.* Let's go and see!"

They ran across the field towards the road, Georges' loping stride taking him ahead of his *copain*.

The road from town turned sharply half a kilometre back, before it reached the farm. There was nothing to be seen yet but both of them could feel the trembling of the track beneath their feet as the rumbling grew louder and louder.

Then there was another sound. A rapid *rat-tat-tat* which, even for his tender years, Jacques knew well. He had seen his uncles and older cousins practise with their guns many times. They were supposed to belong to some secret group that would drive the Germans out of France, but in four years they had not succeeded.

The slightest pause in the rumble, a staccato response, and then the convoy appeared in sight, the sun glistening off the leading jeep. There were many of them. The front jeep and the first lorry seemed to be going faster, pulling away from the lorries following.

Jacques was not old enough to understand that he should not like the Germans. Indeed the few he had come across had smiled and spoken kindly to him in harsh Teutonic French. Some had even given him pieces of *chocolat*. But this was different. This gave him a troubled feeling in his seven year old gut. The approaching jeep contained four uniformed men; one of them in the front was half lying over the side, arms flopping like a marionette.

Georges was transfixed, staring at the vehicles down the road.

"Georges? Georges!" said Jacques urgently. "Quick! Come. We'd best get out of here. I don't like it."

Uncle's farm was on the other side of the road. Jacques did not run to the farmhouse where he knew he would find Auntie, Great Aunt and a few cousins not old enough to work the land. Instead he headed for the barn, instinctively seeking solitude.

Georges pulled himself out of his reverie and followed hard on his heels.

Jacques gave his pal a hand up into the hayloft and they lay still, flat out on the sparse hay.

Georges' breath rasped through his teeth and Jacques whispered for him to be quiet. He peeked out through the small window and saw the jeep and lorry turn towards the farm, the dead man bouncing as the jeep hit the cobbled dirt track. They pulled up beyond the front door.

Great Aunt, still a stout and formidable woman despite her eighty years, appeared from the farmhouse, wiping her hands on her pinafore. She mumbled something Jacques could not hear and motioned with her arms.

The back flap of the lorry was flung back. There were soldiers inside.

Without hesitation a soldier raised his machine gun and blasted Great Aunt from their path. She performed a pirouette, bits of pinafore and something red spraying outwards, before she fell heavily.

The Germans leapt from the vehicles and charged into the farmhouse. There were few shouts or screams from within, just the eerie *crack-crack-crack* of gunfire.

A cat ran from the front door. A single *crack* from within and it somersaulted and lay still.

To the boy watching fascinated from the hayloft it seemed like eternity, but it was in fact just one minute later that the Germans came back out. Their faces were business-like, a job that had to be done, vengeance for their dead *Kamerad* in the jeep. Death to the Resistance! How long till we reach the Fatherland?

A horse grazing near the barn looked up at the men just ten seconds before its eyes and brain were blown away by another gunburst. It fell to the ground, legs stiff and shaking in its death throes.

Jacques quickly pulled away from the window. Beside him, Georges had his face buried into the floor, whimpering in fright.

There was a minute's dreadful silence, then he heard a few foreign voices. Did they know he was there? Were they going to come for him? He heard the vehicles start up and pull away.

He risked a look out. The whole thing had taken so short a time that the main convoy had only just reached the farm entrance. The jeep took its place at the head, the lorry eased its way into line, and they drove off as if nothing had happened, save for the dead man in the front passenger seat.

Jacques could not count more than the fingers on his hands, so he could not say how many lorries, jeeps and cars passed, but it was at least three handfuls.

After the rumbles had faded into a distant hum, Jacques roused Georges and together they descended the wooden ladder.

Hesitantly Jacques looked out of the main door of the barn. All was quiet. The sun still shone, the trees still rustled in the breeze, a bird flew nearby. Life went on. But in the farm there was now only death. A crow screeched.

In front of them the horse still trembled, excreta flowing unrestrained from its arse like lava from a volcano.

Out by the track Great Aunt lay in a heap, her blood running wetly over the grey cobblestones, in some places already settling between the cracks, a macabre grouting.

Jacques looked at the scene. He did not faint or feel sick, in fact he did not feel anything. He was not afraid of the death all around him, he was fascinated. He could see a small, dead hand poking out from the farmhouse doorway.

Georges dashed over to Great Aunt. He stopped and stared, bewildered. He cried softly. Then he sniffed and bent down and began to lick her warm, fresh blood.

"Georges!" cried Jacques, his face stone. "Georges, stop that! Come here! Bad dog, Georges! Bad, bad dog…"

Algérie, 1958

They say that at the moment of death, life flashes before your eyes. At that moment, staring up into the darkness at the twin glints from the Arab's knife and sneering teeth, Jacques believed it.

And it had been such a marvellous day, as well. First a thirty kilometre forced march over the uneven, sandy terrain of Algeria. The big, burly Jacques Mesrine had relished the trip while his French army colleagues had weakened under the debilitating sun. Then, while the others collapsed in their bunks exhausted, an illicit AWOL from barracks for an evening's pleasure at the local brothel. He had enjoyed three journeys inside Camilla, the hundred and ten kilo darling of the establishment, noted not only for her size but for the profusion of hairs on her breasts, up her belly and down the inside of her thighs.

Perhaps it was that that had put him off his guard, made him less careful than usual. After all, a French army uniform in the seedy quarter of Constantine in the spring of 1958 was inviting trouble.

It was in the darkest part of the darkest alley where the Arab, a member of the FLN [*Front de Libération Nationale*], struck him from behind. The blow would have broken the skull of a normal man but, although he was sent sprawling to the ground, Mesrine's hair was not even ruffled.

The Arab swiped downwards with the knife. Mesrine scuffled back on his rear. *Merde alors,* Jacques, you let yourself in for this one...

Expelled from the Oratory School, Juilly, in 1951.

Expelled from the Lycée Chaptal, Paris, in 1953.

Asked to leave technical school in 1955. Troublemaker, they said, ringleader of the bully boys. Ha! He wanted to see life. He wanted adventure, excitement. If everyone else wanted to sit behind a desk reading boring books or being lectured at all day, that was fine, each to his own. But not him, not Jacques Mesrine...

Mesrine lashed out with his right foot but it was deflected by the Arab.

Married Lydia. Ah, ma belle Lydia, big and black from Martinique - and already one month pregnant with another man's child when he met her. But Lord, how she could love...!

Mesrine leapt to his feet, avoiding another stab from the blade and punching the Arab in the right eye.

Then the staleness setting in, the drunken evenings with Lydia in the Latin Quarter. Evenings which always ended in a blazing row.

Then making-up, then visiting heaven in that exquisite ebony body…

The Arab staggered and Mesrine broke his hooked nose with one expert chop, following up with a kick to the groin. The Arab gasped and dropped the knife, clutching his balls.

Her jealousy, her laziness. Expecting him, him *Jacques Mesrine, to earn money to keep* her. *She even gave up her university course. The baby was born. How he hated it, it was not even his, the half-black little bastard…*

Mesrine swooped down for the weapon, but as he went to rise the Arab leant forward and butted the back of his head.

Mercifully call-up. Quick divorce. Army life…

Mesrine sank to his knees, groping again for the knife. It was gone. He looked up as it came spearing towards his throat. This is it, Jacques. The end -

The Arab's hand exploded.

Literally, when it was only centimetres away from his face, it blew up, blood and shards of bone splattering over Mesrine's head and into his mouth. Only then did he hear the report of the gun.

A scream from the Arab as the Frenchman chopped his legs away, kneed him twice on the nose and then stood up, his hobnailed right boot pushing hard across the man's throat.

The Arab gurgled. The stump of his shattered hand pounded uselessly on the ground as his good hand clawed in vain at the Frenchman's leg. His feet flailed in the dust.

Mesrine stood victorious, hands on hips, confident, tough face beaming. He spat out pieces of the other man's bone, wiped his mouth and looked around.

The alley was dark, deserted and noiseless. He could see or hear no one. The shot had obviously driven any observers away or indoors. *No comprendi effendi*, hear nothing, see nothing, say nothing, slit your throat for a *sou*.

A little way back, a dim lamp hanging on the wall creaked in a sudden breeze.

Mesrine looked. Nothing. If there was anyone there they were hidden in the darkness beyond. He chuckled and spoke without raising his voice. "M'sieur, whoever you are, wherever you are, I like your style. That was an amazing and efficient piece of shooting." He looked down at the Arab still clawing uselessly at the boot that was slowly crushing his windpipe. "And you saved my life. I, Jacques Mesrine, will not forget that. May I have the pleasure of knowing to whom I am indebted?"

Silence. Did something move in the shadows?

"I feel like a gladiator," Mesrine was now playing to the audience he knew was there. "You are my Emperor. What shall I do with this shit melon beneath my foot? Does it live or does it die? You threw me the lifeline, you must decide the fate of the vanquished."

This time there was a definite movement. A shadow appeared, but Mesrine could not make out any distinct features. There was just a dark silhouette in front of the wall lamp.

Mesrine gave a half bow. *"Ah! Bonsoir m'sieur, ça va?* Of whom do I have the pleasure?"

There was silence. Then a voice said, "Richer."

He was French and he appeared to be in uniform. Rank? Couldn't see. A conscript like himself?

"Monsieur Richer?"

"Captain Richer."

"Ah." Mesrine nodded. *"Alors, Capitaine.* What is your answer?" A dry wheeze ruckled from beneath his foot as he applied more pressure on the Arab's windpipe.

The figure in the shadows remained still. The voice said, "You are a Frenchman, he is an Arab."

"Yes...?"

"That is your answer."

Mesrine smiled. Slowly he took his foot from his assailant's throat. The Arab looked up in disbelieving relief. He did not even have time to cough once before the heel of Mesrine's boot smashed back down again, instantly breaking his neck with as much concern as a child treading on an ant.

The death was instantaneous but the limbs still twitched for a full thirty seconds afterwards.

"You should be careful, my friend," said Richer from down the alley. "You have been very lucky."

Mesrine looked up from the now still body and wiped more of the dead man's blood from his face with the back of his hand. "Very lucky?"

"Lucky that there was only one of them, they usually hunt in packs."

"Like the animals they are."

"Lucky because you should not even be out, you should be in barracks."

"Pah! Rules, regulations. Why waste a night? We are not prisoners, we are not in jail. We are French soldiers on French soil." He held himself erect.

"You were lucky for another reason."

"What was that?"

"Look in his robes."

Cautiously he bent over. He came back up with a .45 automatic in his hand.

He concealed his surprise carefully. "Hah! He probably didn't know how to use it. These *fellaghas* never do."

"Maybe. Maybe not." The figure moved back into the shadows, out of sight. Mesrine just caught a glimpse of a tall, fair man in uniform as he passed beneath the light, then he could see nothing.

"Hey, Captain Richer!"

"You seem to like danger, Mesrine," came the voice from the dark. "You are not frightened of it, hmm?"

"Me? Frightened?" Mesrine guffawed. "Jacques Mesrine is frightened of nothing."

"You would be interested in getting involved in something a

bit different, perhaps? Something dangerous?"

Mesrine smiled. "What did you have in mind, *mon ami*?"

"At the moment, nothing. But we may have a use for you in the future."

"We...?"

The question floated unanswered into the air and was carried away on the night breeze. The silence of the night had descended again.

"Captain? Captain! Are you there?"

Silence. No one, just Mesrine and the corpse. Time, reflected the Frenchman, to make himself scarce. He turned to go.

"Just one more thing," came Richer's voice, but from further away, almost distant. "You had one final piece of luck."

"Really, *Capitaine*, and what was that?"

"I saw the Arab was about to kill you. I thought you would rather die at French hands than at a melon's. I was not aiming at his hand, I was aiming at your head."

France 1958 - 1960

Mesrine left the army as a fully-trained soldier, an adept combat machine, expert both unarmed and with weaponry. He took with him the Military Cross for Valour, the Commemorative Medal for Operations for the Maintenance of Order - and a certificate of good conduct.

But life in civvy street did not come easy. Army life with its tough physical demands had fitted Mesrine like a glove. Back in the real world, the job his father had lined up for him (a travelling salesman for a lace manufacturer) grated and rubbed like a too-tight shoe.

But he always had his gun, the one he had taken from the dead Arab that night in Constantine. Each night in the privacy of his room in his parents' home in Clichy, Paris, he would dismantle the weapon, clean it, oil it and put it back together again. It made him feel good.

There were women, plenty of them, but nothing permanent, nothing more than the casual lay. He had one marriage behind him and was determined not to make the same mistake again.

Money was transient. It came on pay day and went on wine, women, food and gambling.

He began to meet people he had met in the army, some of the more undesirable conscripts, people to whom crime was a way of life.

Jacques was restless, unsettled... and depressed. Normality was not the life for him, not Jacques Mesrine. He did not always want to have to scrape to make ends meet. He was not like the others, the professional poor of Paris who would not know what to do with one thousand francs if they had it. He did not want to order *vin ordinaire* when *Château Rothschild* was his to be had. If only he had one thing: more money.

He began quarrelling with his mother. God help it, he didn't want to, it wasn't her fault, but he couldn't help himself, she was just getting on his nerves. Her scolding, her chiding, "You are a grown man. What are you going to do with yourself?" Followed by the contradiction of her constant concern, "I love you, you are my son. I want the best for you. You must do something with your life."

Inevitably it got too much. Soon he left home with only the clothes he stood up in, and his gun. He stayed with his army 'friends', and to pay for his keep helped them out with little 'odd jobs'.

He found the little odd jobs easy, almost boring – and, frankly, the beating of a shopkeeper for being late with his 'insurance' payments was not his style (although a unilateral helping of a handful of cash from the till for himself helped ease his *ennui*). But this work did have potential. If he was allowed to do it *his* way, if he was to work for himself, this could be his future. This could feed his craving for adventure, give him that adrenalin rush, pay for the good things of life - and satisfy his demand for *style*.

And it was style that formed the backdrop to his first crime, as it would every crime he ever committed - a breaking and entering, in broad daylight, carrying a huge bunch of flowers. Whilst it could be argued that such an approach, rather than the usual stealth in the darkness, would be a perfect disguise, it was also true that anyone noticing the big, burly man with the big flowers would not fail to remember him...

Europe 1960 - 1978

The crisis in France began around 1960 when relations between the de Gaulle government and the army deteriorated.

Algérie Française, said the army - and they had hoped that the supposedly supreme patriot Charles de Gaulle would support them. But after echoing the cry, he reneged. He wanted a 'political solution' to the Algerian problem, and everyone knew what that meant. As always, for 'political solution' read 'sell out'. A negotiated independence was mooted.

Many members of the army considered de Gaulle a traitor. They did not want independence for Algeria, not at any price. They would fight to keep Algeria French. Together with the French settlers in Algeria, they formed the OAS [*Organisation Armée Secrète*]. It was headed by General Raoul Salan.

Inevitably with his army and criminal background, Mesrine was recruited. Little is known about his OAS activities, but it is thought that the Organisation sent their prized, brave, skilful, flamboyant recruit back to Algeria to fight in Degueldre's notorious Delta Commandos. He might also have been involved in the standard OAS activity of demanding money with menaces from known right-wing sympathisers in France.

What is known is that in the autumn of 1961, in the still hours of the night, Mesrine climbed one of the towers of Notre Dame Cathedral in Paris and hoisted the OAS flag. A daring and courageous feat in itself, made even more outrageous when one realises, of course, that Notre Dame is just two hundred metres opposite, and facing square on to, the *Préfecture* - police headquarters. *Encore le style Mesrine!*

Through his army experiences, both legitimate and secret, Mesrine had learnt everything there was to know about weaponry and things subversive. The OAS had within its web some of the best criminals, smugglers and craftsmen of things illegal, not only in France but in the whole of Europe and beyond.

Again women came and went in Mesrine's life. Another marriage, for five years to the beautiful latin Soledad who gave him an equally beautiful daughter, followed by a succession of girlfriends, usually innocents dragged into Mesrine's criminal circles and, once there, captivated by the man.

Mesrine tried on several occasions to go straight, but one of the requisites to leading a normal life is that you must be at least part way normal yourself. Jacques Mesrine was never normal, indeed he would have scoffed at the suggestion. He was *special*. He knew it, the police knew it and, by the end, nearly the whole world knew it. Going straight would not give the lifestyle this special man required. Crime was the only job that not only paid well but also gave Mesrine his regular fix of the only drugs he ever needed: excitement, danger, adventure.

In March 1962 Mesrine was arrested for burglary. Eighteen months later he was released from Orléans jail. Through the next sixteen years his crimes were to become the talk of Europe. The kidnappings, the burglaries and especially the bank robberies, all carried out with the Mesrine flair, the Mesrine panache, the Mesrine style. Such as stopping to chat with a cashier of a bank he had just robbed whilst the hysterical alarm bells deafened all around him, then a casual stroll outside, turning his reversible jacket inside out, producing a hat, perhaps walking with a limp, certainly altering his expression and posture to look twenty years older, and mixing with the ever-growing crowd looking to see where the din was coming from. Even, it is said, some minutes later approaching the policeman now guarding the doors to the bank to ask him what was happening. Of such stuff, which would not be tolerated in a work of fiction, was the real-life Jacques Mesrine.

It is not the purpose of this book to detail the life and times of Jacques Mesrine. That has been brilliantly done by others, including Mesrine himself in his autobiography *L'Instinct de Mort [Editions Jean-Claude Lattes 1977]* and Carey Schofield in *Mesrine - The Life and Death of a Supercrook [Penguin 1980]*. Some questions which remain unanswered to this day – such as the ease with which Mesrine obtained official identity documents, his smooth escape from jail on 8 May 1978, and the fact that some areas of public authority appeared not to want him recaptured in 1979 – might be answered herein.

Suffice it to say that by 1978 Mesrine genuinely merited the often misused expression 'notorious'. Secretly admired by the public, openly loathed by the police and the Establishment of whom he constantly made fools, Mesrine was truly France's Public Enemy Number One…

Majorque, les îles Baléares 1965

In view of the story that follows, one other incident in Mesrine's career must be mentioned.

On 2 December 1965, Mesrine broke into the residence of the

Governor in Palma, Majorca. He was arrested therein. He had entered the house to steal a document, concerning what and for whom he was never to reveal, which was unusual for the great self-publicist. Perhaps it was something to do with the OAS, perhaps it was not.

When questioned by the Spanish *Guardia Civile* he claimed he was just a simple thief. The *Guardia* suggested that he was an agent of the French government. Mesrine fell into paroxysms of laughter. He was seen by the French Ambassador, brought to court, given a six months suspended sentence and then deported to Paris.

But despite Mesrine's laughter, he never did deny the suggestion made by the *Guardia*...

Subsequent to his breakout from prison on 8 May 1978, Mesrine committed many crimes, some of which are not even known to this day (and some have been attributed to him which he could not possibly have committed). In order for this account to be seen in the perspective of the time, many of the crimes have been reported herein as they happened.

Although the OAS was considered to have collapsed in the sixties with the arrest of General Raoul Salan and the banishment of his successor, Georges Biddault, in 1978 it was still alive in France. No longer an overt terrorist organisation, it had gained the respectability of age and familiarity, a brotherhood who considered themselves the only true Frenchmen. Its members belonged to every major profession, including the public services.

1^{IÈRE} PARTIE

‡

L'ENLÈVEMENT

‡

1. Voleurs

Au cours de l'hiver passé

At 02:00 in the morning the streets of the 16th Arrondisement in Paris are still and almost deserted. Occasionally a taxi might cruise past carrying home a resident of this most exclusive quarter of the French capital. Here and there a solitary figure may be walking, having missed the last metro. Once or twice a week revelry may be heard from within one or other of the fashionable residences, an all-night party which the givers could not afford but had to hold for appearances' sake: for even in this day and age, appearances among the super, nouveau or manqué rich were everything.

That night a lone figure hurried nervously down the wide Avenue Henri Martin. He was self-conscious, aware, for he knew that this area of Paris was not a place for a one ninety centimetre, one two five kilo black man. He looked up at the occasional still-lit windows and bared his teeth, embracing all the residents of the *quartier* with that one sneer of hate. He was a man with a mission: he was going to collect his pension.

Thirty years he had worked for them. *Thirty years!*

He had been their darling, their pet nigger, picked up in the Caribbean during the 40's and brought back to Europe, their butler-cum-handyman-cum-bodyguard. He had served them well. And, he had to admit, they had served him well: good food, good clothes, good accommodation for half a lifetime. Not so good wages, but they were noted for their parsimony.

The boss, 'The Little Man' as lady-boss sometimes referred to him, had died six years ago. But 'Peaches', lady-boss, had kept him on even though the cost of upkeep of the rented house grew year by year. He saw his fellow servants 'let go' one by one until only a minimum had been retained.

Then it had happened. At the beginning of this year. He had heard word that his only brother was dying in Florida. Politely, he had asked lady-boss for time off to go and see him. Her reaction had been to dismiss him summarily. Not even a reprimand, not even a chance to retract his request. *Out.*

Okay, so she was old and frail, half the time *non compos mentis*, living in the past, the Europe of the late 40's and 50's. But that did not excuse her. She had had three facelifts that had tightened her throat so much that she could swallow nothing exceeding one centimetre in width. A hairdresser came in every day to paint over any grey hair that might show, lest she wake (some days she did not), look in a mirror and have a raving fit.

He could allow her her tetchiness, her meanness, her lapses of memory ("Who are you, nigger? Get away from me, get away! I'll call my husband!"), but to be sacked after thirty years with no pension, no severance pay, nothing, was not on ("Be grateful I'm letting you keep the livery you're wearing. Now get out of my sight.").

Okay, so he had been lucky and had found immediate employment on the staff of a diplomat up in Neuilly, but that did not assuage the wrong that had been done. Tonight he would have his pension.

And how would he have it? He touched the bump in his pocket. By the simple expediency of the keys. One by one she had picked off her staff until now she had only one secretary, three contract cleaners and two caterers, and six nurses (two at a time on a 24 hour basis). As each employee had gone, he had retrieved their keys. In the end, the old woman had more keys than staff. When he went he had handed his in - but nobody had asked him for the collection of spares. He had a key to every lock in the house.

Not for him a breaking and entering. He would enter through the door he always used to use, round the side. There were three mortice locks on it but no bolt. From there it was a simple walk up to the old lady's bedroom and the single key safe (no dial or combination) where his pension lay.

He reached the Place de Colombie. Over at the Porte de la Muette, leading into the Bois de Boulogne, a man was propositioning a tart dressed as a nun. Her skirts were open, revealing the goods, and a wad of money changed hands.

As he headed south on the Boulevard Suchet, it began to spit with rain. The house he wanted was on the south-eastern corner of the junction of the Boulevard and the Square des Écrivains Combattants mort pour la France. Number 24...

It was dark, but the night entering from the unshuttered window gave a diffused greyness to the regal ornateness of the bedroom.

The old lady lay flat on her back in the centre of the wide double-bed, painted hair spread out roughly on the bolster, mouth hanging open. Her throat was too tight to permit any snoring. She looked dead, only the slow rise and fall of her chest showed that life was still present. She looked like a queen lying in state – something history had decreed she would never be.

The safe was free-standing against the wall opposite the bed. It opened with a click which reverberated around the large, ornate room. He froze, slowly turning his head.

She did not move.

Carefully he pulled the door open, praying it would not creak.

He shone his pocket torch inside and smiled at his pension. Resting the torch on a bundle of letters tied with pink ribbon, he began to empty the jewellery boxes, fondling each expensive piece in his black-gloved hands as he put them into his pockets.

He did not hear anything, but when he was halfway through he turned and looked back at the bed. He got the shock of his life.

The old woman was sitting up, staring straight at him.

Could she see him? He remained still, but his hands began to shake and he almost dropped a diamond-encrusted gold lizard.

In the dimness he could see her lips moving, and then the voice spoke, croaky but almost girlish in manner. "David? David, is that you?"

He was confused. Could she see? Should he keep quiet, pretend there was no one there?

"David?"

He spoke in a whisper, but he could not disguise the Caribbean accent. "Yes… P-Peaches?"

"What are you doing, you naughty boy? At the bar again? Well, pour me a vodka while you're there, then come to bed, I'm cold."

"Y-yes, P-Peaches."

"What have you been up to, my little man? Out with that floosie again? Little tramp! You know what the doctor said last time. Put on the light and tell me all about her. I'm awake now."

She sank back on the bolster.

He did not move. After half a minute he said, "Peaches?"

There was no response.

"Peaches?"

Her chest rose and fell. She was asleep again.

Holy Mother of God! He grabbed the torch, picking up some tied letters with it, and swiftly but silently closed the safe door.

By the time he was back out in the street, he was perspiring freely, despite the chill of the early morning. A-*men* to that! Still, he had his pension and plenty of it. But can you believe that old woman! If she had not gone back to sleep, what would he have done? The thought that he might have had to get into bed with her did not bear thinking about. The paparazzi would have had fun with that had they been around, but even they had deserted her in the twilight of her life.

He turned left into the Square and walked quickly into the Bois, resisting the urge to run.

It was the last mistake he ever made.

The Bois de Boulogne runs down the entire south-western side of Paris. During the day it is a huge, welcoming, attractive park with something for everybody, from duck ponds and playgrounds for children, through cycle and horse riding, to the race courses of Longchamp and Auteuil. It is always heavily populated, especially at weekends when Parisians descend *en famille*. But even the most novice of tourists knows not to frequent the park at night. Come dusk, every element of Parisian low life crawls out of the woodwork, and you do not go there. Unless, of course, you are after vice in any form, in any position, with any animal from human to aquatic, and are willing to pay for it - in which case it is the place for you.

He should have known that. He *did* know that, so the fact that he went there is even more inexplicable.

He still held the torch and letters in his hand as he crossed the Avenue du Maréchal Maunoury and scurried through the line of trees. The threatened rain had not materialised, but nevertheless it was damp under foot…

They picked him up as he reached the Allée des Fortifications and began to walk north. There were two of them, blatantly homosexual, one tough and aggressive, the other a bitch-queen. They followed the big, black hunk across the appropriately-named Allée des Dames and made their move as he walked along the edge of the Lac Inférieur.

He was aware of nothing until something grabbed his crotch in the darkness. *"Bonsoir, petite,"* said an effeminate voice. "Who's a big boy then?"

"What the - ?"

He felt his genitals being pulled savagely downwards and he had no alternative but to sink to his knees. As he went down, something hit him in the neck.

He drew his left arm back to hit out but stopped as he felt something wet on his chest. He dropped the torch and letters and raised both hands. Something was spraying. *God, was he being pissed on?*

He was not, and as his head flopped the last realisation he had before he fell was that his throat had been cut.

The one with the knife wiped it on the victim's suit as his mate complained. "It was too quick, idiot! You hit the jugular. He's sprayed all over me!" He knelt down and began feeling the pockets, the body still twitching underneath him.

"I'll spray all over you later, sweetie, that's a promise." The one with the knife stood up. "What's he got?"

"A big one."

"Bitch. Find his wallet."

While one searched, the other picked up the torch and letters.

The one kneeling down gasped. "My God, look!" He held up a diamond necklace, glittering even in the faint light from way down the road.

The other stopped undoing the ribbon on the letters and grabbed the necklace.

"Is it real?"

"How the hell do I know? Has he got anything else?"

The rest of the jewellery was removed, two double handfuls in all.

"Je-SUS! We've hit it here, LouLou. If this stuff is real, we're rich bitches!"

"What've you got there?"

"Just his torch and some old papers, nothing. C'mon, let's get out of here. Chances are this stuff is hot, and now we've got it it's hotter still. We've gotta get rid of it and quick."

"What about him?"

"In the lake, he'll never be found. Give me a hand."

"But he's all messed up."

"You're usually not so fussy, sweetie. Come *on*."

It was an effort. In death the black man seemed to weigh a ton. But eventually the body slipped into the water with barely a splash.

They left the Bois at the Porte de la Muette. Under a street lamp, the girl dressed as a nun exposed herself to them until she realised they would have no interest in her.

They shuffled across the Place. As they took a right into Rue de Franqueville, LouLou's chum dropped the bundle of letters. He turned to retrieve them.

"Leave them, Butch," urged LouLou. "Come *on*!"

"Okay, okay," Butch grabbed the bundle. "You never know, there might be something here. If not, I'll chuck them later. And take your jacket off, there's blood all over it."

"What? Oh fuck, another job for the dry cleaners! I suppose red makes a change from white!"

Holding hands, they hurried off.

‡

2. Flics

Mercredi 12 Avril

To call 11 Rue des Saussaies in Paris a turn-of-the-century apartment building would be wrong, although it looks like it and once was. To call it a police station would be wrong, although in effect it is. To call it simply a government building would be wrong, although it could be argued that it is. In fact, the whole of the north side of the Rue des Saussaies is part of the Interior Ministry, each building inter-connecting and in turn joined to the Ministry's *hôtel particulier* (main building) in the Place Beauvau at the southern end of the street. The building that is number 11 is the headquarters of the Sûrêté Nationale.

Although staffed by police, the Sûrêté Nationale is an administrative unit which at that time controlled the five divisions of France's national crime force: the *Police Judiciaire* (PJ), *Renseignments Généraux* (RG), the *Bureau de Sécurité Publique* (BSP), the *Corps Républicain de Sécurité* (CRS) and the *Direction de la Surveillance du Territoire* (DST). The head of the Sûrêté is the Director-General.

As well as the administrative unit, there was one other branch in the Rue des Saussaies. A relatively new section, born just at the end of the presidency of Georges Pompidou, it was known as the *Bureau de la Coopération Politique* (BCP). It was responsible for the protection of, liaison with, and the general comfort and happiness of all foreign government interests in

France, primarily the embassies and the consulates and also the various Important Foreign Citizens granted residential status (either short or long term depending on their political ambitions). The BCP was a small section, officially coming under the DST but in fact independent, reporting directly to the Minister, by-passing even the Director-General.

The BCP was the only section in the whole of the Saussaies complex to have detectives on its staff. Even these, it was argued by the five 'proper' divisions of the Sûreté, were simply glorified public relations men with guns. (There is never any love lost between the police units of France.)

Chief Inspector Paul Richer walked down Rue du Surène, crossed Saussaies and walked through the iron gates of number 11, passing the public entrance on the right. At that same time, Commissaire Charles Fleury-Goujon closed one of the tall wooden doors of the office of the Minister of the Interior in the main building and walked less than enthusiastically back down the maze of corridors that led through to the Saussaies building.

The Commissaire sighed and hefted the file under his right arm, a treatise on the curious sexual proclivities of a certain senior Italian civil servant at the embassy. The Minister had not been interested, "I leave it to you, Charles." Instead he had wanted to talk about the phone call he had received that morning from a certain house in the Bois de Boulogne.

Fleury-Goujon listened to what the Minister had to say and wondered why on earth it should concern a Commissaire of Police let alone a Minister of State. It was a simple theft, and even if the articles were valuable she could afford it. But, as on several occasions in the past, when *Le Bois* barked Saussaies or des Orfèvres (or sometimes even The Elysée) jumped.

"Take care of it, Charles," the Minister had instructed. "Personally if you are able. If not, assign your top man. I want this cleared up, quickly and quietly. And with no publicity. She doesn't often kick up a fuss nowadays, so when she does we must accommodate her."

Chief Inspector Paul Richer entered the elevator and jabbed the button for the sixth floor. Something, he had decided, must be done. He did not like working in a school playground.

It was all the fault of that bastard Claude Gerard. Ever since Richer had joined the section on promotion three months ago, Gerard had made his life hell. They had started off on the wrong foot, Gerard lambasting and Richer strenuously defending Richer's previous section, the CRS anti-riot squads. And they had been at loggerheads ever since. Gerard, also a Chief Inspector, had carefully contrived to leave the messy assignments to Richer, either deliberately not being around when a particularly sticky case was looming, or feigning overwork to the Commissaire at the daily briefing.

After the initial contretemps, Richer and Gerard had hardly spoken to each other, except on official necessity, a supreme example of the testy sulkiness of middle-aged men.

Two days ago had come the last straw. Richer had been in the lavatory, trousers down, when he had heard two others enter. One was Gerard, he could tell instantly, and the other was young Inspector Bauer. They were laughing as they entered.

"Bent as a six franc note," Gerard was saying. "Must be."

"Mais Monsieur l'Inspecteur - !"

"Consider." There was a double zzzz followed by faint splashing. One of them farted. "Mid forties, unmarried, lives alone *and* in Montmartre. I ask you! Never mentions any women friends."

"Well, he has never troubled me."

"Pray he doesn't."

"He seems to be a very fair chief."

"At a work level. But keep him at arm's length, Victor, do you hear? Or is a promotion worth a prick up the rear?"

"I will keep your advice in mind, Inspector."

"It's not your mind you have to worry about, son."

Richer had gritted his teeth and ignored Gerard when he returned to their shared office. For an instant he considered taking Gerard outside and teaching the fat, lazy slob a lesson he would never forget. So, he had never married. That did not mean he did not enjoy women, many and various, even *les girls* of the Rue St Denis or Pigalle whom he frequented whenever he felt lonely. Who wanted to be married with a nagging wife and five kids like that *con* Gerard?

But violence would achieve nothing. Gerard was the senior man, and whatever justification there might be, whatever extreme provocation, as in all government departments throughout the world seniority would decide the victor.

But it had got to the stage now, after three months, when something had to be done.

Richer had just put paper in the typewriter when the Commissaire poked his head round the door. "Morning Paul, Claude in?"

"Morning Commissaire. He's not on till this afternoon. Could I see you for a - "

"*Merde*. Paul, come in will you?"

Richer sat opposite the Commissaire, the window looking out onto the Rue des Saussaies behind the chief's left shoulder.

"Something urgent has come up, from ministerial level. Cigarette?" The Commissioner indicated a silver box on his desk.

"*Merci*." Richer shook his head.

"Usually I would give the case to Claude, he handles these problems," the Commissaire blew smoke out between pursed lips. "But as he is not here and the Minister has stressed the urgency... well, it will be something for you to cut your teeth on."

Richer nodded dutifully. "Actually sir, I wanted to discuss - "

"You may have heard Claude talk about our resident in the Bois de Boulogne, *oui*? He has successfully handled matters there in the past."

"You mean La Dame?"

"*Naturellement*. Well, there's been a hue and cry on. Some sort of robbery. At least, things have gone missing. Only just discovered. Possibly a break-in."

"Light fingered staff?"

"Not likely, she has so few. But you will check, of course."

"No other information?"

The Commissaire shrugged and spread out his hands. "*Non*. One hopes she is not wasting our time, it has been known. She might have put whatever it is that's gone missing into another drawer."

"*Je comprends*."

"As quickly as possible, Paul. This very morning. Drop whatever you've got on, leave it for Claude. I'll have a word with him when he comes in."

"He's not going to like it. She's his lady."

"Too bad. La Dame cannot suit her domestic distress to his hours. Let me know tonight how you get on. The Minister will probably be content just to have her off his hands, but you never know. Bonnet is noted for picking on the most innocuous of things and blowing them up into a proportion they do not deserve."

Richer rose.

"And Paul?"

"Sir?"

"I needn't stress the need for the utmost tact and diplomacy. Humour her if you must. And above all keep it quiet. You do speak her language, I recall?"

"Rusty, but yes sir."

"*Bon*. Now, you wanted to see me about something?"

The Commissaire did not notice the briefest of pauses before

Richer replied, "No sir."

"*Alors*, I'll see you this evening."

"*D'accord, monsieur le Commissaire.*"

When the portly, balding Chief Inspector Claude Gerard came on duty that afternoon he was, predictably, less than pleased that the upstart Richer was trespassing on his territory. La Dame and her problems always fell to him, not to some bungling novice who wouldn't know how to handle her.

Nevertheless, he put on his bravest, most ingratiating face when the Commissaire casually mentioned it *en passant*, and he agreed that the experience would do Richer good.

Back in the privacy of the office, he kicked over a waste bin in petulant disgust and sulked for the whole afternoon.

‡

3. Flic et Victime

Richer walked east along Rue du Ranelagh. It was an overcast day and, to be on the safe side, he had put on an open fawn raincoat above his brown suit.

A train thundered overhead as he passed under the railway bridge. He crossed diagonally across the grand Avenue Ingres and turned right into the Boulevard Suchet. He was surprised to see that the Louis XVI-style *grand maison* on the corner had no driveway to separate it from the road. The front door was right there, accessible to all. He would have expected some form of security, or at least some privacy from prying eyes. He looked up as he pressed the bell next to the large, black wooden door. No cameras.

After an age he was ushered inside by a smooth, well-outfitted gentleman who announced himself to be madame's secretary. Madame's hairdresser was with her. Monsieur l'Inspecteur would wait?

Richer looked around the large foyer. La Dame had always been noted for her sense of design and decoration, and it had not left her even in her later years (he hesitated at even thinking the word 'dotage'). The place was plush and tasteful. Above his head a chandelier tinkled.

Some minutes later a thin, wiry Italian bounded down the stairs, case under arm, and let himself out. The secretary appeared and indicated that Richer should ascend and follow.

As the secretary knocked on the bedroom door and opened

it, he said quietly "Please do not take too long."

The lady looked younger than her 82 years. Propped up in bed by pillows too numerous to count, her hair was jet black, dropping down to touch her black housecoat. Her face was heavily but expertly made-up. She stared at Richer as the door was closed behind him.

She held out her right hand, but it dropped back before Richer could reach it. "Monsieur Gerard, how nice of you to come." Her voice was high, speaking in her original language, still with a trace of American accent.

"Madame - "

"It is such a long time since we've seen you - "

"I - "

" - but you have not changed. Do sit down." She indicated a space near the foot of the bed. There was no chair.

Richer stood in the space allocated. "You called the Minister, madame?"

"Yes. How are your wife and children?"

"Fine. Fine, thank you."

"Good. I would so loved to have had lots of children myself, but it was not to be." Her eyes clouded over at her memories.

Richer fidgeted. *Christ.*

She came back into the present. "Well, what can I do for you, monsieur?"

"The Minister?"

"Oh yes, how is he?"

"You rang, madame. Something has gone missing."

"Ah." She sat forward, a tangible change descending on her, another spirit entering the body. "Yes indeed. In fact Robert - my secretary, you met him - phoned you. I discovered the loss yesterday evening. Or was it the day before? Anyway, the long and short of it is, someone's been at my safe."

"A burglary?"

"Must have been."

"Without you knowing?"

A sheepish expression passed over her face. "I sleep a lot, you know."

"You keep this door locked?"

"No, my servants come in and out."

Richer sensed that he had to keep the questions coming before he lost her. "Are there any - how do you say? - signs of a break-in?"

"You will have to check with Robert, I don't think there was any trace of breaking and entering."

"I noticed you have no cameras. Do you have alarms?"

" Alarms? I think we used to have them..."

"Madame, what has gone missing?"

"Missing...? Has something gone missing...?" Momentarily she looked bewildered. "Oh, yes. Jewellery. Two diamond necklaces, a gold watch and - what was it? Three gold bracelets set with diamonds. And my lizard."

Her *lézard?*

"What is their value?"

"Value? Heaven alone knows. That doesn't worry me, they're of sentimental value, presents from my husband. The two necklaces were handed down from his great grandmother."

Richer raised an eyebrow. Her husband's great grandmother? That was easy to work out. And that would make the necklaces alone priceless.

La Dame moved a weak hand to indicate the bedside table. "Pour me a drink, there's a good boy."

Richer poured what looked like water from a jug. It was vodka.

"Thank you." She wetted her lips with the liquid, hand shaking. "How are your wife and children, Monsieur Gerard?"

"Was anything else taken, madame?"

"What?"

"Taken. From your safe. Anything else besides the

jewellery?"

"My God, yes." A dribble of liquid ran unnoticed down her chin. "For goodness sake sit down monsieur, I can't keep looking up at you, it will strain my neck."

Richer made a pretence of looking around for a chair, and remained standing.

"Some documents," continued the lady. "Mostly letters from David, my husband. You know him, of course."

"*Naturellement, madame.* They were of value, these letters and documents?"

"To me, yes. But there was a document which, if it was made public, would give the game away. And we can't have that, can we? Not after all these years. Not when everything has become normal again."

He frowned. "Game, madame?"

"That's why I called you in, Monsieur Gerard. The jewellery is precious. But I can do without it. But the document… It has an importance greater than you could possibly imagine. You must find it. It *must* be returned!"

Shakily she drained her glass. Quickly Richer refilled it. Taking a tissue from a box on the bedside table, he leant forward and wiped her chin. She did not seem to notice – or perhaps she was simply used to people tending to her.

She looked quite frightened. "My family have never known. David's sister-in-law knows the secret, the rest of his side are dead. No one else must know."

"Madame," said Richer gently, placing the tissue back next to the jug. "What is it? What is this game that must not be given away, this secret? What is this document?"

Her eyes were clear, all faculties intact. "I shall tell you…"

Halfway through her story, Paul Richer involuntarily sat down on the edge of her bed. It was either that or fall down. He could not believe what he was hearing, but he was convinced it was true. At that moment she was completely in control, lucid and cogent. Perfectly sane.

At the end he sat there stunned, unable to say a word. What *could* he say...? One thing was certain: the document must be found, whatever it took, whatever had to be done.

Its value was incalculable.

After a while Richer realised where he was and on whose bed he was sitting. He leapt to his feet but offered no apologies.

"*Madame, qu'est-ce qu'on peut...?*" His voice was hoarse as he lapsed into his native tongue. "What can one say?"

La Dame squinted her eyes as she stared up at him. "Nothing. Precisely nothing, monsieur. You are very privileged to have heard the story. Nobody else must know, especially not the Minister. There must be no police snooping around here. You may not ask my staff questions. No investigations whatsoever are to take place in this house."

"But madame - "

"You will do as I say." Her voice was sharp and nasty. "Do I make myself clear? Nothing is to happen that indicates in any way that anything has gone missing from this house."

"But the jewellery is priceless!"

"I don't care. The document is the only consideration. It must be found and in complete secrecy. Here - more."

She held out her glass.

Richer poured more vodka.

He looked at the lady. When she took the glass away from her lips, her face had changed. She smiled sweetly up at him. She asked in a little girly voice, "How is Madame Gerard and your children?"

‡

4. Flics

It was a serious and thoughtful Richer that returned to the Rue des Saussaies late that afternoon. He was in no mood for Chief Inspector Claude Gerard, who was gleefully awaiting him.

"Well, well, so the blue-eyed boy is back!"

"Stuff it, Gerard."

Gerard took his feet from the desk top and flicked ash from his Disque Bleu. "Have a nice time? Sort it out? Mountain out of a molehill as usual?" He frowned in momentary discomfort and then reached down with his left hand and pulled at his balls.

Richer stared at him.

"Did she give you tea and biscuits?"

Richer sat down, drawing a pen from his pocket and tap-tapping it on his notepad.

Gerard came round, shook his left leg and sat on the edge of his own desk. "Hope you didn't upset the old baggage, she needs careful handling at her age."

"Hmm."

"Tell you what, as a special favour to you, how about if I took it on? Hush hush, Fleury need never know. You'll get the credit."

Richer looked at him in silence, not caring if Gerard saw the contempt in his eyes. Then he asked, "Is the Commissaire in?"

"Think so. What about my offer?"

"He's given it to me. I'll have to see it through."

"What's it about? Her cat escaped again?"

"You could say that." Richer picked up the phone and tapped out three figures. He said to himself, "If *this* cat ever got out of the bag... Richer, sir. Is it convenient? *D'accord*."

"Hey!" complained Gerard as the door closed. "Aren't you even going to tell me what it's about? She *is* my case, you know!" He stood with his hands on his hips, cigarette in his mouth, squinting as the smoke went into his eyes.

Bastard. Damn CRS bastard. Should stick to his riots, that's all he was good for. Well, we'll see about this...

"Everything all right?" Commissaire Fleury-Goujon looked up from the thick file in front of him as Richer entered.

"Yes, sir. Some jewellery missing, nothing much. She's not too worried. I think she just wanted someone to talk to."

The Commissaire humphed and sipped coffee, Arabica with cream. "As always. So I can leave it in your hands?"

"Absolutely."

"*Bon*. I'll tell the Minister we have it under control. Well done, Paul."

"Thank you, sir."

He saw Richer was not moving to go. "Was there anything else?"

After a moment, Richer nodded.

‡

5. Flic

Lundi 17 Avril

Five days later. A sunny but cool Parisian spring morning.

Richer left the headquarters of the Police Judiciaire at the Quai des Orfèvres, turned left and swore softly to himself. His final lead, his only lead, had just gone up in smoke.

Despite La Dame's instructions to the contrary, during the end of last week he had interviewed the small staff retained in Boulevard Suchet and had examined the place for any sign of a break-in, all unbeknownst to herself who stayed in her room, asleep for most of the time.

Having no date for the alleged robbery did not help, but he was convinced the staff knew nothing. The house was normal, no sign of forced entry.

Therefore the thief or thieves had keys, it was the only possible explanation. Therefore who had keys? It had not taken him long to learn of the dismissed black butler. Tracing him to the diplomat in Neuilly was easy.

But the suspect had disappeared nearly two months ago. Simply upped and left one night, leaving his few personal belongings behind. No note, not a word to anyone.

Richer had felt a nasty sensation in his stomach. If the man had *taken* his things, he would have been elated, and the case would have become a simple manhunt. As the man had *not* taken his things, it probably indicated that he had intended to return. Why then hadn't he?

Now the PJ had just confirmed that a black Jean Dubois had been fished out of the Lac Inférieur in the Bois de Boulogne three weeks ago in a state of ripe decomposition. No identification, indeed nothing at all, in his pockets. Cause of death? The autopsy report said basically that it appeared he had bled to death as a result of a knife wound – consistent with his throat being cut. As with all deaths in the Bois, it had minimal investigation and had been recorded as person unknown murdered by persons unknown.

Thank you PJ. Richer had not told them the reason for his enquiry, but he knew he would have to help them clear their books sooner or later. Make it later.

So, the black butler, peeved at being sacked, had returned to help himself to the old woman's jewellery and some letters. Why the letters? Did he have a market or was it just *en passant*? Richer would check into his background, but the chances were that the letters were just grabbed in the rush. It was the jewellery that he would be interested in.

On his way from his crime he had cut through the Bois de Boulogne - and met his death. The mugger had been mugged, the fear of every investigator, for it meant a short, sharp and often permanent halt to any enquiries. The lead had run out.

So, Richer knew what had been taken and he knew who had taken it. But he did not know who had it now. It could be anywhere.

As he crossed the Pont au Change a *Vedettes du Pont Neuf* pleasure boat passed underneath him, only half full with tourists.

The situation reminded him of one of the adventures of the supercriminal Jacques Mesrine. During a chase with the local gendarmerie somewhere in the north, Mesrine had stolen a car. It had been traced once it had been reported missing. But then Mesrine had ditched it and had stolen another vehicle - a vehicle that was already stolen. Obviously the first thief did not report the theft, so end of trail. Mesrine had got clear away.

Richer glanced over at the Tour St Jacques on his right as he headed towards the Rue de Rivoli.

So now what? The document was esoteric, and the chances were that anyone in the criminal underworld in possession of it would not know or understand what they had. Maybe it had simply been thrown away with the letters. But if it still existed it had to be found. Speed was not of the essence – the document had been around for a long time - but secrecy was.

Not only had La Dame insisted that he worked alone, but the information – the secret – she had imparted to him could not be told to anybody. La Dame was asking the impossible. She didn't need the police, she needed a private detective (but, of course, she would have to pay for that). She wanted someone with deeper underworld connections than any *flic* in the country, even those lucky few with their own supergrasses. Someone who could move where no *flic* could. Someone -

He stopped, staring back over at the Tour St Jacques. Fifty-two metres high, it was a tower without a church. A curious incongruity. Originally the belfry of St James-the-Butcher's, the church had gone in 1802 but the tower had survived.

An idea had occurred to him, linked to his previous thoughts. An idea so preposterous, so outrageous, so *impossible…*

An impossible person for an impossible task?

He was aware that people were looking at him, and he walked on. He turned right into the Rue de Rivoli and caught a bus 72 heading west.

‡

6. Flics

"Two hours!" moaned Chief Inspector Claude Gerard. "Two hours and all you've done is sit there with your diary open in front of you tapping your bloody pen."

"Do I annoy you?" Richer did not look up.

Gerard sat back, hands clasped in front of his protruding stomach. "You look like a man with problems."

"Nothing I can't handle."

"That's what Napoleon said on the eve of Waterloo."

"Hmm."

"What is it? La Dame?"

Richer did not reply.

"She's an awkward cow if you don't know how to handle her. Look," ash fell down Gerard's tie from the cigarette in the side of his mouth, "final offer, no strings attached: shall I take it on?"

Richer still did not reply.

"Hey!"

Richer looked up. "What?"

"I'm talking to you."

"Look, I've got work to do, do you mind?"

Gerard shrugged. "Up to you, sunshine."

Five minutes later Richer tidied his desk, locked the diary in the drawer, scribbled something on his notepad, ripped off the top sheet and went out of the office.

Gerard sighed irritably and lit another Disque. Then he frowned, got up and went over to Richer's desk. He picked up the notepad and stared at it closely. Then he snatched the blank top sheet off the pad, stuffed it into his pocket and hastily returned to his own desk.

‡

7. Flic et Voleur

Vendredi 21 Avril

In some ways Rue de la Santé, which forms the boundary between the 13th and 14th Arrondisements in southern Paris, is ironically named, almost with a sense of the macabre. *'Santé'* means 'health' and for sure the *Groupe Hospitalier Cochin* and the *Clinique Chirurgicale Péan* are situated at the northern end of the long street. However, just to the south, on the corner of the Boulevard Arago, is *Maison d'Arrêt de la Santé*, La Santé Prison, the most famous prison in France.

Said to be escape-proof, La Santé is the home of some of France's most notorious criminals. Only fitting then that in the spring of 1978, La Santé housed the most famous criminal in the whole of Europe: Jacques Mesrine.

Mesrine was at the beginning of a twenty year stretch for crimes ranging from murder to passing dud cheques (at the trial it had taken two days to read the list of charges against him). Even as he was being taken down at the end of his trial, Mesrine had vowed to escape from the inescapable La Santé, if it was humanly possible - and one of the several tenets Mesrine lived by was that everything was humanly possible, at least for him if not for mere mortals.

The prison authorities had taken his outpourings seriously and a special top-security wing had been built in which Mesrine now languished.

At 09:50 that morning, Mesrine was on his way to the exercise yard when he was intercepted by three warders. He was wanted in the interview room. Who was it? Who knows? Probably one of his many lawyers conducting his many appeals.

The interview room would have been better termed an interview cupboard. Two metres long by one and a half wide, it contained a small plank table which could be raised flat against the wall on hinges, and two chairs. Nothing else. A reinforced plate glass window looked out onto the corridor.

The plank table was down and a tall, fair man stood behind it.

Mesrine arrived, more like a king attending an audience than a convicted criminal. *"Merci mes amis,* I won't be needing you now," he grinned at his retinue of screws.

"Allez Jacques," retorted one, nodding at the room. *"Et ferme ton bec."*

Mesrine stopped as he entered, frowning at the man on the other side of the table. *"M'sieur?* Do I know you?"

Richer nodded to the guards. The heavy steel door was closed. One guard remained outside by the window, the others dispersed.

The two men stood facing one another, only the table between them. Richer pulled a full packet of Gauloises from his coat and threw them onto the table. He followed it with another package, similar in size but heavier.

Mesrine did not touch either. *"Naturellement, Monsieur Le Flic.* As if I did not know. Broussard send you?"

"Sit down, Jacques," Richer indicated the cigarettes. "Help yourself."

"Filthy habit," Mesrine took the packet as he sat down, opened it and threw one back at Richer. "But, like so many filthy habits, enjoyable. You have a light?"

Richer lit his own cigarette and swallowed smoke into his lungs. Then he took back Mesrine's cigarette and lit it from the tip of his own.

"A cautious man," observed Mesrine, taking a full centimetre off the *sèche* with one inhalation.

"With you, Jacques, always. Keep the packet."

"I was going to."

"And, if you don't mind…" Richer nodded at the other item.

Mesrine opened it. "A remarkably recent picture, Chief Inspector Paul Richer," he tapped the card. "Which tells me one of two things. Either your old photograph was out of date and needed replacing, or you are new to… to what?"

Richer accepted the wallet back. "Very good, Jacques, very good. Very perspicacious. Still as mentally agile as ever - "

"As *agile* as the *lapin*."

"I'm glad a couple of years in jail, with eighteen more still to come, has not weakened your faculties."

"Only the bromide does that."

Richer gave a rueful smile. He said, "So tell me, you are content to spend another eighteen years here, huh? You'll be - what? Nearly sixty when you come out."

"Inspector, Inspector," Mesrine's voice held the patience of one talking to a child. "I will not be here for another eighteen years. Not even for another eighteen months. I have told them all, even the Governor himself. There is not a gaol that can hold Jacques Mesrine."

"But no one has ever escaped from La Santé."

"There is not a gaol that can hold Jacques Mesrine."

"Hmm! Are you a little - forgive me for saying this - foolhardy for publicising your intentions?"

"Hah, everyone knows!" Mesrine pushed out his chest. "Some of my previous escapes from custody - "

"I know, I know. The Master of Invention, the Master of Disguise, *et cetera, et cetera*."

"You mock?"

"As if I would! You - yes, even you – cannot escape from La

Santé alone. You will need help."

Mesrine stubbed out the cigarette on the table top. Smoke drifted from his nose and mouth as he said, "Maybe. But, *Monsieur l'Inspecteur*, we are getting into the realms of name, rank and serial number. What do you want? I am a busy man."

Richer sat back. "What do you know about La Santé, Jacques? You've obviously done a lot of research, seeing as it's taken you two years already and you haven't escaped."

Mesrine chuckled. "What do you *want*?"

"Is this room clean?" Richer looked up at the ceiling. "No fleas? Swept every day?"

"Ha! You, monsieur, are a member of the Establishment. Don't give yourselves credit for more guile than you have. No, this room is not bugged."

"*Bon.*" He looked into Mesrine's dark, deep set eyes. "I want to help you escape."

Mesrine's face was expressionless. He looked at Richer coldly. For thirty seconds he did nothing. Then his brow creased in the slightest of frowns. He took another cigarette from the packet. He did not offer it up to be lit but instead he began rolling it between the fingers of his right hand, gangster-style. It seemed to take up all his attention.

Richer just looked at him.

After a while, Mesrine asked "Am I being set up?"

"No."

The cigarette moved back and forth, Mesrine staring at it.

"Am I being mocked?"

"No."

"I do not like being mocked. Makes me angry. Makes me want to kill."

"You are not being mocked."

With a flick of Mesrine's right thumb, the cigarette jumped from his right hand to his left. Immediately on landing it began rolling between the fingers.

"Then why?" He stopped moving the cigarette and looked up at Richer.

Richer kept his voice low. "I need a man with special talents."

"You have maybe one or two in the whole of the Sûreté."

"I need a man with *extra* special talents. Someone outside the police. Someone with contacts, someone with connections in the criminal world that a *flic* can only dream about."

"There are more criminals out there than there are in here."

"I need *you*."

"And no free lunch."

"*Comment?*"

"There is no such thing as a free lunch. For what do you need *me*, m'sieur?"

"To retrieve something."

"To retrieve something?" Mesrine looked bewildered. "Kidnapping, theft, robbery, even murder - those I can understand. But *retrieval?*"

"In return I will assist in whatever way I can, in whatever way you want me to, in your escape."

"And what makes you think I need help?"

Richer sighed. "Don't piss me around, Jacques. I too am a busy man. A damn sight more busier than you. I'm giving it to you straight."

Mesrine sat, eyes half closed. "And what," he asked at length, "is to stop you and a whole army of *flics* mowing me down in the road outside? How do I know this is not an Establishment plot to finish Mesrine once and for all? Why the hell should *I* trust *you?* What the hell *is* this? Monsieur, I think I have heard enough!" The chair scraped back as he stood up.

"Sit down, Jacques, sit down. And don't be so bloody dramatic." Richer flapped his hands. "For Christ's sake."

Mesrine eyed the other man suspiciously. Only when Richer looked away did he resume his seat.

Richer then said, "You owe me, Mesrine. I've come to

collect."

He frowned. *"Owe* you? *I* owe *you*? Monsieur, I have never met you before in my life. How can I possible *owe* you?"

Richer blew out smoke. "I saved your life."

"You? You saved the life of Jacques Mesrine?"

"You don't remember? Think back. Algeria 58. We were both in the army. The Arab. In the alley at night, when you should have been in camp..."

Mesrine held up the cigarette. This time Richer came round the table and used his lighter.

"You told me then, Jacques, that you liked danger. That you would be interested in something different. Well, we recruited you and trained you, did we not? But you never repaid me personally for saving your life. Now I'm calling."

Mesrine's voice was soft. "It was *you* that night?" He thought back over the years. He could hear and smell Algeria of twenty years ago. "Richer... Richer... *Richer! Captain* Richer!"

"I was then. I am now, as you know, Chief Inspector Richer."

"But... you belonged to the Organisation."

"I did. I still do."

"And you are truly a Chief Inspector in the Sûreté?"

"Oui."

"And you belong to the *Organisation Armée Secrète?"*

"Oui."

"Then you are one of us!"

"Not quite, Jacques, not quite. My beliefs still concern France. I work for France, not for my own ends."

Without warning, Mesrine was up. Richer did not even have a chance to move his arms before the big man had hold of him. *"Mon ami, mon ami,* after all this time." The bear hug was excrutiating. *"Mon dieu!* I do not believe it. But I know it is true! Comrade! *Capitaine!"*

"Jacques - " Richer tried unsuccessfully to avoid the double kiss on each cheek. "Jacques, sit down please. Christ Almighty.

Mesrine, sit down!"

"Sir! *Mon Capitaine!*"

Richer made the thumbs-up sign to the warder frowning in at the corridor window, hand on the door.

"I will give it to you straight," Richer straightened his tie. "At this moment I am talking to you as a Chief Inspector of the BCP. There has been a robbery. Something has been stolen. I want you to get it back."

"That's all?"

"Let me finish. This robbery took place about six or seven weeks ago at a house in the Bois de Boulogne."

"A house?"

"*The* house."

"Ah!"

"Something very important was taken. *Very* important, Jacques. So important that I cannot tell you what it is."

Mesrine raised his hand. "*Un moment, mon ami, un moment.* If I understand right, you want me to retrieve something and you won't even tell me what it is!"

"Correct."

"*Mais c'est impossible.*"

"For the police and for most other people, yes. But not for Jacques Mesrine."

He grinned. "True, true. You know me well. What leads do you have?"

"The only thing we know is that this robbery took place. And I think I know who did it."

"You know who did it? I am confused."

"He was found dead in the Bois. It's pretty certain he died the same night as the robbery."

"Killed by his colleagues?"

"I think he worked alone."

"*Alors,* I am beginning to understand. He tried to take a shortcut through the Bois at night?"

Richer nodded.

"*L'imbécile.*"

"*Oui.*"

"And you have a trail that vanishes."

"*Oui.* He took jewellery worth easily ten million francs, probably a lot more. La Dame is not too worried about that. But he also took some letters. In those letters was a document. I cannot tell you what is in that document. That is between me and La Dame. I do not believe the thief knew the significance of what he was taking. He probably just grabbed the letters along with the ice."

"Can't you give me any clue as to what it is?"

"All I can say is that if it fell into the wrong hands its disclosures would cause chaos in France and Britain. It would damage both governments - no, both *countries.* It would cast black clouds in America. And - needless to say - it would upset La Dame.

"That's it, Jacques. That's what I've been asked to recover. That's what I'm asking *you* to recover. I cannot tell you anything further about what is in it, in case you don't find it. It is dangerous to have the knowledge. All I can offer you in return is assistance in your already well-notified escape from here. I can give you no immunity from recapture or future prosecution, not even a guarantee for your safety. And it *will* be an escape. I can, of course, assist with any hardware you might require, any contacts you may wish to make. You will not be assisted by the police, you understand. You will be assisted by the OAS.

"Just one more thing. If you find the document, take no chances with it. Bring it back at all costs, and only to me. Our mutual friends may have an interest in it."

Mesrine stared at the table, running a nail along the grain of the wood. He said, "So what you are saying is that I will ostensibly be working for the Sûreté on behalf of the government, but in reality I will be working for the OAS?"

"If you like. From your point of view you should regard yourself as working only for Jacques Mesrine. To everyone except me and our friends you will be just an escaped criminal.You will have to watch your back. It will not be easy. But if it was, I wouldn't be asking Jacques Mesrine."

Again the flattery, albeit the truth, pleased Mesrine. He drew on his cigarette. After a minute he said, "Under no circumstances would I do it for the Sûreté."

Richer said nothing.

Mesrine continued. "I might possibly do it for the French government - I am, after all, as patriotic as the next man."

Richer knew the game was being played out now. He watched as Mesrine finished the cigarette.

"I *will* do it for the man who saved my life, and for the OAS."

"Thank you."

"But you must understand, *Capitaine*, that it is my intention to escape from here anyway. I will pursue the document in my own time and at my own pace. I will not be hurried, I will not be intimidated. Neither will I delay any other activities I have planned."

"I understand. I will come to see you again next week. Let me know what you need and what you want me to do. I will see our friends. Once you are out, we will not meet until you have the document. And Jacques?"

"*Inspecteur?*"

"I trust you. I trust you to do it and do it well. In effect I am paying you in advance, with no way of recollection if you default."

"No way? How about a bullet in the head?"

"How will I know where you are? How will I know *who* you are? All I ask is for a regular progress report. I have two telephone numbers, one at Saussaies, one at home. Try Saussaies first. I will answer with my name. If I do not, or if it is someone else, hang up. Then try me at home. At all times use a false name - which?"

"Bruno."

"Okay, Bruno. Memorise the numbers, do not write them down." He gave him the Saussaies number first then the one of his apartment in Montmartre. "Got them?"

Mesrine repeated the two seven-digit codes.

"Good." Richer stood up and walked round the table. "The best of luck, Jacques."

They shook hands, Mesrine's broad back hiding the action from the sight of the guard outside. "Who needs luck, *mon ami*? I am Mesrine. I am luck itself!"

"Of course you are." The steel door slid back upon Richer's rap on the window. Richer said, "You haven't heard the last of this Mesrine. You did it and you know you did. I shall be back."

"*Sale flic!*" spat the prisoner. "You want to pin every unsolved crime in France upon me, huh? Shitehawk!"

"Shut up Jacques, for God's sake," advised the guard as Richer turned and went down the corridor.

"Bastard!" shouted Mesrine over his shoulder as he was led off in the opposite direction. "Damn bastard pig!"

‡

8. L'Organisation

The three men sat in a row behind an old wooden table that had long since seen better days. Paul Richer sat in front of them. The bare room was dingy and smelled of dust and rotting meat. It was a place rarely used nowadays, but in the fifties and sixties the room above the butcher's in Rue Fessart in the 19th arrondisement was a frequent meeting place of the OAS High Command. It had never been discovered to this day.

A lightbulb hung above Richer's head. The men on the other side of the table were in shadow.

"What you are suggesting is preposterous," scoffed the man on the left, the one wearing the cap. "We have not indulged in active operations for years."

"I do not see that as a hindrance. Or as an excuse," countered Richer.

"Oh you don't, do you?"

"Captain, I think you should remember where you are and whom you are addressing," advised the man on the right, the chain smoker.

"If I appear insubordinate sir, that is not my intention. However, we have here a golden opportunity. If we could secure this document for ourselves, I promise you it would give us leverage beyond anything we have hoped for in the past. We would have a direct line into our own government and the governments of at least two other countries."

"But you won't even tell us what this supposed secret is!"

complained the man in the cap. "How do you expect us to order active duties when we do not even know what we are after?"

"Sir, I have already explained. It is better that you do not know. Not until the document is ours. It is not safe. The fewer people who know, the better. With the knowledge I have now, even only verbally, I might be in danger."

"So you do not trust us?"

Richer took a deep breath. "I find that comment insulting, both to me and to everything this organisation represents. Of course I trust the High Command. But you have lives outside of this room. You could be vulnerable. I am protecting you. This is literally a case of what you don't know can't hurt you. When the document is ours, all will be revealed. Do you, sirs, trust *me*?"

"Now who is being insulting?"

"Gentlemen, gentlemen," soothed the man in the middle, the Colonel, the head of the OAS. "Please. Let us not get into squabbles. I know Captain Richer - we all do. I trust him. So do you." It was not open to debate.

The man on the right dragged on his cigarette. "Two questions," he said.

Richer turned to him. "Sir?"

"What about La Dame? She is expecting her document back, *non*? I do not think she would be pleased with just a photocopy. And we would want a provably authentic original."

"She is old, as you know. I have interviewed her. She is very frail, not always there. Leave her to me."

"What will you do?"

"If she proves a problem? I will kill her."

There was silence. The men looked at each other.

The Colonel breathed out very slowly, very audibly. After a while he said, "You will take no action in that respect unless it is first authorised by the High Command."

Richer nodded. "As you wish, sir."

"My second question," continued the man on the right. "Why

on earth Mesrine? Of all people. Why can't we use one of our own, someone whom it is not necessary to break out of jail?"

"Mesrine *is* one of our own. He served us well in the troubled years. We used him before, in Spain. As you said, sir," he addressed the cap man, "the Organisation has not indulged in active operations for years. Who else is there? I've explained the problems of tracing the document. Who else can do it if even the police cannot? I believe there is only one man. Unless you know of any alternatives? In which case I would be pleased to co-operate with them."

The question hung in the air with the smell of the meat from downstairs.

Richer continued. "As to breaking Mesrine out of jail, that is not what I am asking. He has vowed that La Santé will not hold him - *merde alors*, that is why they built the wing especially for him. For sure he will attempt to escape. Rather than have him killed in a battle with the guards, let us help him. Then he will help us. Help, that is all I am asking for. Subtle help, untraceable help. I am not asking for a battalion of OAS veterans to storm the gates of La Santé. I just want help. A door open here, a key in the exact place it should be, some equipment to hand, that sort of thing. With your authority I will organise it." He looked along the table. "Gentlemen?"

The Colonel sat with his hands together in front of him. He looked at his colleagues and then at Richer. He said, "We will need time to consider your proposal, Captain. Return in two hours."

Two hours later, Richer entered the room when beckoned. There was a full liqueur glass on the table and a bottle of calvados. The OAS High Command were standing, glasses in their hands.

The Colonel handed the remaining glass to Richer. He nodded. "It is agreed. Assistance will be arranged. After that it is just you and Mesrine. This is a gamble. Do not fail us, Captain."

"The consequences," said the man with the cap, "might be severe."

"I will not fail," said Richer. "And neither will Mesrine."

"Then gentlemen, a toast," proposed the Colonel.

The four men stood in a circle and raised their glasses.

"Charles de Gaulle," said the Colonel.

They spoke together. "May the traitor rot in hell."

‡

9. Flics

Mardi 25 Avril

Claude Gerard was on duty an hour early that day, a most unusual occurrence. His arrival coincided with Paul Richer's return from his second visit to La Santé Prison. Richer kept the look of surprise from his face as he entered the office and saw Gerard lighting up his first Disque Bleue.

"Afternoon Paul, how's things?"

"Busy. How's things with you?"

"Managing, managing. There's rumbles of an embarrassment with a South American diplomat, got a bit too excited with the gee-gees, lost a packet, might have to go home. Did you clear up the business with La Dame?"

"Yep," Richer sat down and pulled a file and a notepad from a drawer.

"Clever boy."

"Thank you."

"What was it about? Usual something about nothing?"

"Yes."

"Pussy up a tree?"

He was fishing, but Richer's silence told him there would be no biting.

Gerard said, quite calmly, "She was - is - my case, you know. Just because you happen to get *one* job - "

"Yes?"

"Why not confide in me? We're both Chief Inspectors in the BCP, for Christ's sake. Maybe I can help you write it up. In *my* file."

"Don't want you spouting about La Dame's business in the lavatory, do we?"

"What?"

"You heard. Fond of giving advice to junior officers in there, aren't you?"

Gerard understood. "You shit."

"Precisely. And that's what you should have been doing too, arsehole. Rather than slagging off your colleague to a junior. Is Fleury in?"

"See for yourself." The half-smoked Disque was crushed into the glass ashtray.

Richer went to tear off the top sheet from his notepad then changed his mind and picked up the whole pad. Without a further glance at Gerard he left the room, leaving the door swinging open behind him.

On his own, Gerard cursed again, stood up, closed the door and went over to Richer's desk. There was a file in the In Tray and he flicked it open, scanning it briefly. It concerned a grass Richer had contacted in République, something about a plot to bomb Marks and Spencer in Boulevard Haussmann. Nothing about La Dame.

Quickly, Gerard went through the drawers of the desk. Nothing of consequence. But the top drawer on the left was locked.

He swiped a paperclip from the tidy on the desk top, twisted it into shape and bent down level with the drawer.

Richer came back in.

"What're you after?"

Gerard was on his hands and knees looking under the desk. "Nothing."

Richer snatched the file from the In Tray. "What do you mean 'nothing'?"

"I dropped my fucking pen and it rolled across, don't mind do you?"

"You should use it to write with and not keep tossing it about and playing with it." Richer hurried back out.

"*Con.*"

With two or three deft twists Gerard had the drawer open, eyes lighting like Aladdin in his cave of treasure.

The light soon went out. All Richer had under lock and key was an English *Parker* fountain pen, twenty francs in small change, a packet of tissues, an apple and his leave chit. *Shit!* Hold on, what was beneath the tissues? A diary!

Quickly flicking through the pages, Gerard's eyes skimmed over the entries, mostly appointments both official and social. The letter 'M' appeared on 21st, today and Friday 28th. Around Friday 5th May was a faint red circle.

Gerard replaced the diary and locked the drawer as skilfully as he had opened it.

He picked up his own telephone and keyed the front office. "Chief Inspector Gerard. Can you tell me where Chief Inspector Richer was this morning?" He heard the thumbing of a page.

"He was logged down as being at La Santé, sir."

"Right. Is he back yet?" Cosmetics.

"Saw him in about twenty minutes ago, sir."

"*Merci.*"

You bastard, what are you up to? A visit to La Santé... The letters 'M' in the diary... A mark for ten days hence...

Gerard pulled the folded piece of paper from inside his pocket, the one he had taken from Richer's notepad last week. He opened it. From a distance, where he had lightly rubbed his pencil over the surface, it looked like a drawing of a grey rain cloud. Only close up, peeking palely through the cloud, could he make out the two letters. The first was a J, definitely a J.

J.M.

‡

10. Flic

Samedi 29 Avril

Richer was not on duty that day, so Gerard had time to rifle his desk at leisure.

For a long time he examined the diary, turning the pages back and forth, staring at the entries again and again in case they might change. It was only a fit of coughing that made him realise that he had smoked half a packet of Disques and that the room was getting heavy. Lighting another, he stood up, stretched and coughed again. He pulled his left butt cheek outwards and farted. Quickly he opened the window.

What he was thinking was crazy, preposterous. He had not an ounce of proof. 'M' could stand for *'mère'*. Perhaps Richer had been visiting his mother a lot? As CI with responsibilities for personnel, Gerard knew that the lady was in her eighties and was permanently ensconced in a clinic in Issy. But that would be giving Richer the benefit of the doubt. It was too easy. Richer had been at La Santé last Tuesday. Richer's mother was not in La Santé! But someone with the initials J.M was.

Was there a link, either in the present or in the past, between the two men? Couldn't be, Richer would never have risen to where he was today had there been the slightest doubt about his background.

Gerard went over to his own desk and opened the big envelope that had arrived for him in the last internal post.

Inside, in another sealed envelope, was a pink personnel file. He took it out.

From a locked drawer of his desk he removed a thick blue casework file he had obtained from central registry that morning. It was one of a series of files with the same number.

He sat staring at the two files. As he lit another cigarette, he opened the blue file labelled *Mesrine J R* and began to read.

It took him an hour to get to 1956. When he did, he put the file still open to one side and pulled over the pink file. The label on the cover read *Richer P J*.

‡

11. Le Directeur

Mercredi 3 Mai

The direct telephone line to the office of the Governor of La Santé prison was at that time 336-40-50. It rang that afternoon, logged at 14:30 hours, and was answered by the then Deputy Governor Monsieur Jean Fagianelli.

The message consisted of fourteen words.

"Mesrine will escape on Friday 5th May. I repeat, Mesrine will escape on Friday."

Naturally the caller did not identify himself.

The Deputy discussed the matter with the Governor, Monsieur Hubert Bonaldi. It was decided to note the call but to take no further action as a consequence. Nobody had ever escaped from La Santé, and the grey world of the Parisian criminal fraternity (from where it was thought the call had originated) is always rife with rumours, plots, counterplots and tip-offs which come to nothing.

‡

12. Voleur

Vendredi 5 Mai

A discreet extra watch was kept on Jacques Mesrine on 5th May, but he did nothing out of the ordinary.

The authorities of La Santé prison never knew that the only reason he did not escape that Friday was that it rained all day.

Lundi 8 Mai

[The following is a factual account of the escape of Jacques Mesrine from La Santé prison.]

At that time there were only three other men considered dangerous enough to share the top-security wing of La Santé prison with Jacques Mesrine. Two of them, François Besse and Carman Rives, were taking their exercise with Mesrine at 09:50 that morning.

At 09:55 two guards came into the exercise yard and escorted Mesrine to the interview room. Madame Giletti, one of his many lawyers, awaited him on legitimate business.

Prisoner Besse was taken back to his cell at 10:00. Rives, who was not in on the escape, followed, suspicious of this break from routine.

After a few minutes in the interview room with the lawyer, Mesrine knocked calmly on the inner window. One of the two guards opened the metal door.

"Albert," smiled Mesrine as if speaking to a close friend. "Forgive me, I need some papers. They are in a file I left in François' room. I wonder if you would be so kind as to get them for me?"

"Certainly, Jacques." The guard was only too pleased to assist. "Excuse me, madame," he nodded at the lawyer.

Besse's cell was a mere ten metres along the corridor.

"François, you have some papers of Jacques'? He needs them." Albert unlocked the outer wooden door.

Besse was fiddling with a toothpaste tube. *"Papiers? Ah, oui. That Jacques is an idiot! Why did he leave them here?"* He took a large box file from the table in the corner and tried to push it through the bars of the inner door. As intended, the box was far too big.

"Pah! Hang on, hang on." Albert unlocked the inner door. As he pulled it open, Besse simultaneously whacked him on the chin with the box and squirted soapy water into his eyes from the toothpaste tube. Albert shouted out. Besse kneed him in the groin.

Although talking to his lawyer, Mesrine's gaze was glued on the window. He saw the second guard dash to his left.

Besse saw the second guard coming and quickly rammed his foot into the face of the moaning, prostrate Albert. The moaning stopped.

"Madame, this room is bugged!" To his lawyer's astonishment, Mesrine suddenly jumped up onto the plank table.

Pulling a pair of nail scissors from his shirt pocket, Mesrine undid the retaining screw of the ventilation grill in the ceiling with one fluid twist.

"Monsieur!" gasped the lawyer.

From inside the shaft, Mesrine pulled two pistols and a grappling iron with blue mountaineering rope attached. "Madame," he announced triumphantly, "the bugs in La Santé are huge!"

Besse struggled, pinned against the wall by the big, beefy second guard. Albert was still on the floor but slowly moving. Besse kicked out, trying to make contact with the second guard's shins or more vital areas.

The guard held him tightly. "What the fuck's got into you, François? Want to get rough, hn?"

Then he felt something hard press into the back of his neck.

"Do not move." There was no mistaking the voice of the most dangerous, most notorious killer in France. "Let him go."

The guard relaxed his grip.

"Sensible, Charles, sensible."

"Jacques, you'll never - "

"Silence!" The gun pushed against his skull.

Besse grabbed the guard and swung him into the cell. Albert was now on his knees, perplexed and bewildered.

Mesrine filled the doorway. "Right, messieurs, take off your clothes."

"What?"

"*Vite!* Or are you in such a hurry to meet your maker?"

Mesrine and Besse covered the guards in turn as the other stepped into the discarded uniforms of navy blue jacket, pants, cap and tie, and light blue shirt.

Charles' clothes fit Mesrine with a stunning exactness. The criminal was transformed, every inch the warder. Once Besse was ready, he said "*Adieux, messieurs.* One way or another, you will never see me in here again." He slammed the cell doors shut, locking each of them.

Besse had the mountaineering rope and grapple wound round his shoulders. *"Allons, Jacques."*

"Oui, François, oui. But remember, we are warders. Warders do not hurry."

They headed for the staff office at the end of the corridor, passing the cell of Carman Rives. The convict was at the bars of the locked inner door, staring out. Mesrine had an idea.

"You want to come?" he asked the astonished Rives, unlocking the door. Rives was out in an instant.

At the staff office, Mesrine calmly opened the door and walked in. Inside were two assistant governors, the Chief Warder and five of his men. A convenient meeting at a convenient time.

"Good morning, gentlemen," greeted the unmistakable moustached figure. Quickly and deliberately he gave the nearest warder a savage smash around the head with the butt of his gun. The man staggered and then sat down untidily on the floor. "That is a warning. If anyone tries anything they will be shot."

While Besse covered the men and Rives looked bewildered, Mesrine relieved them of their guns, keys and papers, and ripped the telephone wires from the wall.

He was handing a gun to Rives when the door to the office opened. Two nurses from the prison infirmary came in, their smiles dropping to looks of horror. They froze.

"Mesdames, welcome," greeted Mesrine. "Close the door and be quiet."

One of the nurses looked at the warder sitting on the floor, his head bleeding. "He will live," said Mesrine. "And so will you if you behave."

Besse tugged at his sleeve. "Take them hostage, *Le Grand.*"

"No." The look in his eyes said more than the simple negative. "Ladies, if you will excuse us?" The prisoners backed out of the office. Mesrine locked the door and threw the key down the corridor.

He knew exactly which of the other keys would fit the main double doors of the top-security wing, and the three men were out into the yard in moments.

On the other side of the area, the Chief of Works was standing at the base of a ladder. Up above, a workman was fitting new bars onto the window of an empty cell.

The Chief of Works was aware only that two warders and a prisoner were approaching across the yard. He thought nothing wrong with the request of the big warder, the one with the moustache, to move the ladder into the outer courtyard between the inner and outer walls. It was needed urgently.

Exchanging banter with the warders, the Chief of Works and the workman dutifully carried the ladder between them.

As they approached the iron door in the inner wall, five men came round a far corner: three prisoners escorted by two genuine guards.

Rives gasped a nervous warning, but Mesrine and Besse already had their guns raised. "Gentlemen, good morning," Mesrine gave a little bow. "Yes, it is I, Mesrine. If you would be so kind as to join our little group?" It was an invitation they could not refuse.

The door leading to the outer courtyard was open. Mesrine looked at the Chief of Works. The Chief of Works looked back at him blankly.

Across the courtyard, a sentry box stood in front of the outer wall. Although prison regulations forbade sentries leaving the reinforced bullet-proof box whilst on duty, the man was already outside, rifle slung casually over his shoulder, smoking a cigarette. He saw four warders and assorted other men approaching.

"*Merde alors*, what is this?" He made no move for his gun, but the half-smoked cigarette was stamped out.

The largest of the warders strolled over to him, smiling. The smile disappeared as he raised the pistol in his hand. "I am Mesrine. You may have heard of me. Hand over your gun or I will kill you."

As he passed the surrendered rifle to Rives, Mesrine ordered the other men to place the ladder against the wall. He did not notice that one of the warders had gone missing, sneaking back through the inner door…

Besse climbed the ladder first, reached the top of the wall and straddled it. Fixing the grappling hook in place, he went down the outside with the aid of the rope and jumped the last couple of metres into Rue Messier, narrowly missing some dustbins by the foot of the wall. He looked up, waiting for the next man to come over.

Then an alarm began to scream.

"Merde! Vite!" Mesrine nodded for Rives to climb the ladder.

The young man hesitated, his nerve failing at the last moment. "I don't know, *Le Grand*."

With a curse, Mesrine climbed the ladder himself. He reached the top of the wall and looked back. Armed guards were rushing into the courtyard. A bullet skimmed past. "Carman. Carman!" he shouted. "Now or never!" He disappeared over the top.

Making the decision, Rives ran up the ladder. Wood chipped off the rungs as the guards fired. He had the sentry's rifle and, as he reached the top, he stopped to return fire. Then he threw the rifle into the road below and began to slide down the rope.

As Mesrine hit the street, armed policemen appeared from the front of the prison. A little way down the road, Besse was running. He stopped abruptly as he saw the policemen.

As far as the policemen were concerned, they saw two armed

warders in the street.

"Quick, over here!" shouted Mesrine. "It's Mesrine trying to escape!"

Rives was halfway down the rope.

Mesrine raised his pistol and fired, deliberately missing Rives. Rives stopped to look round, holding onto the rope with both hands.

Besse had resumed his run.

"I'll cover the front!" Mesrine screamed at the policemen. "He should give you no trouble. Take him back, will you?" He nodded at the frozen figure halfway up the rope.

As Mesrine disappeared left into the Rue du Faubourg St Jacques, completely in the opposite direction to the front of the prison, one of the policemen, in a state of panic, fired at Carman Rives.

In the Place St Jacques, Besse was waving down a white Renault 20. The driver stopped the car sharply for the rather anxious-looking man in uniform.

Mesrine ran up, fury on his face. "They shot Carman. The *bastards!*"

He pointed the pistol through the side window and his finger tightened on the trigger. "OUT!"

Paul Richer obeyed.

With Mesrine driving, the Renault shot away, across the Place and through the red light at the intersection of the Rue St Jacques. Overhead a metro thundered along the railway, its passengers oblivious to the drama below. Soon enough they would read about it in the papers and see it on the television.

The Renault headed south on the Rue de la Tomb Issoire. Although furious about Rives, more than anything furious with himself for involving the young man, the driver managed to smile. Jacques Mesrine and François Besse had done it.

They had escaped from 'the great unbustable', La Santé prison.

The 7.65 bullet hit Carman Rives in the chest, probably killing him instantly. His head lolled and bashed against the wall of the prison with a dull, hollow sound that echoed halfway down the road. His grip on the rope slackened and his body crashed to the street below, landing on the dustbins and scattering them like tenpins.

The policeman who had fired the shot came over, his panic turning into a triumphant grin. Was this Mesrine? Had he actually shot Mesrine? If not, those two warders would get the bastard round the front.

The death rattle groaned from Carman Rives' throat and his dead eyes stared upwards. He seemed to be looking at something. On the wall, just above where his dead head had hit, was a plaque. It remembered eighteen men of the Resistance executed inside La Santé by the Germans in the Second World War. It read:

EXECUTED ON THE ORDERS OF A GOVERNMENT SERVING THE ENEMY

2ᴵᴱᴹᴱ PARTIE

‡

LA POURSUITE

The escape of Jacques Mesrine from La Santé prison is timed at 10:25 on Monday 8 May 1978, the time that Mesrine's feet touched the ground outside the prison.

The police were in a state of panic. In the aftermath of Mesrine's escape, roadblocks were set up on all major routes out of Paris, and railway stations and airports were hastily put under surveillance. One thousand extra police were immediately called into the capital, and in the coming days others would be recalled from leave.

Commissaire Serge Devos, on his very first day as the new Head of the **Brigade de Répression de Banditisme (BRB)** *was given the task of recapturing Mesrine and Besse.*

All French television and radio programmes were interrupted with news of the escape. Special programmes on Jacques Mesrine were hastily assembled.

Soon the switchboards of every major police headquarters in France, both regional and national, were jammed. People had seen Mesrine. By 13:00 he had been seen in Lille, Dunkirk, Bordeaux, Lyons, Marseilles, Nice – and even Vienna.

‡

13. Flics

"Have you heard?" Commissaire Fleury-Goujon poked his head round the office door. "Mesrine escaped from La Santé half an hour ago."

"*What?* Bloody hell!" Chief Inspector Gerard stood up, ash falling from the cigarette in his lips. "I didn't actually believe it."

"When's Paul on?"

"He's on now. Out somewhere. The office'll have it logged. Shall I - " He reached for the phone.

"No, no. I'll see him when he comes back. *Merci.*"

Gerard followed the Commissaire out into the corridor. "Broussard taking it on?" [*Broussard was Head of the* Brigade de Recherche et d'Intervention, *the man who had arrested Mesrine in September 1973.*]

"No, they've given it to Devos and his new gang."

"The BRB?"

"Yes. Poor bugger. Apparently Peyrefitte [*the Minister of Justice*] is breathing down his neck already. Giscard's taken an immediate personal interest. He wants him caught and caught now. Paris will be saturated. Everyone remotely suspicious will be questioned. All his old haunts and old cronies will be watched. If someone so much as mumbles Mesrine's name in their sleep, they will be arrested."

"Easier said than done with the resources we have. And Mesrine is popular, there will be plenty of people willing to help him. It is *us* the public doesn't like. He's a d'Artagnan. Or who's that English fellow... Robert Hood?"

"*Oui*. Except Mesrine robs the rich to give to himself." The Commissaire stopped by the door to his office. "Was there anything, Claude?"

"No, sir, no. Got to wash my hands."

"What about that South American diplomat?"

"Think we sorted him out. It'll be in my weekly report, or you can have a special sooner if you like."

"No, it's your case. Ask Paul to see me when he's back, will you?"

"Yes, sir."

Gerard pushed by a civilian clerk coming out of the WC, and unzipped in front of the nearest porcelain. He pissed like an elephant.

You bastard, Richer. Did you actually do it? Did *you* spring Jacques Mesrine from La Santé? No, that was impossible. *N'est-ce pas? Ou pas n'est-ce pas?* And if so, why?

What are you up to?

Gerard rezipped, flicked the pee off his shoes, didn't even think about washing his hands, and went back to the office.

‡

14. Voleur

"Forgive me for asking, monsieur, but may I use your bath oil?"

In response, the kindly grey head of the seventy year old homosexual looked round the kitchen door and smiled. Mesrine was naked except for a short towel around his waist, and he was wiping away the dredges of shaving foam after taking off his moustache. Behind him the bath water ran furiously, splashing the portable television that he had balanced on top of the bidet.

"But of course, *mon ami*," said the homosexual, quietly admiring the big, muscular man. "This apartment and the things in it are yours for as long as you wish. Dinner will be ready in one hour."

The master criminal had known the old queer Marcel (or Marcelle as he liked to be known) for some years, he was a friend of a mutual friend. A swift phone call by someone on Mesrine's behalf yesterday afternoon had ensured that Marcel was prepared for his special guest.

The apartment in the Rue Jean Nicot, near Les Invalides, was a typical piece of Mesrine cunning. Les Invalides is on the western edge of Paris' *quartier* of central government. Nearby is the Assemblée Nationale and just to the north is the Quai d'Orsay itself. Mesrine's principle of never fleeing but sheltering in the eye of the storm had seen him through on many occasions. The police would think he was well away from the capital by now - and even if they didn't, the apartment was clean. Mesrine knew for certain that the police did not know of the place or of Marcel.

Similarly, Mesrine always believed that searching for one needle in a haystack was harder than searching for two, so he and Besse had split up after abandoning the commandeered Renault 20 in the Rue André-Theuriet down near Malakoff. The police would establish it as a hired car and their enquiries would reveal that the hirer had used false papers. End of trail.

He stepped into the bath and lay back in the *Floris*-scented water. He felt pleased with himself. It had all gone smoothly, as he had been promised. Keys, people and things had been in the right place at the right time - except for poor Carman Rives. He should never have invited him along, it had been a foolish impetuosity. He had never intended for Rives to escape, of course. He was to be a decoy, to be recaptured and throw attention away from the 'warders'. He had obviously underestimated the venom of authority. To shoot Carmen in cold blood. Somebody would pay for that. In the meantime, Mesrine would ensure that Rives had the best funeral money could buy.

And at some stage he would have to figure out how to obtain a document. An anonymous document, subject unknown. How would he know if he had the right item? *Merde alors*, if it was that important he would certainly know it when he saw it.

Now, plans. He would phone the *Capitaine* and confirm his safe arrival. Then he would lie low for as long as it took for the immediate fuss to die down. He reckoned on a month. Marcel would be accommodating. Money would be needed, though, and he might have to make one small excursion out at sometime.

He let the water flap around his neck and grinned as he saw his face flash up on the television screen. Not bad, taken a couple of years ago, moustache, no beard.

"Marcelle, cherie," he called over his shoulder, "you don't have such a thing as a cigar, do you?"

He settled down to listen to details of his past exploits in the news bulletin. If they got any facts wrong he would contact the producer in the morning.

Mardi 9 Mai

The second casualty of the Mesrine escape (after Carmen Rives) was Monsieur Pierre Aymard, the Director of Prison Administration. While the hunt continued, with police forces throughout France visiting every address of every person who had ever known Jacques Mesrine, Monsieur Aymard received a call from the Chief Secretary's Office of the Ministry of Justice that morning.

As Aymard looked for the last time out of his office window over the Place Vendôme, he was told that he had been removed from his post. The escape had damaged the credibility of the French penal system and the reputation of the Ministry of Justice.

‡

15. Flic et les Anglais

Lundi 15 Mai

At 14:30 on the day that Jacques Mesrine entered the second week of his self-imposed seclusion, Claude Gerard entered foreign territory over on the Faubourg St Honoré. The Chief Inspector had been asked, if he would be so kind, to pop across to the British Embassy when he had a spare moment, on a completely informal basis, naturally.

Behind the diffident, reserved Anglo-Saxon manner, Gerard recognised a summons when he heard one. He did not like 'visiting'. Meant he had to do his shirt collar up. Nearly bloody strangled him.

"Claude, old chap, how nice to see you." Small, stocky Ron Becker came to meet him at the ornate Reception.

"Ronald, 'ow are you?"

"Can't complain, old duck, can't complain." Becker was Gerard's usual liaison. Supposedly just a normal Foreign Office executive officer, beneath the veneer that fooled no one Becker was a member of the British security service.

"There is somesing I can do for you?" queried Gerard. "You are 'aving problems?"

Becker smiled at the slovenly Frenchman with the dog-end hanging from his lips. His collar looked tight enough to strangle him. "Problems? No, no, not at all. Just something that's come up from back home. Nothing much. Actually, not really my baby. There's someone who'd like a word, Claude old love."

"A word?"

"Or two. This way."

Gerard was ushered upstairs, along plushly carpeted corridors with old paintings of long-dead Englishmen on the walls, and into a small but comfortably-furnished office.

The man who stood up from behind the large desk was tall and immaculately dressed. His woollen suit probably cost what Gerard earned in a month. But he was almost painfully thin, suspicious eyes sunk into his skeletal face. "Chief Inspector," he shook Gerard's hand with the warmth of a midwinter's day. He did not introduce himself but apologised in surprisingly good and well-accented French for asking him to call on a public holiday and please would he sit down?

As he sat, Gerard turned to see Becker leaving the room. Gerard shifted back, noticing the examination he was getting from the sunken eyes. He pulled out his cigarettes.

"I'd rather you didn't." It was the statement of a man used to being obeyed.

Gerard stopped with a fresh Disque halfway to his lips, the old *mégot* between his fingers. Who was this damn *rosbeef*?

He lowered his arm and replaced the Disque and butt tenderly into the packet.

Without preamble the man said, "I believe you have special responsibility for La Dame?"

Gerard replaced the packet into his pocket. "I think you had better ask my superiors, m'sieur, through proper channels."

The face did not react. "You *are* the BCP official charged with UK interests?"

"Among many others, yes."

"Then these are the proper channels."

"Nevertheless - "

"Nevertheless nothing."

Gerard inhaled, bit his tongue, and just decided against

standing up and walking out. Instead he asked, "What do you want, m'sieur?"

"You have not answered my original question."

"And until I find out what this is about, neither will I."

This time an eyebrow was raised. "I see." Then he asked, "A drink?"

"I beg your pardon?"

"Would you like a drink?" The man actually smiled.

"Er… thank you." Gerard's fingers fiddled with an imaginary cigarette. "Do you have cognac?"

"Certainly." The man stood up and walked over to a glass-fronted cabinet. He spoke as he selected and poured. "Word has reached us from London that La Dame lost something not so long ago. Something important."

"I see."

"We have been asked - very discreetly and unofficially you understand - to (a) see if the rumour is true and (b) ask what is being done about it."

"I see."

Gerard accepted the generous glass of liquor.

The man waited, standing in front of him. Gerard sipped the drink.

"Well?"

"M'sieur?"

Lightening flashed in the eyes and then was replaced by amusement. Now it was the Englishman's turn to say, "I see."

Gerard put his glass down on the rim of the desk and again reached for his cigarettes. This time no curt command stopped him before he lit up.

Through smoke Gerard said, "I thought you people regarded La Dame as purely an embarrassment, the sooner she departed this life the better. I am surprised you have taken an interest."

"Therefore you are confirming my point (a)." The man sat back down.

"Possibly." Gerard surveyed the top of his Disque and blew on it. "I am still surprised at your interest."

"Frankly, so am I. But I am a mere pawn of my masters, I simply do as I am bidden."

And I'm the Sun King, thought Gerard. He said, "Monsieur, I will confirm your point (a). There was a robbery, things went missing. But I am interested to know how you found out."

"The walls, monsieur, have ears."

Gerard looked around.

"Oh no, not here. I was speaking in metaphor."

"Ah. One of your little British *tournures familières*, hmm?"

"The loss has got to the ears of someone in London. Cards on the table - "

Gerard glanced at the desk top.

" - I know nothing about this other than what I am told. La Dame has, apparently, lost something. London is asking questions. So, if you wish to enlighten me further…?"

"Monsieur, with respect, I do not."

"I see. Just as well, perhaps. As to my point (b)…?"

Gerard put down the empty glass, noting that there was no offer of a refill, and looked around for an ashtray. Finding none, he tapped his Disque into his cupped hand. "As to your point (b), I am not in charge of the enquiry."

"You are not?"

"*Non*. Usually I would be, but on this occasion a colleague was assigned the task."

"Oh."

"However, I can tell you that the matter is being looked into. But, to be frank m'sieur, robberies occur every day, throughout France, throughout Europe, throughout the world. Notwithstanding the owner of the goods in this instance, enquiries are enquiries and the chances of a successful outcome are… remote."

The man was nodding. "Naturally, I understand. Which

brings me to point (c)."

"Point (c)?" Gerard sat with a palmful of ash in one hand and his cigarette stub in the other.

"Point (c). I am to ask, unofficially, that London - through me - is kept informed of *any* developments, and that if it is humanly possible the missing articles be retrieved."

"I understand."

"And I hope that means more to you than it does to me."

"Really, m'sieur, no. I have said that it is not my case. You are speaking to the wrong man."

The man sniffed. "I think not. You are our BCP liaison officer. When your department was set up at the instigation of your late President himself, we were promised the fullest co-operation from yourselves. A report to the contrary at ambassador level would not, I am sure, be well received."

Nasty.

Gerard was silent.

He made a show of looking around. Then he calmly tipped the palmful of ash onto the carpet. "I understand, m'sieur. So your point (c) is?"

"Keep us informed, Chief Inspector, keep us informed."

"*Bien.*" Gerard stood up, resisting the urge to stub out the cigarette on the polished desk top. "*If* I find out anything, I will let you know. For whom shall I ask?"

"Becker, your normal contact."

They walked over to the door and out.

"Not you?"

"Becker will know even less of what it is about than I do. Just leave a sealed report with him.

"Shall I address it to you?

"No, just leave it blank, he'll know."

They reached the top of the stairway which led down into the wide, echoing foyer. Three steps down, Gerard turned. "Monsieur, I do not know your name."

"No, you don't," said the Englishman as he turned and walked away.

Jeudi 18 Mai

Ten days since the escape. The hunt for Mesrine continued. The failure of the prison officials and the police was discussed in Parliament. The Press showed the authorities no mercy.

The police were angered by the negative publicity. But what could they do? Everyone whom they thought Mesrine might contact was being watched – there were even police marksmen on the roofs of buildings surrounding the home of Mesrine's daughter, Sabrina.

To cover their embarrassment and plunging morale, the police made frequent announcements that Mesrine was about to be recaptured.

But in reality there was nothing. All the sightings had proved false. There had not been one reliable tip-off.

Mesrine had vanished into thin air.

‡

16. Voleur

Samedi 27 Mai

Deauville is a stylish resort in Normandy, a meticulously clean seaside town much frequented by well-to-do visitors from both France and throughout Europe. The place is littered with high quality, expensive villas, usually open for only three or four months a year when their rich owners take their summer break.

As with most haunts of the wealthy in France, Deauville is heavily policed, a state protection which the residents are only too pleased to pay for because of the ever-present threat of robberies or, worse, kidnapping.

The casino in Deauville is a huge, ornate building redolent of times when fortunes could be made or lost with the spin of a wheel or a turn of a card, and horse-drawn carriages would pull up outside to collect their ecstatic or suicidal owners. Fortunes could still be won or lost, of course, but in the more careful and less dramatic late twentieth century the chances were that the gentleman, or sometimes lady, win or lose, would still drive away afterwards in his/her Audi or Lamborghini, not too worse for the experience.

Fortunes can not only be won or lost, they can also be taken. It is recorded that on 27 May 1978 Jacques Mesrine and François Besse robbed the casino in Deauville. Their haul was a mere thirteen thousand francs, small even by working class standards. By Deauville standards it was nothing more than petit monnaie.

‡

17. Flics

Mardi 30 Mai

Paul Richer handed over a ten franc note, accepted his two francs change and the kilo of early strawberries, and walked further up through the crowds on the Rue Lepic, Montmartre's food market. It was a warm, pleasant day and, as usual, the old artists' quarter of Paris was swarming with tourists.

He stopped at another stall for carrots, beans and mushrooms, then popped into a boucherie for his weekly treat of a small steak, and then into a boulangerie for a crusty loaf and tomorrow's breakfast croissants.

Shopping complete, he turned right and continued up the hill. On his left, tourists posed beneath the Moulin de Galette.

He first became aware of the vehicle as he turned right into Rue de l'Abreuvoir. There were always vehicles, of course, trying to negotiate the narrow, cobbled streets of the *butte*; usually experienced residents or careless taxi drivers. Therefore one more white Peugeot should not seem out of the ordinary. But this driver was not experienced or careless, but cautious and careful - a sure sign of a novice on the streets of the hill. And he was moving slowly, keeping a steady but regular distance.

Richer nipped right down Rue des Saules. The car followed.

Richer walked on again and then stopped abruptly, pretending to adjust his parcels of shopping. The vehicle stopped.

Shit.

He walked on.

Richer stopped to look in the window of a clothes shop. The car slowed.

Who could it be? Why would they be following him? His CRS days were behind him, he had retired from this sort of skulduggery. Perhaps he was being too suspicious, the paranoia of his last days at des Orfèvres creeping back. It could just simply be a Parisian who happened to be going his way. Not.

Hell, this was ridiculous. Montmartre, mid-afternoon, in late spring, and he, a Chief Inspector of the Surêté, was being followed.

Not breaking pace but casually looking around as he stepped off the kerb, he crossed Rue Saint Vincent. Now it became quieter, off the tourist track. A little way along he turned right, descending the steep steps of the Cimitière Saint Vincent.

No vehicle could come down here, the road was twenty metres above and behind. Whoever it was would have to alight and follow on foot.

It was silent among the graves. The little tombs were about the height of a man, all different in design but each with the same sombre purpose. Some had doors leading into vaults, others were simply exaggerated headstones. Some of the more recent ones contained framed photographs of their occupants.

As in all Paris cemeteries, there were cats; some looking suspiciously from behind the stones, others brazenly walking about and eyeing the intruder with feline contempt. One dozed on top of the tomb of Utrillo. Over in a corner, a ginger tom pissed his territorial boundary.

Richer came to a stop halfway in, in a position facing the steps. Above one side of him was the road, above the other the back of a block of apartments out on Rue Caulaincourt. He rested his bags behind a vault and crouched down. He wished he had his gun with him.

He could just see the wheels of the Peugeot, stationary on the road above. Someone in a raincoat - stupid for such a lovely day - came from the far side. With no attempt at stealth the person walked down the steps, almost falling down the last three where they were broken.

Richer grunted in annoyance and stood up. "What the bloody hell do you think you're doing, you stupid bastard!"

Claude Gerard jumped as his colleague appeared from nowhere. His cigarette popped out of his mouth and fell onto the grass. He bent down, picked it up and replaced it in his mouth without so much as blowing the dirt off. He smiled. "God, this place smells of piss. *Ça va, Paul?* Wanted a word."

"Why all the cloak and dagger?"

"You've been on leave."

"Exactly, and I still am until next week. Can't I have a rest, for Christ's sake?"

"I was coming to see you at your apartment, and I noticed you in the street."

"Ever heard of the telephone?"

"Truth is, I wanted to get out of the office. Fleury's been on my back about our resident Iranian."

"What is so damn urgent?"

"Paul, I..." Gerard actually looked shamefaced. "I wanted to apologise. Make amends. I've been thinking about it while you've been off. You know, we haven't exactly started off on the right foot."

"And whose fault is that?"

"Okay, okay. But I thought we might try to patch things up. Look, do you fancy a drink?"

"Patch things up? Gerard, you were the one who started the aggression in the first place... Oh fuck it, this is bloody ridiculous! Two grown men, two Chief Inspectors of police, skulking about in a cemetery. If one of our lads comes along he'll have us up for gross indecency in a graveyard. Look -

Claude - I'm on my way home. Can't it wait until Monday?"

"If you like…" Gerard turned to go.

"No, hold on." If it was an olive branch, Richer did not want to reject it out of hand. But the chances were this *con* was up to something. "I can't go for a drink laden down with shopping. Come back to my apartment if you like. For a quick *Napoléon*." He shook his head at the proffered packet of Disques.

"Rue Lamarck you live, isn't it?"

"Number forty-eight." As you know damn well. "You'll have to drive out onto Caulaincourt and round."

"*D'accord*."

"And here, you can take one of these bloody bags as well."

Richer's apartment consisted of four rooms on the top floor of the block, facing south. Rue Lamarck skirts the northern side of the Montmartre *butte*, so one half of the view from the *salle de jour* was obscured by the huge whitestone magnificence of Sacré Coeur on the crest. But just to the east, where the Basilica did not extend, one could see at an angle over the ridge with a view sweeping across to the towers of Notre Dame and beyond.

Gerard insisted on helping to unpack the shopping, dropping the mushrooms onto the kitchen floor. As he bent down to pick them up, something black and furry shot out from underneath the fridge and stopped a rolling champignon in its tracks.

"Jesus Christ!"

Gerard jumped back, squashing two mushrooms under foot.

Richer looked round nonchalantly. "Chivas! *Bonjour petit*. No, that's not for you."

"I didn't know you had a cat," said Gerard.

"No? Claude meet Chivas. Chivas meet Uncle Claude." Richer smiled. One brown trouser to you Gerard.

"Er…" Gerard nodded to the animal. "*Bonjour*."

Richer poured two double *Napoléons* and asked if Gerard would like something to eat. "If we are burying the hatchet, let us bury it in a tournedos."

"*Merci bien, Paul.* But will you have enough? Surely you shopped just for one?"

"I can stretch it."

"*Non, non, pas de probleme!*" Gerard stood up. "I will be back in a moment. You - er - prepare the mushrooms." Before Richer could say anything more he was out of the door and his feet were thumping down the stairs.

Richer looked at the cat.

"What do you think, Chivas?" The cat jumped up onto the worktop as Richer opened a can of beef and chicken liver. "What is he up to? We must watch ourselves with him." He forked the food into a bowl. "No doubt his intentions will be revealed in due course."

In reply, Chivas thrust his backside into his flatmate's face and began to eat.

Gerard was back within twenty minutes with an additional steak, two bottles of Le Piat d'Or rouge and some cat treats. "Three bachelors together, hmm?"

Richer busied himself in the kitchen while Gerard admired the comfortable, cosy apartment and enthused over the view.

Thirty minutes later the two men sat down on the easy chairs in the living room and devoured the rarely-done tournedos, lightly fried mushrooms, carrots and beans, bread and special sauce upon which Richer would not be drawn as to the contents. Already with two double brandies inside them, they now had a bottle of the Piat d'Or each.

They mellowed.

The conversation became quite pally.

"I can understand why you've never married," Gerard leant back in his chair and rubbed his generous gut. "You cook superbly, you have Pigalle within walking distance. Why be saddled with one woman permanently? Why the expense of a wife? What one would cost you you could spend once a month on a full night with one of the local lovelies. Now as for me, well I don't mind telling you, sometimes Mathilde and the four brats get me down. That's why I'm enjoying this evening so much."

"But your children must be growing up now."

"In their teens - and that is the most dangerous age, especially for the girl. You know why. One of the boys is at university, he's okay, outgrown it. But the other two are yobs, potential or actual... It's good to get out."

Richer sympathised and cleared away the plates which Chivas had been giving a pre-wash with his tongue. Gerard poured wine into both their glasses and broke open a packet of Disques. He sauntered over to the floor to ceiling window and quietly watched the lights of Paris come on beyond the Basilica.

Richer came back in.

"Want help with the washing up?" Gerard turned.

"It's in the machine."

"Ah! All mod cons. Here," he held out the Disques. Richer took one and accepted a light. "Love this view. If you ever leave here, let me know. I'll ditch Mathilde and move in myself. My own little bachelor pad."

"You'll have to ask my co-occupant."

"Does he go out?"

"I leave a window ajar for him. Perfectly safe. He loves the rooftops."

"More wine?"

"Sure. Coffee's on."

Gerard exhaled a lungful of smoke. "Look, Paul. I honestly wish to apologise for the way things have gone. It was an unfortunate start. I admit there is no love lost between the CRS and, well, any other branch I suppose, but I shouldn't have put it on a personal level. Genuinely, I'm sorry."

Richer waved his cigarette in the air. "Forget it, Claude. Harsh words were said on both sides. We have to work side by side, so…" He extended his hand. Gerard took it. They shook.

Later, over their third cup of Maison du Café, the air heavy with the combined odours of the evening, Gerard asked, "How's things with La Dame? Everything seems to have gone quiet."

Richer drew on his Disque. Ah, here it comes. "It's going to take time, probably a long time," he said.

"Usually she's on the Minister's back if it's not settled within a day."

"This is special."

"What is it?" It could not have been more ingenuously put.

Richer surveyed the empty cup on the arm of his chair. "Another coffee?" He reached for the jug on the warm plate.

"Why not? Any more of your superb brandy?"

Richer held up the bottle. "Should be enough for two. In the cup?"

"Great."

Richer poured the coffee on top of the *Napoléon* and sat back. He felt relaxed. He felt good.

"What about La Dame?" repeated Gerard.

Richer stifled a burp and then said, "She's lost something…"

Claude Gerard left Paul Richer's apartment at 22:30. He was more than a little pleased with himself.

A fruitful evening Claude, you old dog. A very fruitful evening. He had heard the story of the robbery at Number 24. So, the old woman had lost a fortune in jewellery. But was that all it was? Of course she would want it back.

If and how Mesrine fitted into all this he had yet to establish. It was unwise to strain the new détente at its birth. Perhaps he was reading things into things which just did not exist. He had no proof that Paul Richer had anything to do with Mesrine, let alone his escape from La Santé. His presumptions had been guided by two letters scribbled on a piece of paper, some hieroglyphics and a date marked in red in Richer's office diary, and the fact that both men had served in Algeria at the same time.

So? Many men had served in Algeria at that time. And the date in the diary was a day on which Mesrine had *not* escaped.

He climbed into his white Peugeot.

In a way the evening had gone as planned. In another way it had not. He had confirmed part of the information. La Dame had lost some jewellery and wanted it back. That gave him a base from which to work on the request of the British. But also he had modified his opinion about Richer, which he had not set out to do. The bastard had become at least semi-legitimate. He wasn't such a bad bloke after all. And that would make Gerard's task all the harder.

He must cement the new friendship.

He wondered if Paul would fancy going to the next Paris St Germain match?

‡

18. Voleur

Lundi 12 Juin

Jacques Mesrine climbed the steps from the Guy Moquet metro station, looked around casually and began to walk up the Avenue de Saint Ouen. He walked slowly, enjoying the freshness of freedom, letting the hazy sun caress his face. It was his first time out of doors since his excursion to the north coast two weeks ago, and he had forgotten how good the open air tasted, even the open air of a city.

He entered the first bar he came to, just past the Rue Collette, and ordered a kir at the *zinc*. It was mid-morning and there was only a handful of people in the place. No one took any notice of the man with glasses, clean shaven, hair parted in the centre, slightly protruding chin, dressed in a crisp dark blue two piece suit.

Leaning on the bar, Mesrine began to read yesterday's *France-Dimanche*. On page 9 was a picture of himself and an article on his love life. Lurid stuff. If only he had had half the women they alleged! But that would still be ten times as many as normal men!

"Some man, that Mesrine," grunted the proprietor behind the bar, nodding at the paper.

The customer looked up, almost diffidently. "I've never really followed his exploits myself."

"But you've heard of him?"

"Oh yes."

"Naturally, everyone has heard of Mesrine. Here," the proprietor leant forward conspiratorially. "He used to live around these parts."

"No!"

"*Mais oui!* Down in Clichy. Occasionally he would come up here."

"Heaven! In this actual bar?"

"*Oui.* In fact, he has stood right where you are standing now."

Mesrine, who had never been in the place before in his life, gasped.

"But did you feel safe with a murderer around?"

"Pah! Mesrine a murderer? Never. He's killed people, certainly. Thirty-nine of them - "

"Thirty-nine!"

"*Mais oui. Trente-neuf.* But he's not a murderer in the sense we know it. He does not go out to kill. Only if people get in his way. Well, it is understandable, *n'est-ce pas*?"

"*Oh oui, oui.*"

"You're not from these parts?"

"I'm from Nice. I've just been posted to Paris."

"What do you do? No - don't tell me, let me guess. It's a hobby of mine." The proprietor stared long and hard at Mesrine's face. There was not even a flicker of recognition, no mental connection between the customer and the face he had just seen in the newspaper. "I know! You work in a bank? Am I right or am I right?"

There was admiration in the customer's eyes. "How can you tell?"

"Ah, I have a nose for these things. You develop it after years behind a bar."

"And you are so right! I mean, I could have been anything!"

"Ah!" The proprietor nodded knowingly and tapped the side

of his nose. "This never lets me down."

The banker asked, "Don't know of any apartments to let round here, do you? I'm in an hotel at the moment, but I'd like to get my own place. No hurry, the bank's paying, but an hotel's not the same."

"Nothing like your own roof, eh? Another kir?"

"*Oui merci.*"

The proprietor poured one for himself also. "Not many places about nowadays." He made a show of thinking as the banker paid for both drinks with two one hundred franc notes and indicated that he did not want the change. "Try further up near the Porte."

"That's up that way?"

"*Oui.* Out and to the left."

"*D'accord, merci bien monsieur.*" Mesrine raised his glass. "*Salut.*"

"To Mesrine!" said the proprietor.

"Mesrine?" said the banker. "And why not?"

After five places had proved negative, a shopkeeper (with the help of some innocent charm and the purchase of a rather expensive *Cardin* silk tie) directed him to the concièrge of 124 Passage Charles Albert, near the Porte de Saint Ouen.

It was lunchtime and the aroma of coffee floated from a saucepan on an old gas stove in the corner of the *loge*. The concièrge - Madame La Salle, an old harridan with a gruff manner - was about to start on a baguette and a slice of camembert. She did not take kindly to being disturbed, but the charming, apologetic manner of the smart businessman eventually won her round (although she would never admit to it).

Monsieur Lenoir, the banker from Nice, that afternoon paid three months' rent in advance and took possession of the keys to a ground floor studio apartment.

‡

19. Flics

Jeudi 15 Juin

The telephone on the desk of Chief Inspector Paul Richer rang at 10:39 that morning. He answered with his surname.

The voice on the other end was muffled. "Bruno."

Richer looked across at Claude Gerard. His head was stuck in a file and surrounded by a halo of cigarette smoke.

"Oh yes, hello."

"I am now on the move."

"You are in the city?"

"No questions please. I will set things in motion."

"Good. Things are calm."

"I am pleased to hear it. But remember the terms. Me first, you second. In my own time. I will call you as and when. I must go."

"I'm not tracing."

"Of course not, *chef*. But there are half a million other people who might be." The line went dead.

Richer replaced the receiver and lit a Gitanes, throwing one over to land on Gerard's desk.

"Cheers." Gerard did not even look up.

The telephone on Gerard's desk rang. He answered with a grunt.

The voice at the other end said. "Hello Claude old stick. Ron Becker."

Gerard looked across at Richer. He was staring out of the window.

"Oh yes, hello."

"Any news on La Dame's lost possessions?"

"I'm working on it."

"Of course you are, old fruit. But any news?"

"I have progressed. When I am satisfied, I will report."

"You do that, old son. You do that." The line went dead.

"Want some coffee?"

Gerard looked up with a start to see Richer standing over him. Had he been listening?

"Hmm?"

"I'm getting coffee," repeated Richer. "Want some?"

"Yeh, sure, sure."

"You're bloody engrossed. What've you got there?"

Gerard flicked the file. "An English diplomat, involved with a fancy whore."

"Oh? It's not only a stiff upper lip the *rosbeefs* have then? Going to warn him off?"

"Probably. Doesn't seem like anything sinister, no photos or anything. He just likes to screw." He lit the Gitanes. "Fancy coming to football sometime?"

Richer turned, halfway out the door. "Football?"

"There's a pre-season friendly soon. St Germain against some English club with a funny name."

"You got a spare ticket?"

"I can get one."

"Okay, if I'm not on. Tell you what, we'll see the match then you come back for a meal, huh? Mathilde won't mind, will she?"

"Mathilde can go bugger herself. She didn't even hear me come in the other night."

Richer chuckled and left the office.

Gerard smiled, noted the time and wrote something in the

file.

‡

20. Flic puis voleur

Samedi 17 Juin

The knock rebounded between the four doors, echoed along the corridor and fell headlong down the stairway. The second knock did the same. And the third.

Claude Gerard looked through the letter box. "Chivas? Chivas!"

Everyone, it seemed, was out on Saturday night.

He popped a few cat treats through the letter box, slipped a *bonbon* into his mouth and walked back downstairs. To call at Richer's apartment on his way home after a day's shooting out near Boissy had been a spur of the moment decision. He should have realised that the bachelor would be out. Wonder if he was with a woman?

Well, no *levant le coude* with Richer tonight. He would have to get back home to his beloved and the offspring.

Downstairs, even the concièrge was out.

It was getting dark as Gerard drove away, forced along the cobbled sidestreets by the *butte*'s one-way system. He had only a vague recollection of the route as last time he had been, if not drunk, certainly *sous l'empire*.

Eventually he came out under Sacré Coeur in the Boulevard de Rochechouart. He turned right and followed the main road along into Pigalle. In the Place Blanche, opposite the Moulin Rouge, he nearly ran down a maniac pedestrian crossing over on a green light. He slammed on his brakes.

"Watch where you're going, *imbécile!*" Gerard shouted through the side window. "*Andouille!*" He wrenched his gear stick into second and without a second glance drove off west towards his home in Levallois-Perret.

"Up yours, drunkard!" shouted Jacques Mesrine at the disappearing Peugeot, thrusting his middle finger into the air.

Mesrine's crisp new slacks gave the lie to the cap and shabby jacket above, but no one would notice. With the cheap Algerian cigarette hanging unlit from his lips, he would pass as any of the other members of Parisian lowlife hanging around the *quartier*.

As ever, Pigalle was Pigalle. It never changed. The smells of coffee and booze and exhausts, the new heavy frying odours from the hamburger joints, the warmth of the interminably flashing neon lights, the calls of touts outside the topless joints and sex clubs. The hooting of the vehicles and the chattering of people. And the girls.

The girls paraded their wares openly on the street, in amongst the African street traders (handmade goods spread out on the ground in front of them) and the inevitable pickpockets and chancers. Most of the ladies of the night left nothing to the imagination. Some stood in doorways in their night clothes, complete with the obligatory suspenders and jangling keys. Others paraded encased in studded leather, their tight garments revealing every crack and crevice of their body. Some walked dogs, whether for protection or purchase was debatable. Inevitably there were also men for sale, some macho studs, some high-rouged slags.

"Like some?" asked an enormous-breasted girl from a doorway, wiggling her orbs. There was a distinct love bite on one of them.

Mesrine grinned. "Later, *chérie*. You keep it hot for me, eh?"

"Hot? It will be roasting!"

"Good girl!"

Already she had turned to someone else.

This was Paris as Mesrine remembered it. His Paris. Lewd, dangerous but, in its own way, honest. You got what you paid for. But he could not remember there being so many people in Pigalle before, even on a Saturday. There seemed to be more traders, more girls, more customers, even more traffic like that *batârd* who had nearly knocked him over.

He walked into a bar on the south side of the Place, near the small church. It was busy and nobody took any notice of one more punter. Men sat around solving the problems of the world amongst the heady atmosphere of alcohol, tobacco, sweat and stale food. Two pinball machines *ping-pinged* near the front window as some kids in leather jackets tried the impossibility of topping the invented Highest Score on the fascia. At some of the tables girls did business, persuading clients to take them to hotels in the sidestreets where rooms were let by the hour and the porters were on a percentage.

Mesrine ordered a large calvados then sat down near the front window, facing sideways into the bar but with easy access out. Across the Place Blanche the electric lights on the mechanical windmill on top of the Moulin Rouge rotated and flashed, causing alternate red and white dotted reflections on the window and on Mesrine's face.

He waited.

‡

21. Voleur et poule

She came in about 23:30, looking for what was probably her fifth trick of the evening. Tall and of dark complexion, coarse-featured but in an attractive sort of way. She glanced casually at Mesrine, but his shabby appearance obviously dismissed him as a worthwhile client. She settled on a loud and patently drunk couple of Dutchmen at a table further in.

Mesrine watched and admired the way she did business. In twenty minutes she had persuaded them to buy four more rounds (she would be on a percentage), the last supposedly vintage champagne, certainly highly-priced and even more certainly *vin blanc* diluted fifty-fifty with *Perrier*. But the Dutchmen were too drunk to notice, they would have enjoyed it even if it had been sparkling dog's piss, which was not outside the bounds of possibility.

Ten minutes later the *ménage à trois* rose and left. Drunk or not, one of the men, the younger of the two, had a distinct bulge in the front of his jeans. She was going to have to earn her money this time.

Mesrine followed them out, keeping at a safe distance, strolling casually, looking for any watching eyes.

They turned right out of the bar and right again into Rue Fontaine. An argument was developing as they reached Rue de Douai and one of the men, with a dismissive wave of his arms, continued down Fontaine, leaving the woman with the one with the hard-on.

They entered a hotel in Rue de Douai.

Mesrine hung around in the street, knowing he would not attract attention from passers-by. A lot of men hang around in doorways and on corners in Pigalle at night.

He gave the woman and her client enough time to complete the formalities with the porter. The Dutchman would have to pay as much for the room for the hour as he would for the night in a good three star hotel in the 16th. The porter would give him a clean towel for which he would expect another *pourboire*, not obligatory but you would get your balls kicked in on the way out if you did not subscribe.

Another few minutes to get up to the room and for the woman to obtain her money immediately they went in. Then Mesrine entered the hotel.

In his years in the place, the porter had seen it all and his face was trained into showing no surprise or emotion at whatever might come into, or go on in, the hotel. So when Mesrine entered, the porter's face registered nothing. But he looked. He looked at Mesrine hard. And Mesrine looked back.

"*Ça va?*" asked the porter lowly.

"*Ça va,*" replied Mesrine.

"Congratulations."

"*Merci.* What room?"

"*Vingt-et-un.*"

"*Bien.*"

Five hundred francs (from a wallet lifted from an American tourist two hours earlier) sped across the countertop and was gone.

"I do not exist."

"*Naturellement, Le Grand.*"

Mesrine climbed the uncarpeted stairs to the second floor. The stairway and corridors were only dimly lit and the place stank of the familiar bleachy smell. Every fourth step did not creak.

Muffled noises came from three of the five rooms on the corridor. He stood outside 21 for a second, listening. Then he smiled, stepped back and kicked the door in.

A frozen tableau greeted him. The woman was naked except for white suspenders and laddered black stockings. The Dutchman still had on his shirt and socks, but the rest of him was bare. They were by the sink, the woman in the process of washing the man's jutting member. She screamed, once, as the door crashed open.

Mesrine had never seen an erection go down so quickly. One second it was there, the next it was gone, like an icicle in a furnace. The woman was left holding a limp sausage. The Dutchman gasped fearfully and tried to cover himself, like a schoolboy caught fiddling in the toilets.

"Out!" shouted Mesrine, picking up the man's trousers and flinging them into the corridor.

"But - "

"OUT! Now!" He grabbed the man by the hair and propelled him across the room.

"I have paid good money - " began the Dutchman in broken French.

"Shut it, Frans. *Deux s'amusent, trois s'embêtent.* Be thankful I don't take the rest of it off you, you bloody foreigner!" With a shove, Mesrine had him in the corridor. Kicking his trousers halfway down the stairs, he counselled "And don't let me see your face around here or anywhere ever again!"

He stepped back into the room and slammed the door behind him.

He waited, his back against the door. There was a rapid *thump-thump*ing down the stairs outside.

The woman was still by the sink, drying her hands on the towel. She looked at Mesrine expressionlessly.

"How much did he pay you?" he asked.

"A thousand."

"A thousand? But the summer sales don't start till next month."

"Needs must."

Mesrine admired the still firm body and remarkably jutting hard-nippled breasts. He held her eyes with his. "I would pay you a million."

"I didn't think you were coming." Her voice was deep and hard. "Any later and I would have had to have seen him off into the sink."

Mesrine pouted. "You are two floors up. I was as quick as I could be."

She stared at him. Then she smiled warmly. "Jacques."

"Janou."

She came across. Putting her arms up around his neck, she kissed him tenderly, something Parisian prostitutes reserve for friends, not clients. "I knew you would come to me, my love," she said softly into his ear. "My apartment is being watched, but I knew you would come to me."

"Of course. The only woman I have ever really loved." He took her face in both his hands. "I have need of you, *ma fille*."

She touched his inner thigh. "Of course you do."

Moving her hand up over his hardness, she unbuckled his belt as she pulled him towards the bed.

She lay in Mesrine's arms, head on his chest as he smoked. The place was peaceful, the only sound the muffled thumping of the bed and the occasional grunt from the room next door. It had been two hours and the porter had not come to tell them time was up. Nor would he. They had all the time in the world.

Outside, trade still went on in the streets of Pigalle but now it was muted in deference to the early hour, like a market winding down before closing. Lights gradually turned off, there were not so many noises, life began to fade.

"Janou?" said Mesrine, softly in case she was asleep.

"Oui, mon Jacques?"

"It was marvellous. As always. Soon you will retire. We both will. I will set you up with a house of your own."

"With a room reserved especially for you?"

" Mais naturellement."

"And you will test all the girls before they enter my employ?"

"Rigidly."

Her hand moved from its place on his groin and scratched across his lower stomach. "Bastard."

"Ah, you little cat! Stop that!"

"Cats can be vicious." She bit and sucked on his nipple, causing simultaneous pain and pleasure.

"Wicked, wicked girl," he growled. "I shall thrash you."

"Go on then," she turned in the bed and rubbed her rump against him. "I dare you!"

Mesrine gave each cheek a firm slap and then forcibly turned her around. "Listen, you minx - no, no, don't mess, listen. There is something I want you to do for me."

"Mm? What is that?" Her tongue tickled the corner of his mouth.

"You still know the old gang?"

"Of course. But I will not mention you. The streets are riddled with grasses." The tongue darted into the corner of his eye, then made its way down his cheek like a little wet fish.

"I want some information."

"What sort?" The sharp hairs on the shaving line of his neck pricked her tongue.

"There was a robbery. Sometime this year. Don't know when. Certainly before the middle of April. It was kept quiet in the press. From the house in the Bois."

Her mouth worked its way down his breastbone, licking the blood from the nipple she had bitten. "I think I did hear something on the street."

"I want to know who is involved and, more importantly, where the goods are. There is something of importance to me."

Her head was on his stomach which was firm and muscular despite the time in jail. She kissed his navel, mumbling "I will see what I can do. How can I contact you?"

"You cannot."

"You will contact me?"

"Sometime, yes. At work, not at home."

She moved across his pubic line.

"And Janou?"

"Yes, my love?"

"Be discreet, my child. I do not exist. Listen. Only ask if necessary. Be the model of circumspection."

"Am I ever anything else, *mon petit chou*?" She took him in her mouth and manoeuvred her hips over his head.

‡

22. Voleur

Vendredi 30 Juin

After eight weeks the hunt for Mesrine finally cooled in Paris. The police acknowledged that it would have been suicidal for the master criminal to have stayed in the capital after his escape. As a consequence of both their failure to find him and his appearance in Normandy - and although it had done nothing for their flagging morale - they had already widened their net to take in the whole of France, especially the areas Mesrine had been known to frequent: Lyons, the north coast, the Riviera.

Mesrine knew things would quieten, but he also knew that the hunt for him would never be called off. The cry had gone out. The infamous Mesrine had to be caught. It was nothing more nor less than a grudge match between him and the Establishment. With every crime he committed, the grudge became deeper, more bitter.

He could not contact his family or friends, not for a long, long time. It was something he just had to face and accept. Even contacting Janou had been a risk, but his expertise had ensured his safety. Janou was not being watched on the street: he could smell a flic a kilometre off.

Monsieur Lenoir, the banker from Nice, came and went each day at the studio apartment at 124 Passage Charles Albert. He would leave at 08:00 and take the metro, ostensibly to his office in the 8ᵗʰ arrondisement. At night he would return at 18:30. Sometimes he would go back out in the evening and Madame La Salle, the old concièrge, would smile knowingly. Well, he was a man alone in Paris, wasn't he?

In fact, during the day Mesrine would use the apartment in Invalides. Marcel(le) would ask no questions, naturally, and half the time the old poof was out on adventures of his own anyway. From Invalides, Mesrine would set out into the city in any of his many characters. They were not disguises, for the clean-shaven giant rarely used false items or other things theatrical, except the occasional beard or wig which, on their own, would fool nobody. No, the character came from within. From posture, that could vary his height by as much as thirty centimetres; from facial expression, that could make him a youth or age him twenty years. That was the secret. When he was in full character, no one would instantly recognise him.

It was, Mesrine acknowledged, just one of his many talents.

Thievery was another. On 30 June, Mesrine and Besse raided the home of Monsieur Jean-Claude Martigny at Noissy-le-Sec, to the east of Paris. Monsieur Martigny was a bank employee. Whilst Besse held Madame Martigny hostage, Mesrine escorted her husband to collect money from his bank, the Société Générale in Le Raincy. The total haul was four hundred and fifty thousand francs. Nobody was hurt during the operation.

‡

23. Flic et les Anglais

Lundi 3 Juillet

Claude Gerard nodded at the security guard on duty just inside the main doors of the British Embassy and walked across to the pretty receptionist. She smiled in recognition.

"*Bonjour, mam'selle,*" said Gerard politely. "Is he in?"

"I'll see, *m'sieur,*" she replied in French. "*Un moment, s'il vous plait.*" She picked up the handset of her complex-looking telephone and keyed a three-digit number. The other end was quick to respond.

"Reception here, is Mr Becker available? I have Mr Gerard for him." She listened, nodded, then held the handset against her shoulder. "*Je regrette, m'sieur.* Monsieur Becker is in a meeting at the moment. Can I arrange an appointment or get him to call you?"

The policeman did not look too happy. "No, it does not matter. Just see that he gets this, will you?" From an inside pocket he withdrew a white, sealed A4 envelope. There was no name written on it.

The receptionist looked at it. "This is for Mr Becker?"

"*Oui.* He will know what to do with it."

"Any reply?"

"I do not think so."

"*D'accord m'sieur.* I will see that he gets it."

"*Merci bien, mam'selle.*"

The receptionist watched him go. Then she put the handset back to her ear. "Hello? Tell Ron that report he's been waiting for has arrived..."

✝

24. Voleur et poule

Vendredi 21 Juillet

The English tourist sheepishly entered the bar on the south side of the Place Blanche, looking around with the apprehension of a married man let off the leash alone in a foreign city. He was probably a Tottenham Hotspur supporter still lingering after their defeat by Paris St Germain the previous Wednesday. Usually such men travelled in (drunken) packs, but the occasional stray was not unknown.

Not wishing to draw attention to himself, he sat down cautiously at a table for two near the doorway, looking out at the neon lights of the Place, tonight refracting from the puddles of a rainy Paris. He undid his sports jacket and adjusted the cravat at his neck. His suede Hush Puppies streaked dirt onto his slacks as he crossed his legs.

Taking the last of his pack of Players No 6 cigarettes, he lit up, put the match into the empty packet and crumpled it into the ashtray.

The pinball machine opposite was unoccupied. From further inside Claude François, the recently dead pop star, sang *Magnolias For Ever* from the jukebox.

"*Monsieurquestcequevousdesirez?*" The waiter used the usual Parisian trick of speaking at such velocity that the foreigner had not a hope in hell of understanding what he said.

The man blinked up from behind his British National Health

spectacles and guessed what the question must have been.

"A-avey vooz urn beer?" he asked with the dead accent of the English.

Without a word the waiter walked away, giving no indication that the order was received, understood or accepted.

Nevertheless ten minutes later a full litre glass of French beer was delivered, together with a till receipt. Making the mistake of every tourist, the Englishman hurriedly placed a note underneath the bill. The waiter ignored it and walked away.

The tourist took a swig of the beer, blanched at its harshness, and took another. Distorted over the rim of the glass, he noticed the tart at a nearby table. The tough, man-of-the-world expression he adopted fooled no one, but the tart returned his smile.

She came over, the scrape of tightly denimed thighs beneath the open rubber rainmac, low cleavage in the cheap blouse.

They spoke the usual introductory platitudes, the mild flirting before the encounter's inevitable conclusion. The Englishman had trouble with his French, but the intent of the exchange was universal. Perhaps the tart spoke a little too loudly, but no one noticed.

A bottle of the sparkling plonk was in equal parts cajoled, moued and extorted, the tart ensuring that the client drank most of it.

Soon they were out in the street, the Englishman nervous and diffident but forced to huddle against the woman in the rain. Her perfume wafted into his face. She led him into the backstreets.

"God, that champagne!" laughed Jacques Mesrine, still in accent. "I've tasted better stuff out of the sinks in La Santé!"

"I have to drink at least one glass of that every time I'm in that place!" complained Janou. "Think of that!"

"*Ah, ma pauvre petite,* soon you will not have to. I do not forget my promises." As he was still in character, he resisted the urge to hug her.

The hotel porter knew Janou but this time he did not recognise the man with her. The usual procedure of payment for the room plus the 'free' towel went smoothly, Mesrine handing over money like an innocent abroad.

In the room they made love.

Later, as they smoked together, he asked about the robbery on the Boulevard Suchet.

"I had to be careful," said Janou. "I couldn't ask just anyone. And I was being discreet as you asked."

"Good girl."

"The word is that it was not a local job, possibly someone new or the crew from up north."

"The Nenesse mob? I've done a few jobs with them recently - you may have seen it in the papers. They would have told me."

"Apparently not them then. Could be a new outfit. Could be someone from outside France all together, maybe from Holland. It's uncertain, but not local. Not much is known."

"Any mention of some letters or a document?"

"*Non.* But it was quite a haul in jewellery. Actual value some two or three million, according to the *téléphone arabe.*"

"So I understand. You heard nothing else?"

She turned so that she lay flat on the bed. In the half-light from the street lamps outside, he could see a wicked smile on her coarse face. "I did hear something else, but I don't know whether it would be of interest." Coyly she ran her finger up her right breast and made circular motions on the nipple, making it harden.

"What did you hear, you tease?"

"They got rid of the stuff here."

"What!" Mesrine pulled her towards him, her breasts flopping sideways as she leant on her elbow above him. "Where? Tell me."

"I knew you would be pleased," she giggled. "In the shop

near the Gare de l'Est."

He said the name.

"That's right."

"So, they come from out of town, fence the stuff *here*, and then have it away with the proceeds. Little risk of being caught with the ice on them. Very good. Worthy of *me*. Janou, you are wonderful." He crushed her to him, his lips enveloping her whole mouth, tongue darting between her teeth. After a full minute kissing he beamed, "What on earth would I have done without you?"

"But I love you, Jacques," she reasoned with an innocent naiveté, that one principle explaining everything.

"And I you, my princess. Here," he reached over the side of the creaky bed and dragged his jacket from the floor. "A little something I obtained for you earlier on." He handed over a sizeable wad of rolled money, mixed denominations.

"Jacques! There must be - "

"I don't know how much is there. I haven't counted it. What do you think a grocer's in Neuilly takes in a day?"

As she opened her mouth to respond, there came a sudden banging at the door. "Hey in there, your hour is up!"

Janou slid from beneath the sheets, peeled two one hundred franc notes from her roll, bent down from the waist and slid them underneath the door. There was a grunt from outside and then the sound of footsteps retreating.

Mesrine admired her rump as she straightened up, the cheeks contracting with a powerful grip. It was still firm, but not too firm. It would not resist probing.

"Now," she came back over. "We have at least another hour. How would you like me to say thank you?"

He thought of the desirable buttocks. "Take me somewhere Greek," he said.

‡

25. Voleur et receleurs

Mardi 25 Juillet

At 10:15 that morning there were no customers in the small gunsmith shop on the Rue du 8 Mai 1945, up by the Gare de l'Est. The owner was busy polishing his stock while his brother fiddled with the window display of pistols, revolvers and hunting guns.

The shop's busiest days of the week were Friday and Monday. Friday for the legitimate sales and rentals of firearms prior to a weekend's shoot, and Monday for quite another purpose. For the shop was also a launderers, frequented by members of the Parisian underworld. On a Monday they would bring the weekend's spoils, money for laundering at a fifty per cent exchange rate, articles for fencing at a maximum of ten per cent of their true value.

The man in the blue anorak and cream cap who now entered had avoided the busiest days and, having sat on the metre-high wall outside the station opposite for an hour, had avoided any early morning callers.

The owner looked up from his polishing, decided the caller was buying not selling, and smiled *"M'sieur"* in greeting.

"Bonjour messieurs," said the customer jovially. "A pair of handcuffs if you please."

An unusual request, but often such things were required by gamekeepers and such like, and there was no law against selling them.

"Certainly m'sieur, any particular type?"

"It is for a play. I am a teacher, you see. The nearest you've got to standard police issue."

The owner bent down and began to sort through a drawer underneath the counter. He was aware of his brother coming over. He extracted an appropriate pair of cuffs and straightened up. He found himself facing the barrel of a .38 Smith and Wesson.

He stared, not saying a word, handcuffs dangling from his right hand. His brother was already next to the gunman, hands in the air.

"Go round," ordered the man to the brother, softly but firmly. "*Vite!*"

Brother joined brother behind the counter.

"Closer."

They moved together.

Holding the gun actually touching the owner's right eye, arm outstretched, the gunman said, "*Alors messieurs*, if you would be so kind as to put the cuffs on."

"What?"

"The cuffs. Put them on. One on you," he tapped the gun on the owner's nose as he spoke. "And one on you." Tap. "Then put your other hands flat on the counter top, palms up."

It was quickly done, the owner fumbling with the catch on the cuffs but getting it at the third attempt.

When their hands were in position, palms up and open, the gunman relaxed. "*Merci bien.* Now gentlemen, considering your line of business I am sure you do not have any alarms connected to the *gendarmerie* down the road. Why should you? You are well protected with all these guns around!" He laughed. "So I will give it to you straight. Behave and you will live. One false move, even to scratch your nose, and you will die. I cannot say fairer than that now, can I?" He actually seemed to want a reply to the question.

"N - n – n - " said the owner.

Next to him, beads of sweat draped his brother's white face.

"Now then, if you please…" The gunman's first task was to come round and open the till. Inside was twenty thousand francs. He tut-tutted. "So much, at such an early hour! You're just asking to be robbed. Let me look after it in case any thieves come in."

He then went round the shop at his leisure, examining guns, looking down their barrels, experimenting with the safety catches, firing at invisible objects. All the time he kept the two men expertly covered.

Some housewives walked past outside, their loud voices complaining about the price of the loaves they had just purchased from the *patisserie* further along. The owner of the shop looked across, fearful lest they look into the place and raise the alarm. He could tell this man was a professional, an expert – look at the way the arms were being examined. One intrusion and somebody would surely end up dead.

The gunman chose two Smith and Wesson 9mm pistols, seven hundred rounds in boxes of one hundred, and a wicked-looking hunting knife, usually used for skinning. He took a sports bag from the shelves and packed the guns and ammunition into it. He kept the knife in his hand.

"Thank you, gentlemen," he looked across, satisfied. "Very kind of you. I'd love to stay and enjoy your company longer, but you know how it is. I've enjoyed our little chat." He flung the holdall over his right shoulder and made for the door. Then he stopped as if something had just occurred to him. He turned back. "Oh, one other thing. You had some jewellery in here sometime during the last months. Very expensive jewellery."

The brothers looked nonplussed.

"Don't look so bloody stupid!" The friendliness vanished with a frightening suddenness. His right hand holding the gun swept through the air and knocked a display flying. "Jewellery stolen from a house in the Boulevard Suchet. From La Dame. You bought it. Right?"

"What?"

Without a second's hesitation, the gunman's left hand moved upwards then down. With a thump the knife sliced through the brother's left palm, pinning his hand to the wooden counter. There was a scrape of bone as the knife went in and one squirt of blood. It made a pretty red pattern over a display of shotgun cartridges.

The scream echoed round the shop. Instinctively the brother pulled his hand, but it was pinned firm. More blood flowed thickly from the pulled wound.

The owner began to shake as he stared with shock at his brother's hand.

"Now," said the gunman sadly, "that was unfortunate and unnecessary, wasn't it? Be quick or they will find two bodies here. Answer me, you handled the stuff?"

"Th - there was some s-stuff that w-would fit - " The owner was very pale.

"Well I am not interested in it. Something else was taken at the same time. Some letters which might be of interest to me. You have them?"

"Of course not. I never keep things." He spoke softly now, in monotone.

"But you handled them."

"A wad of old letters, m'sieur. Nothing important. But I noticed one or two signatures. I thought they might be of value to an autograph collector or someone."

"Who did you sell them to? Quickly please."

"It - it is a specialised area. I undercut myself. There is a dealer," he stole a glance at his brother who was staring, equally ashen, at his own hand. "In the Boulevard Montmartre... in the arcade."

"Thank you, m'sieur. You will, of course, not be so silly as to phone the arcade?"

"Monsieur, I have no interest. I disposed of them to my gain - just."

"Has anybody else been asking about them?"

"We have our regular visits from the police. They look around, but we never keep things here. We pay them our insurance. They go. They did ask about some jewellery – but, as always, we were found to be innocent."

"And the letters?"

"No, they have never mentioned them."

The gunman drew ten thousand francs from his pocket and put them on the counter top. "You are a man of honour, I can see that. Well so am I. This is to compensate your brother. It will pay to have his hand seen to."

The brother looked up at him, unable to speak. His legs were shaking.

(It was not until many hours later that the owner was to realise that the gunman had given him back his own money and had still kept half the contents of the till.)

The gunman removed his cap. Both men looked at him, expecting something more. All he did was smile. "Messieurs, continue with your good work. You will remember this day." He backed to the door. "Naturally I ask you not to contact the police. I do not think you will. But if they arrive as a result of the scream, I will not hold it against you." He turned and was gone.

The brothers stayed motionless. After five minutes the owner fumbled for a key to the handcuffs. Two minutes later the brother, still attached to the counter and unable to move, had recovered sufficiently to say, "H-he looked familiar. Wh- who was he?"

The owner thought for a moment. "God knows," he said.

‡

God knew that Jacques Mesrine left the shop, turned left and walked quickly down the steps of the southern entrance to the Gare de l'Est metro station, his bag of guns in his right hand, ten thousand francs in his anorak pocket. He paused to buy a *tarte aux fraises* from a little shop in the underground complex and scoffed it in two bites as he queued behind a man renewing his *Carte d'orange*. When his turn came he bought himself a *carnet*.

Ligne 4 to Strasbourg - Saint-Denis, then Ligne 8 to Rue Montmartre. The journey on the most efficient underground system in the world took less than ten minutes. By car it would have taken an hour at least.

It did not take him long to find the shop in the Galeries Montmartre in the Passage de Panoramas.

Pulling himself up to his full height, he adopted a cock-sure pose, made certain the bag with the cap and guns was zipped up, and entered the small premises.

The place was warm and musty, books lining all three walls from floor to ceiling. A bespectacled, middle-aged man was seated at a desk. He looked up over his *pince-nez* as a police identity card (complete with proper photograph) was thrust at him.

He sniffed. *"Monsieur l'agent?"*

"Monsieur...?"

"Buisson."

"Monsieur Buisson, bonjour. I will not keep you long. We believe certain documents recently came into your possession, to wit a bundle of letters containing some famous signatures."

"Whose signatures, m'sieur?"

The policeman told him a name.

Buisson removed his spectacles and absentmindedly began to clean them on the end of his tie. "I think I recall the items. Nothing wrong was there? Not forgeries or anything? The seller seemed genuine, said he had owned them for years."

"No, no," the policeman, sensing co-operation, relaxed his

voice. "We would just like to have a look at them. We believe something might have slipped in there by mistake. Something that was not for sale."

"He hasn't complained, has he?"

"Who?"

"The vendor. He did accuse me of being a criminal, an extortionist. Said I only gave him a fraction of their worth."

"And did you?"

"Naturally. I am not a charitable organisation." The bookseller put the *pince-nez* back on, blinking up at the policeman.

"Did you examine the letters?" asked the policeman.

"I examined the signatures. Seemed genuine. But you can never be one hundred per cent sure. Never. It's like finding a completely unknown Renoir. Is it or isn't it? Majority acceptance decides."

"You did not actually read the letters?"

"I went through them superficially. Nothing much. Mostly letters she sent to and received from her husband. Love letters. Some others. She is a meticulous lady. All on plain paper."

The policeman pondered. "Hm. Doesn't sound as if it's what we're looking for. You don't still have them, I suppose?"

"No. I have a mailing list of clients. There is an Anglophile in Normandy. He snapped them up."

"At a hundred times what you paid for them?"

"Twenty."

"I'll contact him anyway. Can you let me have his name and address?"

Buisson turned and rummaged through a box index. Withdrawing a card, he transferred the information onto a sheet of yellowing headed paper.

The policeman read the name and address and frowned. "You don't happen to know what he does, by any chance?"

"Actually I do. Funny coincidence..."

Buisson told him and it was all Mesrine could do to stop himself exploding with laughter.

‡

26. Flic et l'Anglais

Lundi 31 Juillet

Claude Gerard sat on the benches in front of the *Jours de France* buildings on the south side of the Rond Point des Champs Elysées, facing north, watching the traffic manoeuvre back and forth across the circular crossroads. He sucked on a liquorice-tasting cachou and simultaneously smoked a Disque. The hot sun beamed down on the back of his head. He hoped it would not be as hot as this at Ostend, upon which the Gerard family would be descending at the end of next week.

For the third time he looked at his watch. 13:35. His meet was late.

It was another ten minutes before he saw him, walking past the Matignon Drugstore on the far side of the Point. Gerard rose, stubbed his cigarette under his right foot, and walked round to meet his man as he crossed over the Avenue des Champs Elysées at the lights.

"Afternoon, Claude old stick," greeted Ron Becker of the British Embassy. "Sorry I'm late."

"Pas de probleme," said Gerard. "Sometimes it is nice just to sit and reflect."

"Quite."

"You wanted to see me?"

"Yes. Shall we walk?"

They began to walk up the Champs on the southern side.

"Wondered how things were coming along re the little problem," said Becker without preamble. "It's been a while."

Gerard raised his eyebrows. "I gave you a report."

"Not good enough, old son, not good enough. So I'm told. I didn't read it. Passed it on to the man as instructed."

"Who *is* he?"

"Just a civil servant."

"Of course. Aren't we all?"

"Cigarette?" Becker proffered a packet of Peter Stuyvesant.

"*Merci.*" Gerard shook his head. "Cachou?"

"Trying to give them up."

They passed the Le Paris cinema on their left, at that time twinned and, as usual, not doing very good business (it was to be demolished in the mid-eighties).

"Exactly what is it that you want?" asked Gerard gruffly. "What do you mean, my report was not good enough? I told your superior that he was talking to the wrong man - and now I'm telling you. It is not my case."

Becker chose to ignore the point of contention. "I had a little chat with my superior, as you call him. He put me in the picture, as far as he was able. In fact, he is pleased that there's been no publicity. He says that shows that whoever has whatever it is does not know its significance - whatever that significance may be. Even he does not know. Do you?"

"No. What can be so significant about stolen jewellery? *Alors, bien sûr,* I know it is worth a lot, and there could be some historical interest – "

"It was more than jewellery."

"*Pardon?*"

"Something else was taken as well as the jewellery."

Fuck. "I am not aware of this. What is it?"

"That, old sport, I don't know. I just know it is of great significance. There is firm pressure being applied from somewhere. My *superior* has asked me to remind you of point (c)."

Gerard furrowed his brow. "Point (c)... point (c)? Which one was that? There were so many points."

"Come on, Claude," sneered Becker. "Don't act the innocent. For God's sake be reasonable. You're our liaison man, and we have passed on a reasonable request. The request comes from a very important person in London. Doesn't that mean anything to you?"

"You know what we did to royals in this country, m'sieur."

They stopped outside the *Aéroflot* offices.

"So," said Becker. "You are refusing to co-operate?"

Gerard sighed and looked everywhere but at the Englishman. He said, *"Non.* I will co-operate. I *am* co-operating. I have given you a report. All I knew was that some jewellery was stolen. I will pursue things further. I will give you another report as and when I know something. Monsieur, things take time. Your royal cannot expect results within a day. If I may tell my colleague of your interest, he can liaise with you direct - "

"No, my son, no." Becker stabbed his cigarette in Gerard's direction. "No one else is to know of our interest. It's in your hands. As long as you have our interests at heart, that's all that matters."

"Of course."

Becker looked at his watch, took a final drag on his cigarette before throwing it away, then said "Okay, keep in touch. I must go, I have some shopping to do. Just keep us informed, old fruit." With a nod, he disappeared down the Marignon entrance to the Franklin D Roosevelt metro station.

For a minute Gerard stayed looking at the magazines on display around the nearby kiosk. He muttered, *"Rosbeef* arsehole," then he crossed the Champs and walked off down the Rue du Colisée.

"Stupid frog," mumbled Becker as he waited for his Ligne 9

train to take him to Havre-Caumartin. Absentmindedly he looked at the Pont de Sèvres train standing at the opposite platform. A blonde, middle-aged man looked back at him from inside the train. Their eyes met and then quickly looked away, as strangers' eyes always do.

Paul Richer turned from the window and began to read the adverts inside as the train pulled away towards Alma Marceau. He read the same advert over and over again - details of the *Billet de Tourisme* - until he was distracted by a bunch of tourists alighting at Trocadéro for Chaillot and the Eiffel Tower. He knew this route well but still he looked up at the linear map above the doors. Three more stops to Ranelagh. Then the short walk and he would be at the Boulevard Suchet.

✝

27. Flic et victime

Soon Richer was being ushered into La Dame's bedroom. He had booked his appointment two days in advance, so this time there was no delay for cosmetics (or, as he thought cruelly, for the cracks to be plastered over).

She looked the same as when he had visited her before, propped up in the centre of the bed, housecoat matching her jet-black painted hair. Make-up heavy but tasteful. It was as if she had not moved since his last visit, as if she had been turned off when he left and only switched back on again a few minutes ago.

"Madame," he gave a little bow and spoke in English. "I regret to disturb you. I thought you would like a report on my progress."

Her clear eyes looked at him. She gave a quizzical little smile. "Who *are* you, monsieur?"

Richer coughed. "From the BCP, madame." He pronounced it Bay-Say-Pay. "The Sûreté."

"The Sûreté... the Sûreté..." She frowned. "But where is Monsieur Gerard?"

"He could not come, madame."

"Such a *nice* man."

"Indeed, madame. I thought you would like to know how things were progressing."

"What is *your* name?"

"Richer. Chief Inspector Richer."

"We have never met?"

"Once, madame."

"Oh, you must forgive me. I am an old woman." She giggled like a little girl. "Now, what can I do for you, Chief Inspector?"

"About the document, madame. I thought you would like a progress report - "

"Document? What document?"

"The robbery."

"What robbery? Oh never mind, never mind. Come here, will you? Pour me a drink."

Richer did as he was bidden and stood on the spot he had occupied three months before.

She sipped the vodka. "Sit down, monsieur, I cannot look up at you. I will get a pain in my neck."

Not even bothering to look for a chair, Richer squatted on the edge of the bed. "Although we have had no success yet, madame, I have a good man on the job."

"Monsieur," a feeble hand was raised and then fell back on the bed. "What *are* you talking about?"

"You called us last April, madame. About the robbery. The jewellery that had been taken."

"I did? *Jewellery!*" Another giggle twinkled lightly from her old lips with the incongruity of a mountain stream in a desert. "Did I *really*?"

"*Et je pense que - Pardon.* And I thought that you would like a progress report seeing as August is now upon us."

"Monsieur," she spoke kindly, on the edge of condescension. "Monsieur *Gerard*. I do not know anything about any robbery or jewellery."

"Or the document, madame? The game that must not be given away?"

"I... game? I have a feeling... that this... is a game... monsieur..." She closed her eyes and Richer quickly caught the glass as it flopped from her fingers.

Putting the glass back on the bedside table, he rose, keeping his eyes locked on La Dame. She did not stir.

Silently he walked across to the door. It opened without a sound.

"Thank you for coming," said the old woman's voice suddenly, loud and clear.

He looked back.

She was wide awake, looking at him. "Do call again. It has been so nice talking to you. I hardly have anyone visit me nowadays, you know. Not since David left me." She sighed.

Richer nodded and turned to leave.

"Tell me," she said. "How *is* Madame Gerard and your children?"

That evening Richer sat in his favourite chair in his *salon*, brandy in one hand, stroking Chivas on his lap. A current affairs programme was on TRF1 but, although his eyes stared at the screen, nothing was registering. He was deep in thought.

La Dame could remember nothing. To be more correct, *at this moment* La Dame could remember nothing. But she was notoriously inconsistent. Tomorrow she might remember all.

But if she did not?

Chivas turned in his lap for a belly stroke.

If she did not, then there need be no further police involvement other than a filed report. There need be no lies about the document being destroyed, no stealth.

Tipping Chivas off his lap, he went across to his jacket and removed the article he had taken to the Boulevard Suchet that afternoon. A woman's stocking.

He twisted his hands between the ends and snapped the stocking out sharply.

And he need not murder La Dame, the very important American lady: Wallis Warfield Simpson, the Duchess of Windsor.

‡

28. Voleur

Vendredi 4 Août

It is difficult for the non-French to understand the significance of an August in France. August means vacation. Many factories and offices close for the whole month. The cities close down, the coastal resorts come alive.

Even in Paris every third shop is closed and every second restaurant has the 'Fermeture Annuelle' sign on its locked doors. It is truly a month when Paris is populated only by tourists and the thieves who prey on them.

No self-respecting Frenchman remains in Paris in August unless he has to through personal, occupational or other fiscal necessity. If it was one trait of Jacques Mesrine it was that he was self-respecting. Thus August and most of September saw him on holidays with friends, first touring in Italy then Algeria. Then he left the friends and took a lady to London, staying in an hotel near Marble Arch.

On Friday 4 August, while Mesrine was enjoying himself in Italy, Paris Match published an interview he had given to a freelance journalist a couple of weeks previously. It caused an uproar, embarrassed the police and the Establishment, and led to the arrest of the magazine's publisher Daniel Filipacchi on charges of condoning murder and theft.

The interview put Mesrine back on the front pages and renewed pressure on the police to find him. Frequently the police stated that they had new information, new leads on the master criminal's whereabouts. Undoubtedly at the time they thought they had. But their failure to produce him led to them being pilloried in the press for incompetence and laziness. The press, of course, had their axes out and finely honed after the arrest of Filipacchi, one of their brethren.

Public demand for Mesrine stories was rekindled and satisfied (August is a noted news-less month throughout the western world).

Mesrine was away from the furore, but he kept in touch with events, taking French newspapers at whatever town, whatever address he happened to be staying. He was pleased that he was back where he considered he belonged, on the front pages.

By the time he returned to Paris, at the end of September, things had quietened down again...

‡

29. Flic

Samedi 30 Septembre

Paul Richer stood by his window, brandy in one hand, Gitanes in the other, and watched the floodlights of the Sacré Coeur Basilica blink on. It was mid-evening and the sun was leaving Paris for another day, bequeathing a clear sky which augured well for the morrow. Chivas slept on top of the television.

Richer was busy at work, but thank God his rank and job were sufficient to ensure he never worked nights as a matter of routine. He left that to his staff. Young Inspector Bauer seemed hardly ever to be off duty.

Things were quiet on the Mesrine front. No longer did his picture appear in the newspapers *every* day as a consequence of the Paris Match fiasco last month. No longer were there extended accounts of his exploits in the nightly news bulletins. It was generally accepted in police circles that Mesrine was once again well away from Paris, probably out of France.

But one man in the force knew differently.

Because just a few moments ago Richer had received a phone call. A quickly-terminated phone call from Bruno to say he was back and would soon be taking 'further recovery action'.

At 21:46 on Saturday 30 September, Paul Richer raised his glass in a salute from his window and swallowed his brandy in one.

‡

30. Voleur et flics

Vendredi 6 Octobre

In keeping with the quiet opulence of the rest of the town, the police station in Deauville, Normandy, looks anything but what it actually is. It is more like a cottage, quaint and gabled, with six stone steps leading up to the front door. Inside, the hallway has a mosaic floor, wood panelling on the walls and wooden furniture.

That night, as usual, two officers were on duty in the public reception area. All had been quiet for the first hour of their 22:00 to 06:00 shift.

At 23:00 the outside door opened. The officers looked up from their newspapers to see a big man dressed in a neat but slightly crumpled serge suit, document case under his arm, striding towards the counter. He looked angry.

"Chief Inspector Dorner, Internal Affairs, Paris. Is Inspector Le Bouthillier in?"

Quickly the officers straightened themselves up. "He's not on duty, sir," replied one.

"*Merde alors!*" Chief Inspector Dorner's eyes blazed. "It is imperative that I get hold of him. I have been travelling all day."

"*Je regrette, monsieur -* "

"Why did he not wait for me? Did he not get my message?"

"Your message, sir?"

"Yes, my message! I telephoned from Paris this morning. He

wasn't in *then*! Some rookie took a message. By Christ, this is *typical*! Bloody provincial *gendarmes*." His fist clenched and unclenched around the bottom of the document case, bottled fury on the point of exploding.

"*Monsieur, je regrette -* "

"Yes, yes, yes. Well I'm here and I want to see him. What's his home address?"

"I have his telephone number, sir." The officer who was doing the talking thumbed through his book while the other officer went over to a card index. "Here it is."

"What about his address?"

The second officer called over his shoulder, "I have it here, sir."

"Right." Dorner accepted both the number and the address. Then, as if the thought had just struck him, he looked at his watch. "Hell. Do you have a private phone in a private room? I had better call him first considering the lateness of the hour."

The officers were the personification of help and assistance, not wishing to displease the already irate Chief Inspector from Paris.

"This way, sir."

Dorner was shown into a small unoccupied office behind the reception area. Next door he could hear muffled voices in what must have been the general office.

Left on his own, he moved quickly, dialling the number he had been given. After three rings a man's voice answered, muffled, as if he had been asleep.

Dorner put down the receiver. He did not, however, replace it in its cradle but balanced it on the body just above. Anyone looking in casually would presume the receiver was down, only close examination would reveal otherwise.

It was one of the oldest tricks in the book. The incoming call that could not be cut off. Now, even if Inspector Le Bouthillier replaced his phone, as he would do imminently, the connection was made. If he picked up his receiver again, he would be connected back to this office. And, of course, any incoming calls to the Inspector would receive the engaged tone.

Dorner came back out, closing the door behind him. *"Merci."* His temper was abating. "The Inspector will see me."

"Do you wish a car, sir?"

"No, no. I have my own. Which way do I go?" He was given directions. *"D'accord."* He paused by the front entrance. "Oh by the way, is the Inspector married?"

"Sir?"

Dorner actually smiled. "It is late. I wish to disturb his wife as little as possible."

"Oh yes, sir. The Inspector is married."

"Children?"

"Grown up, not at home."

"Bien, merci messieurs." And Dorner was off through the doors.

Like a thief in the night.

It was not until the officers were nearing the end of their shift six hours later that one, the younger one who had done most of the talking to the Chief Inspector, said suddenly, "That man was Mesrine."

"Who?" The other officer was engrossed in a cup of hot chocolate.

"That Chief Inspector earlier on. It was Mesrine."

"Rubbish. You're going mad."

"It was Mesrine I tell you."

"Mesrine would never return to Deauville after the casino job. The Chief Inspector was fatter and younger than that shit. Besides, Mesrine is out of France by now – haven't you read the reports? You're getting tired, Pierre, hallucinating. I think you'd better go home."

"He didn't show any identification."

"True…"

"I think I'll ring Le Bouthillier."

"What! You *are* mad! He'll have your bollocks. It's five o'clock in the morning, man!"

"But what if it *was* Mesrine? I'll ring him anyway."

But by then it was too late.

✝

31. Voleur et flic

The stolen blue Simca crossed the Pont de Belges and, keeping within the speed limit at all times, passed through Trouville. The street lighting disappeared on the edge of town and Chief Inspector Dorner drove through the quiet, dark lanes of Normandy on full headlights.

A mélange of intermittent farms and houses passed by until he found the one he wanted, a thatched, single-level cottage, with sizeable gardens front and rear, out of shouting distance of anywhere else.

And out of screaming distance.

He cruised the Simca the last few metres with its engine off, parking it off the road, blocking the small driveway but facing outwards. With the headlights off, Dorner had only a half moon for illumination. He climbed from the vehicle, leaving the keys in the ignition and the door unlocked, and strode purposefully up to the double front door.

He gave the bell three short bursts and then kept his finger on it.

After two minutes a light came on inside and footsteps could be heard approaching.

"*Alors, arrêtez, arrêtez!*" shouted a gruff, disgruntled voice. "*Qu'est-ce que c'est? Qui est-là? Merde alors, c'est minuit!*"

"*Monsieur l'Inspecteur?*" called the man outside. "Inspector Le Bouthillier?"

"*Qui est-là?*"

"Dorner. Chief Inspector Dorner. Sûreté Nationale. It is vital that I see you at once."

"From Headquarters? Caen?" There was a fumbling of chains. A bolt was pulled back.

"No, not Caen. Paris."

The door was opened.

"Paris!" Le Bouthillier was a squat, balding man in his early fifties with a surprisingly aristocratic hooked nose. He frowned at the official ID thrust into his face. He gawped at the 9mm Smith and Wesson that followed it.

"Inside and shut your mouth *tight!*"

"What the - ?"

"Shut up, *con,*" Mesrine pushed the dressing-gowned policeman against the wall as he forced his way in. "Shut up and you *may* live to see tomorrow."

"What – "

Mesrine pushed the gun savagely up Le Bouthillier's left nostril. His eyes glared death. The policeman closed his mouth without further sound.

Mesrine span him around to face the wall as he kicked the front door closed behind him. He grabbed the Inspector's right arm and bent it excrutiatingly up his back, held in place by the closeness of his body. He wrapped his left arm around the Inspector's neck and pressed the gun firmly into his right temple. Le Bouthillier struggled but the big intruder was strong, and another hard jab from the pistol pre-empted anything silly.

Mesrine marched him along the smartly-carpeted hallway and into the first room on the right, the *salon.*

"Your wife." Mesrine's hot breath blew into his ear.

"What?"

"Your wife. Where is she?"

"In bed."

"Where's the kitchen?"

"The what?"

"The kitchen - for Christ's sake man, are you deaf? Ah, I know what your little game is! Bedroom, quickly!" He released the neckhold and grabbed a clump of hair at the back of Le Bouthillier's head. The gun moved round from the temple to press into the ear.

The Inspector was pulled into the hallway. Mesrine was breathing deeply, almost snarling. "Madame Le Bouthillier!" he called. "Madame! It is no good. Your telephone is blocked. Please come out. I will have no hesitation in shooting your husband."

There was a silence lasting half a minute. Mesrine said, "*Madame, s'il vous plait*. I will not ask you again. In thirty seconds you will become a widow."

Slowly a door down the hallway creaked open. A middle-aged woman, frightened but defiant, stepped hesitantly out. She was dressed in a flowery pink robe with a nightdress poking out at the neck and ankles.

"*Bonsoir Madame*." The intruder gave a broad grin which, at another time, in another place, would have been received as a charming smile. "I out-thought you. But do not be down-hearted. There are not many people who get the better of Jacques Mesrine."

The Inspector stiffened. "M - Mesrine?" He tried to turn to look but he was still held tight. "What on earth - ?"

"Silence. In a moment, Inspector. *Madame, s'il vous plait*. Where is the kitchen?"

She nodded to her right. "*Là.*"

"Then if you please, madame."

Madame Le Bouthillier led the way, instinctively flicking on the light switch. Two flourescents flashed into life.

Just before he entered, Mesrine paused, the Inspector held in front of him. "The blinds. They are drawn?"

"They are drawn, m'sieur," confirmed the lady.

The two men shuffled in. Mesrine swiftly sized up the place.

Traditional, oak beams, old stove, solid wooden table and chairs, newer cupboards and worktops, a few modern appliances.

"Madame, please sit down. Put your hands flat on the table top, palms upwards. Thank you. Please do not move, not even to scratch your nose. If you do, something terrible might happen."

The Inspector tried again to turn round but he was still held fast. "F - for goodness sake, what do you want Mesrine?"

"Be patient Inspector, please," said the voice next to his ear. "In a moment. Now, I want you to go and join your good lady. Sit opposite her and adopt the same posture. Please believe that I will not hesitate in shooting both of you if the need arises. I *beg* you not to be foolish." He let go of the hair and took a quick step backwards.

But the Inspector was not foolish. He did as he was instructed.

With husband and wife seated at the table, hands in view, Mesrine said, "Now then, I must apologise for calling at this ungodly hour, but I am on a quest. A quest of the utmost delicacy. And it is better perpetrated under the cover of darkness."

Inspector Le Bouthillier frowned across at him.

"I shall not keep you long. Inspector, you recently bought some signed letters from Monsieur Buisson in Paris. Letters of the American lady. I want them."

The Inspector's jowls wobbled as he shook his head uncomprehendingly. "That is all this is about? They are not worth what you might think, you know. Fifty thousand at the most."

"I am not interested in their value. Do you have them?"

"You are not interested in their value? Then why - "

Mesrine moved like a lynx. With two steps he was across the room. His gun slammed down onto the fingers of Madame Le

Bouthillier's right hand.

The lady gasped and went very pale but, through what must have been terrifying pain, she retained her composure. The fingers were black and swollen within two seconds.

It was the Inspector who screamed. "You fucker!" His hands lifted off the table.

Mesrine pointed his gun straight between Le Bouthillier's eyes.

"Easy, easy. I did advise you, m'sieur. Now look what you have done to your poor lady wife. Calm yourself. Please. Come on, calm down."

The Inspector was breathing deeply. He glared at Mesrine.

Mesrine smiled at him, like an old friend. "Better, *non?* Fancy making me do that to the woman you love."

Le Bouthillier let his hands fall back onto the table, palms upwards. Two tears ran down Madame Le Bouthillier's cheeks.

Mesrine went over to the worktop and, with his left hand, unravelled the flex on an old liquidiser. The Inspector, now sweating profusely, looked perplexed. Mesrine pulled the flex from the worktop to the table, satisfied himself that it stretched, and brought over the liquidiser. He plugged the cable into the socket in the wall.

The liquidiser sat, blades glistening, in front of Madame. Mesrine tested it. The machine roared viciously, like a wild beast disturbed from its rest. Both the Inspector and his wife jumped.

"Madame, your self-control is admirable," complimented the gunman as he turned the liquidiser on its side. "I am sorry for what your husband did to you. *Monsieur L'Inspecteur*, please. No more delays, questions - or lies. *Madame, permettez-moi.*" He took the woman's now paralysed black fingers. She tried to tug her arm back but did not have the strength.

As casually as if he was loading meat into a mincer, Mesrine pushed her hand into the liquidiser. He held the wrist on the table and, gun pointing in the Inspector's direction, held the ON/OFF switch with the third finger of his right hand. *"Monsieur?"*

The Inspector was open-eyed. "You - you *animal*, Mesrine. How *can* you? Everything they say about you is true."

"And more so. Believe it, m'sieur. Now, let us make this unpleasantness as brief as possible. You have the letters?"

Le Bouthillier was staring at his wife's hand in the obscene machine. "In - in the *salon*. I - I am a collector of autographs - in a small way, you understand. More out of interest than any financial investment, though they could be a hedge against inflation. I have others also. There's a Pasteur, a Piaf - take them please. Take them all." A nervous giggle jogged from his lips.

Without warning Mesrine thumped Madame Le Bouthillier across the back of the neck. She slumped forward soundlessly, head on the table, hand still in the appliance.

"You bastard!" The Inspector leapt to his feet. By the time his legs had straightened, the gun was pressing into his left eye.

"Easy!" snapped Mesrine. "Easy, Inspector, easy. She is asleep, that is all. Control yourself, you're a police officer."

The men stared at each other.

"She will be fine," continued Mesrine. "A dull headache when she awakes, no more. The letters, if you please."

"But - "

"Please."

The Inspector led the way back into the *salon*, all the time covered by Mesrine's gun. No words were spoken as he fumbled in the top of an escritoire for a key and then unlocked a drawer lower down.

"Be careful what you pull from that drawer, m'sieur." It was wise counsel.

A bundle tied with pink ribbon was held out to Mesrine.

"Into my hand please. *Merci bien.* Now Inspector, if you would be so kind, remove your dressing gown."

"Quoi?"

"Please do as I ask. Let us not spoil our new-found co-operation."

With a sigh, the Inspector did as he was asked.

"Now, sit down on the couch. *Bon.* And wrap the gown around your ankles. Come along. Thank you."

Mesrine sat on a chair behind the couch next to the escritoire, the back of Le Bouthillier's head a mere metre away. "I do not have to tell you, *Monsieur L'Inspecteur*, that a bullet from this range would ensure that your widow would need to completely redecorate this room."

Mesrine untied the ribbon and began to read the letters. Occasionally the silence was punctuated with comments like "You know, you really should keep these somewhere safer. There are thievés about." And, "It is a pity your wife is not awake, she could make us some coffee."

There were nine of them in all. Mostly from 'Peaches' to 'David' and back. They were all in English. He read each one carefully. He did not fully understand some of them, but his time in Canada had given him a fair command of the language.

At the end of the ninth letter, he frowned and then read them all again in reverse order. Then he held each one up to the light and then shook each envelope out, the ageing glue complaining and parting.

They all seemed straightforward, completely non-controversial, nothing earth-shattering. It would help, of course, if he had some idea of what the hell he was supposed to be looking for. But the Captain had said he would know it when he saw it. Well, he hadn't seen it here. *Merde.*

Then he asked sharply, "Where are the others?"

Le Bouthillier jumped at the sudden breaking of the silence. He began to turn his head until he felt the coldness of the gun against his face. "Oth - others?"

"You heard what I said."

"I have no others - "

"*D'accord!*"

Le Bouthillier was pulled upwards by the collar of his pyjamas. He stumbled with the dressing gown still round his ankles and Mesrine dragged him into the kitchen on his knees, the cotton of the pyjamas tearing, the opening in the front gaping, exposing him lewdly.

Mesrine let him fall at the feet of his unconscious wife. "I have had *enough!* Let us see how your wife looks without her fingers."

Le Bouthillier snuffled, trying to cover himself and rise at the same time, still entangled in the robe. He slipped, his head landing on his wife's lap.

The liquidiser roared as it was switched on.

"NO!" screamed Le Bouthillier above the roar. "IN THE NAME OF CHRIST!" His head came above the table, eyes half closed, not wanting to see what he must see. "I'll tell you. Let me explain. *Oh my God!*"

His wife's hand was intact. Mesrine held her wrist, the fearsome blades one centimetre from her fingers.

Mesrine said nothing for a full minute, letting Le Bouthillier appreciate the drama of the moment. Then calmly, almost amicably, he said softly "Please do not think that this reprieve is any sign of weakness on my part. I switched the machine on without looking. Madame's hand must somehow have fallen backwards. I will not miss this time."

"You *bastard.* You *cunt.* You're a madman."

"It has been said. Now, you were going to explain?"

"I thought you must be after those. My dealer advised me to sell. Said the police had been enquiring after them. But how did you know? How could you have possibly found out?"

"Where are they?"

"*Ecoutez!*" There was desperation in the Inspector's voice. "Perhaps we can do a deal. I belong to the - "

He never had time to complete the sentence.

Mesrine was always to swear that it was an accident, that he never had any intention of doing it. Whether his finger slipped or not, the result was the same. The liquidiser roared again.

The top of Madame Le Bouthillier's second finger disintegrated, and her whole hand disappeared from sight as the centrifugal force coated the sides of the jug in blood. She moaned in her unconsciousness.

Le Bouthillier screamed and leapt for the gunman.

Mesrine, shocked himself, stepped back and easily knocked the policeman to the floor. On his back, Le Bouthillier made a wild sweep for his legs. Mesrine kicked his arm away and stepped on his throat.

Memories flooded back. Memories of years ago when he had had an Arab in exactly the same position. That night in Algeria. The night he had met, and been saved by, Captain Paul Richer. The man who was responsible for him being here in Normandy tonight.

The smell of Africa came back to him.

He pointed the gun straight down into Le Bouthillier's face. "One chance, melon," he murmured. "One chance before I blow you away."

Le Bouthillier's face was turning purple, water streaming from his eyes, breath cracking.

"Who has them and where?" Mesrine eased his foot just enough.

The Inspector gasped a name and a place.

"Repeat," ordered Mesrine, leaning forward to confirm his ears. "*Encore.*"

The Inspector repeated the name and the place.

Then it happened.

Mesrine had not even been aware of a movement, let alone the sound of any drawer opening. Perhaps it had not. Perhaps she had had it on her all the time. Whatever, it did not matter.

What mattered was that at that moment, with a speed belying her age, Madame Le Bouthillier lunged forward and stabbed Jacques Mesrine with a carving knife.

‡

32. Flics

Samedi 7 Octobre

"Did you hear?" Claude Gerard burst into the office, tossing a bag containing a slice of warm quiche at Paul Richer. It was 14:00 on a sunny Parisian day. Gerard was on lates.

"Hear what?" Richer laid the greasy bag down gingerly on a piece of scrap paper and tore it open.

"Mesrine. He's surfaced."

Richer looked up sharply. "Where d'you hear this?"

"On the radio. One o'clock news."

"What did they say?"

Gerard attacked his quiche with gusto, a piece of onion lodging on his chin and bouncing up and down as he spoke. "Killed an inspector and his wife up in Normandy last night."

"A *police* inspector?"

"*Mais oui.* Strangely enough, nothing seems to have been taken."

"Then - ?"

"A straight case of murder. Revenge probably. You know what a vengeful bastard he is. Always swearing to get even with those who put him inside. He robbed the casino up there in May."

"They didn't give the inspector's name?"

"No, but we can find out." The last half of the pie was crammed into his mouth. Richer had not even started on his.

"How do they know it was Mesrine?"

"No details," mumbled Gerard. "Seems he was recognised by a young officer earlier that night."

"Earlier? *Je ne comprends pas.*"

Richer picked up the telephone as Gerard asked him if he wanted coffee.

"Something stronger." Richer tapped out the three figures of the General Office. "Fancy coming downstairs? - Hello, Bauer? What's this I hear about Jacques Mesrine? You don't? Okay, leave it, *merci*. I'll be out for about half an hour."

Gerard was grinning. "You're starting early today. Just afternoon and you want to booze already."

"You complaining?"

"No, let's go. What's up? Something wrong? You had a shock?"

"I just fancy some cognac, that's all. If you don't shut up you can buy your own."

The telephone on Richer's desk shrilled. Both men turned from the doorway. Gerard looked at him inquiringly. He nodded at the phone.

"Leave it," said Richer bluntly.

They went out.

Commissaire Fleury-Goujon put down his telephone then picked it up again immediately, keying the General Office.

"This is the Commissaire. Where's Chief Inspector Richer?"

"Just logged out sir."

"Did he say he'd be long?"

"Half an hour, sir."

"I want him immediately he returns."

"Yes sir."

They stood at the *zinc* of the bar at the corner of Rue de Penthièvre and Rue Cambacérès.

"Anything wrong, Paul?" asked Gerard as he lit their cigarettes. "You seem… pre-occupied."

Richer opened his mouth to say something, thought better of it, paused and then said, "No, I'm having problems, that's all. On a case." He swilled his drink down in one.

"Can I help?"

Richer smiled. "Claude, you offered already. *Henri! Encore!*"

"La Dame? Is the old bitch causing trouble again?"

"No, just trying to retrieve her damn jewellery. Enquiries drawing a blank. You know how it is."

"I thought you'd written it up as closed."

"I did. To keep the Minister happy. I lied."

"How many men you got on it?"

"Just one. And you know it can't be full time. There are other, daresay more important, things."

"Of course there bloody well are. I told you, it's a PR job. Smooth her over, charm her up. Chances are she'll forget about it."

Richer stared at the bottles on the shelf behind the bar. For some reason his eyes rested on an ornately-designed bottle of chocolate mint liqueur. On its label was an ebony maiden carrying a pannier on her head. Why on earth did she remind him of Mesrine?

He called to the barman. *"Henri! Deux petites!"*

As they tucked into the sausages and bread, they spoke about other things: about Claude's case of the British diplomat and the whore that was occasioning frequent visits to the embassy; about the vicissitudes of Paris St Germain; about Mathilde Gerard; about Jacques Mesrine.

Lydia.

It hit Richer like a bolt from the blue. Mesrine's first wife, the black girl from Martinique. That's who the girl on the bottle reminded him of. How strange.

He asked, "Fancy another meal sometime?"

Gerard was halfway through his *petite*, crumbs down his tie and over the *zinc* in front of him. He nodded. "That's good. I'd like to. When?"

"When are you free?"

"God, any time. Mathilde probably thinks I've got a woman anyway. You know what she said to me the other day?" A piece of half chewed sausage shot out of his mouth and landed like a limpet on the side of his glass. "That I was turning queer, spending all my time with you. *All my time!* I ask you! I only go round your place - what? - once a month? And already we are lovers!"

Richer slapped Gerard on the back. "Come along then, *chéri*, let us finish off with a beer. *Henri! Deux bieres!* What do you say? Tomorrow night?"

"Suits me, *mon ami*," Gerard wiped his mouth on his sleeve. "And wear your suspenders and that wispy little thong, there's a good chap."

The young officer heard the chatter of the two Chief Inspectors in the corridor and poked his head out of the General Office. "Chief Inspector Richer, sir?"

"*Oui?*"

"The Commissaire, sir. Wants to see you immediately."

"Shit."

"Yes, sir." The officer disappeared.

"La Dame?" asked Gerard.

Richer shrugged. "Shouldn't be. But I'll soon find out."

Fleury-Goujon motioned for Richer to sit down. "Heard about Mesrine?"

Richer accepted the proffered cigarette and reciprocated with his lighter. "Third hand, sir. From the radio."

"Strange happenings," the Commissaire swallowed most of the smoke, a trickle flowing down his nostrils like a resting dragon. "Apparently it was quite a deliberate act of murder. The Inspector was shot once through the heart at a distance of no more than one metre. The wife was different. She was battered brutally about the head and then shot behind the left ear. Seems she put up a struggle. Also the top of one of the fingers of her left hand had been chopped off."

"Torture?"

"Possibly. But the strange thing is, there was not a drop of blood anywhere but on the bodies. Not a speck. And nothing was out of place. The whole house was neat and tidy. They were discovered stretched out on the kitchen floor next to one another. Had it not been for the manner of their deaths, it could have been a suicide pact."

Richer stared at the top of the cigarette in his hand. "No weapon?"

"*Non.*"

"And nothing missing?"

"*Non.* But two unusual things. Firstly, there were deep marks on the Inspector's neck - "

"Attempted strangulation?"

"Boot marks. And secondly, placed on the floor next to the bodies was… a melon."

Richer stared at the Commissaire. "A melon?"

"A melon. And underneath that melon was an old letter, written some forty years ago. From La Dame to her husband."

Richer did not react. His face was stone.

"Devos has been on to me already," continued Fleury. "Wanted to know if we knew anything about it or if it meant anything."

"What did you say?"

"I said no. Our only interest was in some jewellery that was taken many months ago."

"How exactly do they know it was Mesrine?"

"He went into the local station earlier asking for the

Inspector. Passed himself off as a *flic*. You know he's noted for doing that. It was only hours later that one of the lads on duty realised who he was. They'll have the poor buggers balls, of course."

Richer sniffed. "The Inspector anyone we know?"

"An Inspector called Le Bouthillier."

‡

33. L'Organisation

"An Inspector called Le Bouthillier," answered Richer to the question from the man in the cap. "Just a provincial *flic*." They were seated as before in the room above the butcher's in Rue Fessart.

"So Mesrine has the document?"

"I don't know. This murder may not even be connected with the quest. Remember, Mesrine said he would get it in his own time. He might have been leaving me a sign with the melon. I don't know. He will let me know when he has it."

"Meanwhile we just sit and wait," grumbled the man.

"Is there no other way we can get it?" asked the chain smoker on the right.

Richer shook his head. "How? The reason I involved Mesrine in the first place was because of his special talents. If something needs sniffing out, he'll sniff it. If something needs retrieving, he'll retrieve it."

"And you're sure this letter under the melon was not the document we are seeking?"

"Absolutely not. Mesrine would not do that. He is contracted to bring the document to me."

"And you trust him?"

"Mesrine is a man of honour." Richer ignored the cap man's cynical laugh. "He has a quest for which he has been paid in advance. He would not play games. And he would not take kindly to being withdrawn - even if I could contact him, which I cannot."

"So all we can do is sit and wait," echoed the chain smoker.

"And what if this secret - which you have deigned not to let us in on - breaks?" The cap man. "The document will be no good to us then. All will be lost, and we will have freed Mesrine for nothing."

"The secret will not break." It was the first time the Colonel had spoken. "If it was going to break it would have done so long ago, long before La Dame even got round to reporting the theft to the Minister. No, whoever has it is keeping quiet for his own purposes."

"Or does not know what he has," said Richer.

The Colonel nodded slowly. "*Oui*. That is the alternative."

"I still think we should try some other way to obtain it," said cap man.

"How?" Richer could not keep the contempt from his voice. "Who do you suggest? Some OAS geriatric?"

"Captain!" The Colonel frowned.

"Pardon me, gentlemen," Richer looked at each man in turn. "All I'm saying is Mesrine's not only the best we have, he *is* the best. But we must be patient. He is looking for a needle which is not even in a haystack. It could be anywhere."

"What about La Dame?" asked the chain smoker.

"I visited her two months ago. She remembers nothing."

"You are certain?"

"I will, of course, make further visits. But she cannot even remember losing her jewellery."

"Then it will not be necessary to kill her?"

"It is an option we must keep open," reasoned Richer. "But I don't think so, no."

"That," said the cap man, "is a pity."

‡

34. Concièrge

Mardi 10 Octobre

Madame La Salle, the concièrge of 124 Passage Charles Albert, stood in front of the old sink in her *loge* preparing some potatoes for her evening meal. Her shaky, arthritic hands could barely hold the knife, let alone peel, but somehow she managed, the chopped skins falling onto the newspaper in front of her. It was yesterday's *Le Figaro* which she had picked up from one of the tenants this morning.

She never read the headlines. An old woman could do without the wars, the crimes, the accidents, the rapes. She read the inside pages, particularly the stars and agony columns (for neither of which was *Le Figaro* noted). Consequently she had not noticed the picture on the front page and the report of the killings in Normandy.

She noticed it now as a piece of potato peel fell onto the photographed face. Had she had her reading glasses on, the face would have appeared fully in focus and she would have thought nothing of it. As it was, she saw a blurred image of a round head, hearty, confident face, deep set eyes and a moustache.

The image reminded her of someone, but she could not put her finger on it. She brushed away the piece of peel and squinted.

No, she would have to get her glasses. But later, it was not important, do the potatoes first.

The next piece of peel fell onto the picture, covering the blur of the moustache.

She stared again.

Good heavens! What a remarkable resemblance!

With the moustache covered up, the blurred image looked just like Monsieur Lenoir from the ground floor studio!

She chuckled. With her glasses on, of course, the picture would look nothing like him. But what a coincidence! Monsieur Lenoir was a charming man, always ready with a quip (if she had been thirty years younger!). He would see the funny side of it when she told him. He was back home in Nice for a time, but when he returned she would have a little joke with him. Would he laugh when he found out who he looked like!

‡

35. Voleur et filles

Mercredi 11 Octobre

It was a dream.

He lay on the bed, eyes half closed, trying to recapture the sleep that was quickly fading - but at the same time trying to focus on the dream in front of him. They were hazy at first, just two blurs, but slowly they came into focus. He must be in Heaven.

There were two women standing at the end of the bed. And they were both completely naked.

Jacques Mesrine smiled and winced at the same time as he moved onto the tender spot.

Janou came over. *"Bonjour mon amour,* you are feeling better?"

"Bonjour ma petite." He reached out and caressed her smooth thigh. "How long have I been asleep?"

"Off and on for four days. You had a fever." She smiled towards the other woman. "You remember I introduced you to Sylvie?"

Sylvie pulled a robe across her shoulders - an act which concealed nothing - and grinned. There was naughtiness in her eyes. "Hello. It is nice to have you back with us again. We were worried about you."

"Hush!" said Janou. "He'll get big headed!"

"But it is true!" Sylvie's voice was rich and golden. "You

should have seen her. She was worried to death about you."

"Sylvie, *hush!* Go and prepare breakfast, you wicked child."

Sylvie moued at Mesrine, poked her tongue out at Janou and went out of the room. Mesrine saw a beautiful, full round bottom beneath the diaphanous robe. He could have sworn it blew a kiss at him.

"How is it?" asked Janou. "Let me see."

"Bloody sore, but I'll live." Mesrine turned onto his front.

Janou pulled back the bedclothes. She could not help grinning but she dare not let Jacques see her. Of all the places to get stabbed! "Looks better this morning," she commented. "But we must keep the cream on it like the doctor advised."

"Pah! It is not deep!" he mumbled into the bolster. "A flesh wound, that is all."

"Six centimetres is not a flesh wound. As he said, six centimetres anywhere else could have been fatal. In your arse it was nothing more than a cut. But still a severe cut. And you have had a fever and shock reaction." She slapped on the ointment. Mesrine flinched.

"And you are very bruised," nagged Janou. "I ask you, fancy driving all day with a stab wound underneath you!"

"Shut up woman. You are worse than a wife. Nag, nag, nag. If I didn't love you, I'd marry you!"

But he had to acknowledge that what she said was true. He had driven the two hundred and forty kilometres from Deauville to Paris all day Saturday after spending a total of three hours cleaning up after the unfortunate 'accident'. He had not intended to harm either of the Le Bouthilliers, not even Madame's finger, but after she had attacked him and the old man had foolishly joined in... well, instinctive self-preservation had taken over.

He had arrived in St Germain-en-Laye to the west of Paris late in the afternoon. The long distance had taken even longer as he had to drive with one cheek off the seat and an increasing temperature. An RER Ligne A train to Charles de Gaulle-Etoile and then metro Ligne 2 to Pigalle and into the bar to wait for Janou.

She had not come in for two hours, during which time Mesrine had become very restless, ill and just a little drunk. When she had appeared she had made no pretence of picking him up, she had come straight across, shocked at his appearance. She knew better than to ask questions, but it was obvious that Jacques needed a doctor and fast.

Even after all this time it was likely that the *flics* were watching her place, so she could not take chances. Her friend Sylvie had a place in Rue du Ponceau off the Rue St Denis. She would put them up. No fear of any clients calling as she was a visiting girl.

Once they were safely in the apartment, a *médicin* of dubious character from Belleville had been called. He was used to treating the combatants of Parisian street fights and he had no reason to believe *le m'sieur* was anything else. He did not recognise the face that in the past months had been plastered over every newspaper and TV screen in the country.

A tetanus jab, an undisclosed tablet and a jar of ointment in exchange for a donation of one thousand francs, and the doctor was on his way, silent for ever.

"Breakfast!" called Sylvie from the kitchen. "Shall I bring Jacques' in?"

"No," called Mesrine rising. "I am not an invalid. I shall have it in there." He rose very carefully from the bed, trying not to show his dizziness. "Do you have a robe?"

"Only a flimsy nightgown of Sylvie's, my sweet," grinned Janou. "I'm not sure it would suit you."

"But I cannot sit down at the table like this!"

"Of course you can," said Sylvie from the doorway, a pot of hot coffee in her hand. "We do not mind. We have seen boys before, you know."

"But I am stark naked!"

"No! Really?"

Mesrine hobbled into the *salle*, trying unsuccessfully to keep one hand over his dick without looking as if he was being modest. The delicious smell of the coffee and warm croissants reminded him how hungry he was. Over by the window, the pot was full and the plate was high.

Janou produced a cushion. "Here, sit yourself down and eat. And behave yourself. We are Sylvie's guests."

Mesrine smiled at his pretty, blonde-haired, big busted hostess. "*Mais naturellement*." He sat down, poured the coffee into his *bol* and dipped in his first croissant. "I like your place, Sylvie. All yours?"

"*Oui*. Originally I rented it, but when my man took me off the streets and moved me up, he bought it for me. I have the deeds."

"That was remarkably kind." For a pimp, he added to himself.

"He was a remarkably kind man." Sylvie had her bowl in her hands and was sipping from it. "He really did love me."

"Did?"

Janou explained. "Sylvie's man was killed last year. Outside on St Denis. A disagreement with a customer over the rates for one of his other girls. A knife..." She shrugged.

"So who protects you now?" asked Mesrine.

"No one." Sylvie put down the bowl and broke a roll. "I run my own business from here. That," she nodded at the white telephone in the corner with the answering contraption beneath, "is my sole employer."

"But this is a rough area. Beaubourg, the old Halles, the street is famous for its girls in doorways. Wouldn't a business be better run from, say, Neuilly or somewhere in the sixteenth?"

"Maybe. But I like it here. I was brought up here, introduced to the trade here. I could move if I wanted to, I make enough. But I shall not go until I retire."

Mesrine looked at her face, surprisingly soft and innocent for a whore. "And when will you do that?"

"When I am thirty or when I marry, whichever is the sooner."

He poured his second bowl of coffee. "You are a woman who knows her own mind. I like that. You have done Mesrine a great favour by accommodating him here. He must think of a way of repaying you."

Janou nudged her friend. "Careful Sylvie, I think he likes you."

"I am grateful to you beyond words, Sylvie. You know who I am. The infamous Jacques Mesrine! Thief! Murderer! The most wanted man in Europe. The most wanted man in the world. Yet you take me in. I will not forget this."

Sylvie smiled. Not the false, lecherous smile of the professional tart, but the smile of an attractive, intelligent woman. *"Tu es très gentil, Jacques."*

Janou began to clear away the bowls, leaving Mesrine's as he refilled it for a second time.

The telephone rang.

"Shall I get it?" he asked.

"No, no, the machine will take it," said Sylvie. "Probably somebody fixing for tonight."

"Ah." Mesrine licked his finger and began lifting crumbs from the table and popping them into his mouth. "You never bring your customers here?"

"I always visit. *Pourquoi?*"

"I may need somewhere to stay. I have a couple of places, but until I see how the land lies may I stay here?"

Janou's voice came above the sound of the running water from the sink. "That's it. You'll never get rid of him now!"

Sylvie laughed, stood up, bent over and kissed him on the top of the head. "He may stay here for as long as he likes," she called back to her friend. Her eyes met his.

She walked away, the gown open down the front, concealing nothing, not even the fact that she was not a natural blonde.

At that moment Mesrine wanted her. Her wanted her very much. It was only after feeling the first stirrings of arousal that he remembered he was stark naked. As his erection peeked above the top of the table, the two women looked at him and giggled.

Jacques Mesrine blushed red as an edam cheese.

Sylvie's phone rang regularly throughout the day. Although Mesrine expected it, he was surprised. If all the calls were for that evening, she was a hell of a busy lady.

In mid-afternoon she had a private session with the answering machine, transferring the messages from the headphones to dates in her notebook. Mesrine would have loved to have heard the messages, but he thought it unwise even to make the suggestion.

One thing he had decided: sometime he would have her. She was gorgeous. Wonder how much she charged her clients? However much it was not enough, not for that body.

Janou returned from shopping as Sylvie was going out to work at 17:30. Sylvie had what she termed a 'double-nighter' - somebody had booked her for two nights and days - and she was carrying a small overnight case. They bade farewell to each other and soon Mesrine and Janou heard Sylvie's car start up downstairs and the friendly ribald comments of the girls out on the street as she drove past.

"Here," Janou handed over *Le Figaro* and *France-Soir* and watched his face fall as he saw that he was not on the front pages. "*Et voici te pantalon.*" She held out the distinctive red and white *Monoprix* bag. "It was all they had in your size. It is not a very big branch in Sebastopol."

Mesrine pulled out the grey slacks. "They are fine, *ma petite,* fine. You had enough money?"

"Certainly."

"Good. But I must get some more. Maybe a spectacular stunt is called for. It would get me back on the front pages. How dare they take the great Mesrine off after only one day!" He was trying to make light of it, but Janou knew he was serious.

"Also I got you these." With a flourish she held up a pair of bright scarlet underpants.

Mesrine guffawed. "*Merde alors chérie*, but you think of everything!" He pulled her to him and kissed her.

"How are you feeling?" she asked after the embrace.

"*Pas mal*, in my self. Physically my arse is sore and, strangely enough, my leg feels a little stiff."

"You should rest, perhaps for a few weeks."

Mesrine looked around. "I might do just that. I like this place. It is safe. I like - "

"You like Sylvie."

"You mind?"

"Of course not! My dear boy, I do not own you. I love you. And I know Sylvie likes you too."

He grabbed her round the back of the neck, pulled her to him roughly, and kissed her again, long and hard. "You are a hell of a woman, Janou," he said softly after the embrace.

"Nonsense." She licked the tip of his nose. "I am a woman, *simplement*. We go back a long way."

He nodded. "A lot of water has flowed through the stable doors since then."

"*Oui, beaucoup d'eau.*"

"But I have things to do. There are places I must be seen in."

"*Je comprends.*" Janou understood, and she would not ask questions. She did not want to know. She had not even read the weekend's newspapers which had yet again splashed his name and picture over their front pages. It was the best way.

"What about food?" she asked.

"If I had my wardrobe from Marcel's, we could go anywhere. I would like to take you out. I have not been to *La Tour d'Argent* for some time. But perhaps going out is not wise for the moment. I shall eat here. Sylvie's freezer is well stocked."

"Shall I prepare you something?"

"*Non, non,*" he took her hand. "I will do it later. When are you going to work?"

"Soon. I need to go home first."

"Then we have time." He raised her hand and kissed it.

"Time? For what?"

"Well, I told you. I have this stiffness…"

✝

36. Voleur et concièrge

Vendredi 13 Octobre

Despite the date, that day in Paris was glorious. Not a cloud in the blue autumn sky. A gentle breeze wafted the smells of the city together: the *patisseries*, the *boucheries*, the fruit on the market stalls, the cigarette smoke, the coffee, the traffic fumes, the musty boiled rice smell of the sewers from the metro ventilation shafts, all forming to make a not unpleasant scent that was uniquely Parisian.

The Passage Charles Albert runs roughly north to south up in the 18th Arrondisement and, as with all roads that run off at an angle from the direction of the Seine, the even numbers are on the right as looked at from the river. Thus it was that the sun did not shine directly on the entrance to number 124 until late afternoon.

Madame La Salle was sitting on a creaky old wooden chair outside the doorway, pinafore over two thick cardigans, glasses on, trying to read last week's edition of *France Dimanche*.

It was quiet in the Passage, but now and then noise would drift through from the Rue Jules Cloquet further up where the shops were. Pedestrians passed by, some (usually the older ones, not these roughneck young) occasionally stopping to pass the time of day.

With her glasses on she could see him clearly when he was still some way down the road. Monsieur Lenoir had returned!

At least - ?

It *was* Monsieur Lenoir, she could not mistake him, he was a big man. Yet he seemed different. He was limping noticeably, and he kept looking about as if he was searching for someone. But it was the clothes, that's what made him look different. Short jacket and grey *pantalon*, shirt but no tie. She was used to seeing him in his business clothes, not dressed casually. But what could she expect? The man was just returning from a break with his family, he would not be dressed for the Bourse!

She chided herself for being a stupid old woman, and watched him approach. She wondered about the limp. The poor man had probably hurt himself playing with the children. It always happened. The unfit father!

The big, charming smile spread across his face as he saw her sitting outside. What a *nice* man he was.

"*Bonjour Madame La Salle!*" he called. "A lovely day!"

"*Bonjour Monsieur Lenoir*, welcome back." Good Lord, he did not look at all well. He was as white as a ghost. "How was Nice?"

"Nice was fine, fine."

"You do not look too brown, monsieur."

"Ah," he nodded sadly. "A little accident. With the dog, you know? I was inside with my foot up most of the time." He helped her to rise, her old elbow shaking in his powerful hand.

"Pah! Men of your age should be careful," she reprimanded. "You try to do too much. You go on vacation and wear yourselves out, so you are none the better for it." They walked slowly into the dark foyer. "Look at me. I have eighty-six years and I have never taken exercise in my life. It is a killer m'sieur, mark the words of an old woman who intends to live for a lot longer yet."

"Madame, you are right. Undoubtedly right."

They stopped by her little *loge*. She patted his arm. "I have something to show you," she confided, the gleam in her eye made all the more mischievous by the gruff expression beneath. "I think it will amuse you. *Ici.*"

Lenoir pulled open the hinged counter and they entered her little sanctum. "What on earth can it be?" he put the incredulity into his voice to humour her. Sweet old biddy. But he hoped it would not take too long, he did not feel good.

A newspaper lay on the small table, wrinkling at the corners where it had been screwed up and then flattened out again. It was *Le Figaro* of a few days ago.

"Look!" she pointed.

Lenoir looked. The headlines were about the Mesrine slayings. The most recent picture (moustachioed, longish hair) stared up from next to the text.

"What?"

"The picture. Look!"

"I cannot see anything unusual, madame. It is that murderer Mesrine."

"Ah, but watch!" She was excited now, like a child with a secret. From a drawer beneath the table she produced a knife and placed it over the upper lip on the picture. "Now!"

Lenoir hoped it was not what he thought. "*Madame, je regrette mais -* "

"True, true. But if you screw up your eyes, so…" She pulled off her glasses and squinted. "Do you not see? It is *you*, it is you! Isn't that funny! You'd best be careful of people who have not got their glasses on, m'sieur. What a catastrophe to be mistaken for *this* man!"

"Oh, madame," Lenoir sighed quietly, despondently. "Oh, madame…"

His hands went to her throat and he murdered her with the least possible pain.

‡

37. Voleur et fille

Samedi 14 Octobre

Sylvie did not return to the apartment in the Rue du Ponceau from her double-nighter until after the early hours. She entered quietly, turning the light on in the kitchen rather than in the *salle* which would reflect into the bedroom.

Opening the door of the *frigo*, she decided against making an omelette and instead grabbed the final piece of a chocolate gateau. Coffee was still warm on the hot plate and she poured a cup.

Carrying her food into the *salle*, she sorted through her bag while she ate. Usually she would make neat piles of the cash, cheques and credit card slips, ready to pay in in the morning, but after two days with one client she just had one, rather sizeable, wad of cash, English money from her diplomat friend.

After working out the current exchange rate (hmm, not bad for two days' work), she tidied up her plate and cup and then walked soundlessly to the bedroom door, pushing it open. A smile spread across her face as she saw what she wanted to see. He was in the bed. Fast asleep and snoring gently.

And the two suitcases in the corner (which, in fact, contained the last mortal traces of Monsieur Lenoir) showed that he had come to stay - at least for a while. She was pleased.

The shower was off the bedroom so she could not avoid some noise as she washed and douched and then rubbed herself with body lotion.

He was awake when she came back in. His sleepy eyes roved over her naked, glistening body, lingering on the large breasts which were suspended at an impossibly horizontal angle but irrefutably were without support.

"Hello," she whispered, the sheets rustling as she slid in next to him.

"*Bonsoir.*"

"I'm glad you are staying."

"Staying?"

"You have your cases."

"*Ah, oui.* You had a nice couple of days?"

"Work is work."

"Of course."

She bent forward and kissed him tentatively, her lips becoming stronger and more confident as he responded.

"You are not tired?" asked Mesrine as he ran his lips over her nose. His right hand came across and grasped one of the amazing breasts. It was solid.

"Not for you, my hero."

Her touched her lips with his index finger. "I'm no hero, I am just - "

"A hero." She sucked on the finger.

" - a man. I have talents, true - but I'm as mortal as anyone else. I have needs, I have hungers, I have - "

"Desires?"

"*Oui.*"

"Then, mortal hero, prove it to me. Or are you too sore?"

"I am *never* too sore. But be gentle with me. Don't hurt me."

She straddled him, her breasts on his head, the rock hard nipples demanding to be sucked. She straightened up, one tit in his mouth, the nipple being pulled. As she guided him into her, she gasped. "That," she said, "is not a mere mortal."

Gently she began to move her hips up and down.

‡

38. Flics

Lundi 16 Octobre

"I have an idea!" enthused Claude Gerard as Paul Richer let him into the apartment. They shook hands.

"*Bonsoir Claude,* and what is that?" Richer looked quite at home in his apron depicting brassiere, pants and suspenders on the front. It had been a gift from Gerard last time they had had a *soirée*.

Gerard nodded at the apron. "Just that! What say we see some of Pigalle tonight?"

"You're joking."

"No I'm not. Not to indulge, you understand. Just for a stroll about."

"If you feel like even *moving* after the meal I've prepared I shall feel highly insulted!"

Gerard sniffed the air. "*Alors,* smells delicious. *Qu'est-ce que c'est?*"

"Moussaka."

"My God, you will make someone a perfect wife one day!" From a brown paper bag he handed over a litre of Monoprix's best and a bottle of *Napoléon.*

"*Merci bien.* You proposing?"

"You'd probably be better than Mathilde. At least you can cook."

"Ah, but what about the other pleasures?"

"What other pleasures?"

Gerard sat down, loosened his tie and broke open a new packet of cigarettes. Chivas came over and flopped by his feet.

Richer called for him to pour two brandies. "And put some music on if you like."

Gerard studied the collection of about fifty cassettes as he poured the drinks.

A few moments later, Brel began to sing about the port of Amsterdam and the bellies of whores. Deciding that perhaps Brel was, after all, a bit on the depressive side, at least for so early in the evening, Gerard stopped the immortal man in mid-crochet and replaced him with Liberace, the American pianist.

"Want your cognac in there?"

"No, leave it there, I'll be out soon. I'll have one of your *sèches* too."

"You're the *chef.*" Gerard sat back down in the comfortable armchair, angled towards the window, and gazed at the byzantine magnificence of Sacré-Coeur on the *butte*. His mind wandered.

He mused on his case of the British diplomat and the whore. On the pretence of other matters, he had spoken to the man personally, explaining how the French government did not like to see a representative of an ally (ally! The British!) compromising himself like this.

The man had made self-deprecating clucking noises, understood completely, and had promised to behave. He had not. He had seen the tart on at least two more occasions to Gerard's personal knowledge, the last time being closeted away with her for two days and nights in a small hotel out near Torcy.

So, it was time for the photographs. Which would mean the man's removal from the embassy. But that was his look-out. Rather removal because of compromising ally photographs than blackmail by Red photographs -

"Fuckit!"

Richer's oath snapped him out of his reverie.

"Paul?" Gerard was on his feet. Chivas jumped away with a squeak.

Richer's furious face appeared in the doorway. "Know what?"

"What?"

"I'm out of eggs."

"Out of eggs? Is that all? I thought some catastrophe had happened."

"It *is* a catastrophe. I cannot make a roux without eggs! What time is it?" He wiped his hands on his apron.

Gerard looked at his wrist. "Mickey's big hand is just poking up Minnie's skirt. Eighteen forty-five."

Richer yanked off the apron. "I might just make it. There's a Co-Op down the road, closes at seven."

"I'll go." Gerard put down his cognac.

"No, no. My own fault. I'll go." Richer pulled on a jacket. "You just relax. Look after Chivas. You can wash up after, as usual." He went out.

Gerard settled down. Chivas leapt silently onto his lap, and Gerard absentmindedly stroked the cat while he stared out of the window. The room slowly darkened as the sun was obscured by the church above. He found himself on the verge of sleep.

Richer had been gone five minutes when the telephone rang.

The sudden, prolonged shrill startled Gerard back to awareness and the cat fled from the room. Bloody hell, the one moment Paul was not here and it had to ring. Should he ignore it?

It trilled again.

Could it be Paul from downstairs? No, he would come up. Could it be Mathilde? He had told her where he was going.

Ring.

He picked up the receiver.

"'Allo?"

"Bruno."

"Yes?"

"I had problems at Trouville, you probably heard. I did not intend to kill them."

"What? I'm sorry?"

The line went dead.

‡

39. Voleur

Mesrine slammed down the telephone. *Merde*. What had happened? A wrong number?

It was this infernal bloody machine of Sylvie's, all strapped up to this glorified tape recorder. She had told him to leave the phone alone if it rang, but she had not said anything about not using it to call out.

You were an idiot, Jacques, an imbecile. The Captain had *said* he would answer with his name.

After five minutes he began to see the funny side of it. Had he got through to one of Sylvie's clients? Now that would have perplexed whoever it was. Could it have been that British diplomat she had been telling him about, the one with the taste for conservative blue knickers, the one she had spent the double-nighter with in Torcy? Serves him right if it was. Shouldn't associate with young girls. After all, Sylvie was *his* -

He stopped himself. Heaven! Had he actually thought that? *His* Sylvie...?

It was an idea. She was a lovely girl. But he had tried permanency before with Lydia and Soledad, and it had not worked. Why should it on this occasion? And what about Janou?

But if you were on the run you were less noticeable with a woman by your side...

‡

40. Flics

By the time Richer returned, Gerard was on his fourth cognac and was feeling the warm, mellowing effects.

"She was closed," said Richer. "But there's a Felix Potin down in Rue Yvonne-Le-Tac, that's why I've been so long. Just caught her." He held the eggs in the air like an Olympian with the torch and hurried through into the kitchen.

Claude blew out a lungful of smoke and assaulted the cognac as if it was going out of fashion. "Had a call while you were out."

"Oh yes?"

"Weird. Think it was a wrong number. Somebody called Bruno."

There was silence. Slowly Richer's head came round the door.

"What?"

"Know him?"

"What did he say?"

"He hung up when he realised it wasn't you."

"He's… one of my snouts."

"Ah, that explains it. He mumbled something about some killings in Trouville. Mean anything?"

"Don't know. Hunting. He goes hunting. Did he say anything else?"

"No, he hung up like I said."

"*D'accord.*" Richer went back into the kitchen.

"Funny," said Gerard above the music, the smoke and the

effects of the alcohol. "Trouville should mean something to me, but I can't for the life of me remember why."

Richer grimaced wryly. God, Jacques, what a time to ring! Of all the seconds in all the days you had to pick one when he wasn't there and someone else was. And what a someone else!

And, my dear Claude, what an expression for you to use. *For the life of you.*

He hoped it wouldn't be.

With half a bottle of cognac inside him (not to mention the half litre of wine, two whiskies from Richer's cabinet and the delicious moussaka), Gerard was too far gone even to walk down the stairs. At around 23:00, in the middle of an intense discussion on the merits or otherwise of women shaving their pudendas, he keeled back in the chair and began to snore deeply.

Richer, not feeling over energetic himself, put the older man's feet on a pouffe, covered him with a blanket and left him to it. He shut Chivas in the kitchen and then went to bed.

Trouville. Would Claude remember in the morning? He hoped not. If Claude put two and two together... but he would not. He might realise the recent Mesrine murders had been committed there, but he could not possibly even guess at the link between Richer and the supercriminal. He had said nothing. There was nothing written down.

There was no way Claude could make the connection.

No way.

‡

41. Flic et voleur

Jeudi 19 Octobre

Richer had a briefing with Commissaire Fleury-Goujon that morning. The Commissaire had hinted that a trip to England might be on the cards. Whitehall were getting snotty about some photos Gerard had of one of their diplomats and a Parisian whore. They needed smoothing over. The personal touch. Couldn't send Gerard, of course, not on a public relations exercise.

The phone was ringing as Richer re-entered his office. He lit up a Gauloise.

"Richer," he mumbled half-heartedly into the mouthpiece.

"Bruno."

"Jesus! Where have you been?"

"I know, I know. I am sorry. There have been difficulties, you've no doubt read about them. Listen, I cannot stay - you know why."

"It's not tapped."

"I still have matters under control. It has been passed about. If only you'd tell me exactly what I am looking for - "

"Bruno, listen! We should meet - "

"No chance, Captain, the heat is on. I must drop out for a while. I am ill and I need a rest. I will contact you when I return."

"When?"

"I do not know. But I do not forget an agreement. I will go now."

"Wait! Jacques - "

He was gone.

‡

42. Voleur et fille

Dimanche 22 Octobre

Mesrine never worried, it was not in his character. So the best way to describe the emotion was *concern*. It had been caused by a simple incident that had happened when he was returning to the apartment last night.

The Rue St Denis has been described as 'the hottest street in Paris'. While recently, with the removal of the market in next door Les Halles to Rungis on the southern side of the city, the hottest street could be said to have cooled a bit, ladies of pleasure still paraded their wares in the doorways nearly 24 hours a day.

It was one of the pretty ones, nipples peeking over the top of her baby doll nightie, small G-string, and the incongruous but ubiquitous bag over her shoulder, who said hello to him as he passed by on his way to the apartment.

It wasn't what she said, it was the way she said it. It was not a come-on greeting, it was a greeting of neighbours. And it was that that concerned Mesrine. For it meant that he was becoming known. Sylvie's guy. And that was dangerous. Tongues wag.

So there was only one logical conclusion. Move. He needed a new pasture.

But what about Sylvie?

Over breakfast he announced that the time had come for him to look for a new place.

A sad smile passed over Sylvie's face, but she had been expecting it. This man, of all men, she could not hold on to forever.

She came over and sat on his lap, raising her negligée as she sat down so that her bare bottom rested against his flesh. Putting her arms around his neck, she kissed him.

"It had to happen," she said softly. "Janou warned me not to get involved, that you would have to leave some day. But I was hoping you wouldn't. At least, not so soon."

"Believe me, *ma petite*, there is nothing I would like better than to stay here with you. But I am a man on the run, and I have things to do. You must appreciate that. I am becoming known. 'The man who lives with Sylvie.' They cannot recognise me from the published pictures, but all it needs is a *flic* to overhear something in the salad basket *[the police wagon used to round up streetwalkers]* and come nosing."

Lightly, he stroked her thigh, the skin smooth and warm and inviting. She smelled of desire.

A tear filled her left eye but did not fall. "I shall miss you," she said at length.

"Really?"

"Really. In my business you do not have chance to become fond of men. Since my man was killed I have had nobody to love me, nobody to love. Not until you. And now you will leave me." Reluctantly, the tear fell.

He licked the tear, licked a dribble of snot from her nose, and licked the valley between her breasts. He caught the faintest of traces of last night's body oil.

"Come with me," he said.

It took a moment to sink in, then she pulled his hair back savagely. "*Qu'est-ce que tu dit?*"

He grinned. "Come with me."

She slammed his head back into her chest, pressing him hard into the solid mounds. "But... I cannot!... I mean... you would not want me... what you say is true... you are important... you are a hero... you do not want to be saddled with *me*..."

"Mmgurph," said Mesrine.

She wrenched his head back. "What?"

"Calm down, my child, calm down. I have already discussed it with Janou. She thinks it is a good idea."

"Jacques - my love - how can I? Do you *mean* it? Honestly mean it?" She pouted suspiciously. "You would not joke with me?"

"Of course I mean it. But it will mean leaving all this, all your clients."

"Fuck them."

"Exactly. But it is your living."

"*Was* my living. As of this moment Jacques Mesrine is my living. *Tout compris.*"

"But think of your future! With a criminal. With a man on the run - "

"With a man I love! Oh, do not change your mind Jacques. Oh say you mean it, please say you mean it." She was jumping up and down on his lap, with the consequent profound effect on a certain part of his anatomy.

"Sylvie," he said softly. "I promise you. I mean it."

With a whoop of joy she leapt from his lap, went over to the wall and yanked the telephone and answering machine from the socket. "*Voila!*" she dropped the lot on the floor with an almighty thud. "Sylvie Jacquot, call-girl, no longer exists. I am *yours.*"

She bounced back, threw a leg over and squatted on his naked lap. "Let us begin the way we mean to carry on."

He feigned astonishment. "Here and now? At the breakfast table?"

"Here and now. At the breakfast table."

"You little animal."

"I have never denied it."

She manoeuvred herself so that he slipped up into her.

Between bites at her breasts, he mumbled "I've heard of having a roll for breakfast, but this is ridiculous!"

‡

43. Flics puis Voleur

Lundi 30 Octobre

"Nice arse, don't you think? I wouldn't mind slipping that one myself."

"Personally I'm a tit man, Chief," said Inspector Bauer looking over Gerard's shoulder.

"She's generous with those as well," Gerard shuffled through the packet of photographs and produced a top torso shot. A bald headed, middle-aged man was hanging by his teeth from her right nipple.

"The Brits don't want to know," sniffed Gerard. "They're even kicking up a bit of a fuss because we took the pictures in the first place. I'll never understand them. They pretend they're the height of sophistication yet underneath they alternate between strict prudery and unabashed savagery. I think the whole country needs to see a shrink." As he spoke he was laying the photos out one by one across his desk.

Bauer was smiling. Work or no work, it was still a pleasure to see a girl getting well and truly shafted. "So no action?" he asked.

"Not against him. But I've found who the girl is." Gerard turned over the last photo - a particularly raw and slightly blurred shot of anal intercourse - and read the particulars. "Sylvie Jacquot, 3 Ponceau, just off St Denis."

"Form?"

"Picked up six times when she was on the streets. Nothing since she moved indoors."

"Want me to pull her?"

"Put the frighteners on. Scare her off the *rosbeef*. If she doesn't co-operate, show her these." He selected three photos and gave them to the Inspector.

"*D'accord.*"

"Take a couple of lads in case you have trouble with her pimp."

"Know who he is?"

"No. Some new guy, so rumour has it. Once he sees their uniforms he'll be off like a shot. It'll be the worse for this little darling when he comes back later of course, but that can't be helped. She shouldn't be a naughty girl."

"Right."

"And Bauer?"

"Yes Chief?"

"No fucking, not even for free."

"Thanks a lot, Chief. How about a blow job?"

"Kind of you to offer but I've just eaten."

Bauer had been hammering on the downstairs door for three minutes with no answer. The two uniformed men remained in the unmarked car with the tinted windows.

Once again Bauer stepped back and looked at the upstairs window. There was no abrupt movement, no curtain quickly closing. The place was still.

A female voice said, "She's gone."

Bauer turned. A little way along, on the corner of Rue St Denis, a girl in a baby doll nightie lounged against the wall.

"Gone?"

The girl pushed herself upright and walked towards him, high heels clicking, handbag over one shoulder, keys jingling in her hand.

"She left this morning."

"When will she be back?" Bauer's eyes rested on her nipples jutting over the top of her nightie.

"No, she's left. Moved. She's never coming back."

"Did she leave a forwarding address?"

The girl laughed. "What do you think, *mon amour*? You'll have to find yourself another friend."

"Fuck," said Bauer.

"Five hundred francs," said the girl.

"Forget it," said Gerard when Bauer reported back. "She could be traced, no problem. She owns the apartment. But why bother? If the *rosbeefs* don't care, I'm sure I don't. She's not worth a toss." Which, considering what he had been doing with the photographs in the lavatory that afternoon, was a lie.

Earlier that day, Monsieur and Madame Renoir ("No, no relation, I cannot even paint by numbers!") had taken over the lease of an apartment at 7 Impasse St François in the 18th Arrondisement. The concièrge had been struck by the charm of *le monsieur*, a tall man with a beard and a mop of curly hair.

‡

44. Voleur

Vendredi 10 Novembre

On this day Jacques Mesrine made a bungled attempt to kidnap Judge Petit, the presiding judge at his last trial.

Whether it was due to lack of planning, underestimation of what the job would entail, or just downright ill-health (Mesrine's knife wound simply refused to heal completely and he was still subject to spasmodic bouts of fever), or a combination of all three, is debatable, but the outcome was a fiasco in which the police were alerted and Mesrine only narrowly missed being recaptured.

He came face to face with the police as he was fleeing down the stairs from the judge's apartment after realising his game was lost. He used his usual trick of becoming one of them. Gun in one hand, handcuffs (which had been meant for his victim) in the other, he shouted that the intruder was still in the block and ordered the advancing men upstairs. As they rushed past him, he continued downwards.

The only policeman to recognise Mesrine was a young officer who had been left to guard the entrance to the building. And it was this recognition which caused the fear that froze all his bodily functions except his bladder, that saved his life. He was found later, handcuffed to a nearby lamppost, sobbing quietly. His pantalon *were saturated.*

Although the attempt had been a farcical flop, when the story burst in the following day's papers Mesrine was again a hero thanks to his lenient treatment of the young officer.

Samedi 11 Novembre

Armistice Day celebrations in Paris always put a great strain on the capital's police forces. With the knowledge that Mesrine was certainly back in town, and the hunt for him now renewed with avengeance, the strain that year was almost at breaking point. But for that weekend all available men were on crowd control, so the hunt for Mesrine would have to wait at least until Monday.

So it was that Jacques Mesrine was able to visit the Gare du Nord that Saturday and book two tickets on tomorrow morning's train to London without so much as a second glance from anybody.

He was displeased with himself. A displeasure bordering on the fury. All right, the newspapers were lauding him, he was popular again. But the popularity did not assuage the fact that he had failed. He had failed himself, as the ransom for Judge Petit could have seen him through many a month.

And he had failed the Captain as he had not yet gotten the document, the item he had to retrieve without even knowing what it was.

He was unwell and he needed to get away, out of Paris, out of France. He loved London second only to Paris. He needed to go there. Maybe he would rent a flat. Sylvie would like the town. They would live well, but not extravagantly. And when the money ran out... Well, he would face that bridge when he came to it.

He was getting tired. If only he had enough money to retire, to settle down, to spend the rest of his life with Sylvie. He would be able to end his life of crime. He would be able to *try* to live like a normal person.

If only...

‡

45. La visite

Vendredi 15 Décembre

"Inspector Richer?"

"Chief Inspector Richer, madame," he said in heavily accented English. "From the Sûreté, in Paris."

"So you said on the telephone. Please, won't you sit down?" Julie Bayfield was an attractive woman in her late thirties, hair long but tied up, dressed in a classic but tight-fitting blue two piece. The Frenchman liked what he saw.

She accepted his offer of a cigarette, *Ma Griffe* wafting in his direction as she leant forward for a light.

"So," she said as she sat back in her swivel chair. "What brings a French policeman all the way to London on a cold winter's Friday? It must be something important."

"Something which needs... discretion, madame. Firstly, my thanks for seeing me at such a time. I am duty bound to point out to you that I have no authority as a police officer in your country. I am here on other business. For the purpose of this conversation I must be regarded as being here as a private citizen."

"Intriguing. Well then, would you like some tea *Monsieur* Richer?"

"That would be nice, thank you."

She spoke into an intercom on her desk and then smiled back at him. "So, in a private capacity, what can I do for you?"

"Madame, I believe you have in your possession certain documents which were stolen from a French resident almost a year ago. I am investigating the crime."

"And what makes you think I have these documents?"

"My investigations have shown me that since the theft these documents have passed through many hands. The last possessor of them confessed to me that he sent them to an auction house in London. Both Phillips and Sotheby's deny any knowledge of the documents and both suggested I contact you. You specialise, I believe, in books, manuscripts, letters, that sort of thing."

"I see. Well, Chief Inspector - " There was a tap on the door and a young boy entered carrying a tray. "Thank you, Clint."

"Miss." Clint put the tray on her desk and ambled off.

"Milk and sugar?"

"Black, just as it comes, please madame."

"Unusual." She poured.

"You know us French!" he laughed as he accepted the china cup and took a chocolate biscuit from the proffered plate. "Do you have the articles, madame?"

She sipped her tea. "We are a small, family firm. Not in the league of the major auction houses."

"An ideal situation if someone wanted to sell something unobtrusively."

"You are not, I hope, implying some sort of criminal action on the part of this house?"

"No, no, no, madame, not at all."

"Good. In which case I will look in our records. You realise if we do find something I am not going to simply hand it over to you."

"Proper procedures will be followed madame."

"Right. Now what are the documents about?"

"I have no idea."

She looked at him quizzically. "Well then, were they signed?

Who was the originator?"

"The Duke of Windsor, the Duchess of Windsor."

She smiled. "Oh yes. In that case I do not have to look in our records."

"Madame?"

"There were a bundle of letters and assorted documents."

"You read them?"

"No. I did not have time to. I just looked at the top one. It was an old love letter. Authentic enough, but there really is no market for them. Not in this country, anyway."

He put his cup and saucer down on the edge of her desk. "So you still have them?"

She moved his crockery onto the tray, next to hers. "No. I was going to include them in my spring catalogue but I had an enquiry for them. From your country actually. From France. The offer was reasonable, so I let them go."

"The offer was only reasonable?"

"I told you, they were of little value. And she is notoriously litigious. To trade in her letters while she is still alive might be inviting trouble. I made a small profit." She shook her head regretfully. "I'm sorry Chief Inspector, but it seems your trip here was wasted."

"Not at all, madame," he smiled a big, charming smile. "I have met you, have I not?"

She looked away coyly.

"And London at Christmas time!" he continued. "All those pretty lights! Might I presume to ask to whom you sold them?"

"Ah, the six-four thousand dollar question."

"Madame?"

"These documents were stolen, you say?"

"They were. And the lady wants them back."

"It is a question of ethics, you see. I sold them to a dealer in Paris. If I tell you his name, will I be implicated?"

"Madame, I can assure you. The French police have no

authority here. You bought the goods in good faith - and from a French policeman, Monsieur Le Bouthillier, *non*? Acting in good faith is not a crime. And you have your money."

"Yes. That is true." She tapped a pencil against her desk. "Do I have your word, Chief Inspector, that I will not be implicated?"

"Madame, your only offence is to unknowingly deal in stolen goods from another country. There is no reason for you to fear. I will not implicate you. The lady wants her letters back. She is not after retribution."

Julie stood up and took a small, thick book from a cabinet against the wall. She flicked through it, transferred certain details onto a sheet of paper and handed it to him.

He looked at it. "You know this man?"

"Not personally. I have occasional dealings with him."

"You would not, for example, be tempted to ring him and tell him of the Surêté's interest?"

"Now why should I do that? It is none of my business."

"No, of course not." He stood up. "Madame, I have taken up far too much of your time. You have been most gracious." He slipped his scarf around his neck and pulled on his gloves. "And most helpful. My thanks." He held out his right hand.

She came around the desk. "You are welcome, Chief Inspector. I always try to stay on the right side of the law." She went to shake his hand but somehow missed it.

"So do I, madame." His raised hand lunged for her throat. She gasped as the fingers sunk into her neck. Before she could even raise a hand in defence, she was lifted off her feet by the big, burly policeman. She tried to grab his arm for support. Her legs flailed. One of her shoes fell off.

His face was no more than half a metre away. He watched as her cheeks turned purple and her bulging eyes went from shock to incomprehension to pleading and to terror. They began to roll and fade.

"Forgive me, madame," he pleaded softly. "One day you will understand. I can take no chances."

His hand made a sudden movement as if turning a key in a lock. Her neck broke with a sharp *crack*.

Gently he placed her back down in her seat behind her desk. Slowly he lowered her forward so she looked as if she had fallen asleep.

Outside, he popped his head into the General Office. Clint was talking to a young popsie sitting behind a typewriter.

"Madame has asked not to be disturbed for one hour," said the Frenchman.

"Okay guv," nodded Clint. "Mind 'ow yer go now."

"I will." Jacques Mesrine turned up his collar and went out into the cold, blustery English wind.

‡

46. Voleur

Mesrine returned to France after only two months in London.

1979 was to become known as 'The Year of Mesrine' in Europe. How many petty crimes he committed is not known, but with each incident to which his name was linked (either properly or by certain members of the police who had no one else upon whom to pin the particular crime) the pressure for his capture increased.

In early January, Mesrine sent a threatening letter to Jean-Claude Lattes, the publisher of his autobiography, claiming that he was owed two hundred and thirty thousand francs. This was rather a forlorn attempt (it has been suggested by some that it was done purely for publicity) as Mesrine well-knew that the profits from the book had been frozen on the orders of the French government.

On Saturday 20 January he held up a supermarket in Massy and came away better off to the tune of four hundred thousand francs. This, together with the proceeds of the many robberies he committed in the second quarter of the year, went towards financing The Big One.

It was planned for months, to the exclusion of everything else. He planned down to the last detail, including intricate notations on the phases of the moon and whether or not leaves would be on the trees at any particular time.

The Big One happened on Thursday 21 June. Impersonating policemen, Mesrine and an accomplice [the rumour that this was Chrastny, his protegée, has never been proved] *kidnapped Henri Lelièvre from his house in the village of Maresche near Le Mans. Eighty-two year old Monsieur Lelièvre was an ex-banker and* industrialist, one of the richest men in France.

At a rented house in Breuil, near Blois, the victim was held for over five weeks. On Saturday 28 July he was released safe and well near a taxi rank in the 17th Arrondisement in Paris. The ransom paid was six million francs in used fifty franc notes.

Never one for modesty, Mesrine was pleased with himself to the point of jubilation. He had done it. This time he had really pulled it off. For the first time ever he felt financially secure. He could fulfil his dreams, he could plan his retirement. He would buy a property somewhere. He would marry Sylvie.

But later.

First there was a slate that needed to be wiped clean.

3ᴵᴱᴹᴱ PARTIE

‡

LE RECOUVREMENT

‡

47. L'Organisation

Vendredi 15 Juin

"How do you know he hasn't given up?" asked the man on the right, the chain smoker.

"I know him," answered Richer. "He will fulfil his debt. I told you it would take time."

"It is all a con," snapped the cap man. "He tricked us into getting him out of jail and now he is laughing at us. All these crimes he is committing, without one word to you. He will not fulfil any debt. There is no honour among thieves."

"But there is honour," said Richer calmly, "amongst the OAS."

There was silence. Then the Colonel smiled. "*Touché*, I think."

"Why don't we send someone else after it?" asked the chain smoker. "I don't mean some OAS James Bond. Just someone who knows about the subject."

"Someone who could make discreet, knowledgeable enquiries," suggested the cap man. "Someone who will not run amok over France and have the entire bloody judiciary gunning for him!"

Richer finished his cigarette and immediately lit another. "That is at your discretion, of course. But Mesrine wouldn't take kindly to it."

"Mesrine wouldn't take kindly to it!" scoffed the chain smoker. "Fuck Mesrine. He is a simple conscript - like yourself,

Captain. He obeys orders. Like yourself, Captain."

"Could you call him off?" asked the Colonel.

Richer shook his head. "I have no way of contacting him. He contacts me. And in the present climate, with everyone wanting his blood, he is not likely to. He suspects my phones are bugged."

"And are they?"

Richer shrugged. "You tell me. There is no reason why they should be." He held the Colonel's eyes.

"Tell us what the secret is," urged cap man. "Then we can ask someone else to look for it."

Richer transferred his gaze. "That order must come from the Colonel himself. Otherwise my answer is no."

The Colonel looked from cap man to Richer. Then he looked at the man on his left. He said to Richer, "You do not want to tell us?"

"Not yet, sir. Not till we have the document. Be patient. Let Mesrine get on with it. He will not fail."

"He'd better not," came a mumble from the left.

The Colonel breathed out long and slow. "And La Dame?"

"She is unconscious most of the time now. I have managed to speak to her twice this year. She doesn't know who I am or what the hell I am talking about."

"*Alors,*" the Colonel nodded. "For now, Captain. For now we will leave it. But our patience is wearing thin. We must have a return on our investment soon."

‡

48. Voleur et receleur

Mardi 31 Juillet

It was overcast, warm yet with a sharp breeze that whistled along the boulevards and gave spasmodic reminders that summers can never be guaranteed. The big, tall man with the dark, deep set eyes did not look out of place in the open beige trenchcoat as he walked along Boulevard Montmartre and turned into the Passage de Panoramas.

He had expected the shops in the Galeries Montmartre to be closed for the *'Fermeture Annuelle'*, but a phone call earlier that morning had revealed that the one he was interested in did not shut until the end of the week.

The bell on the door *ting-a-ling*ed as he entered the small, musty premises. The lights were on, there was the smell of cigarette smoke, yet no one was there. He closed the door behind him and looked around.

A scuffling sound came from somewhere. As if by magic some papers rose in the air from behind the desk. They were followed by a mumbled "Oh dear", and then the bespectacled Monsieur Buisson came into view.

He jumped as he noticed the visitor. *"Ah, monsieur! Pardonez-moi!* I did not realise there was anyone here. What can I - ?" He frowned at the man on the other side of the desk. "Do I not know you?"

The visitor's hand went towards the right pocket of his

trenchcoat, the one that looked like it had something heavy in it.

"Undoubtedly."

"Let me think," Buisson looked hard into his eyes. Then he nodded. "Oh yes. I know you."

The visitor's hand went into the pocket.

"It was a while ago, wasn't it? Sometime last year…" His upper lip wrinkled, then his face cleared and he said, "The police."

"The police?"

"I am not wrong, am I? Are you not from the police? Were you not here before?"

The visitor laughed. "You remember?"

"Indeed. I am right then."

"I was here last year making enquiries about autographs of La Dame."

"La Dame… yes, I recall. Didn't something happen? Did I not read…?"

"Yes, the name you gave me. Inspector Le Bouthillier. He died."

"Yes, yes. That is right. Poor man."

"Well, you know how it is," said the visitor chattily. "When people don't co-operate."

"Yes indeed. Well, what - " The smile fell from Buisson's face as he realised what had been said.

The visitor still grinned at him.

"Y - you mean the *police* killed him?" The shopkeeper removed his pince-nez and began rubbing them on a dirty handkerchief.

"No, no, you're missing the point. Not the police. *Mesrine.* Jacques Mesrine." The hand came out of the trenchcoat pocket holding a gun - a weird-looking object with a round, bulbous knob on the end which resembled the glans of a penis. "You may have heard of me."

Buisson's mouth was open. It stayed that way, a single strand of spittle joining his upper and lower teeth.

"Let me introduce you to my little friend," said Mesrine.

Buisson went cross-eyed as he stared at the gun no more than thirty centimetres from his face. His jaw trembled.

"Although her beauty leaves something to be desired, her physical performance is excellent. She is a foreign lady. Russian. You have not met her like before, hmm?"

"N - n – n- "

Mesrine ran the circular tip down the edge of Buisson's face. "She likes you. I can see that. Pray that she does not want you. She is like a Black Widow. Deadly. And she is silent, did you know? She doesn't go *bang*, she doesn't even go *phut*. She just goes *click*." He came round behind the shopkeeper. He could smell his fear as he said softly into his ear, "*Click*, monsieur. And if you are her mate, you do not even hear it."

An involuntary fart shot out from the seat of Buisson's chair. "I - "

"You will co-operate, yes? Then you need soil yourself no further."

"Y - yes."

"*Très bien*. Now, m'sieur, you have been very naughty, have you not?" The gun tapped lightly and rhythmically around Buisson's face. "After I had been here last year – my God, what did you have for breakfast? - you contacted your client, the late lamented Inspector Le Bouthillier. You told him, no doubt, of the police interest and you advised him to sell the document. Make a quick profit before the police seized them."

"I did not - "

The gun prodded sharply into his lips, breaking two of his front teeth. The obscene bulb slid into his mouth like a cock. "Do not talk to me if you are going to lie." Buisson screwed up his eyes in agony. "Now, the Inspector took your advice. He sold them to a dealer in London. He told you. And here you pulled what you thought was your master stroke. After the fuss of the death had died down, you contacted the dealer and bought them back. You realised that if they were important enough for a thief - a thief identified publicly as the great Jacques Mesrine - to kill for, then you were onto a very, very big profit margin indeed."

The gun came out of Buisson's mouth and slowly wiped spittle and blood across his cheek. One of his front teeth had been snapped at the gum.

"But you came unstuck, did you not?" continued Mesrine. "You couldn't shift them. Weren't you surprised at the price the London dealer let them go at?"

"I didn't - "

"Shut up. Did she not tell you they were of very little value, especially over there? People look at the signatures you see, and they do not want their's. They are not fashionable. People do not look at the contents of one document slipped among a handful of namby-pamby love letters. I suspect you have not been able to sell them, m'sieur. I believe they have been here, in this shop, for the last seven months. Am I right, m'sieur?"

At last that horrible, tormenting gun left Buisson's face. His mouth was swollen and sore. His throat was dry and tight. "N - n - near enough, m'sieur. You are correct. Yes."

"Good. Then I will take them off you now, if you please."

"No."

"I beg your pardon?" The gun came back towards him.

"Y - you were almost right. They hung around here for ages. But I sold them. Two weeks ago."

"*You did what?*"

"A collector. I had offered them to him before but he was not interested. Then two weeks ago he changed his mind."

"Why should he do that?"

"Said something about a wedding present for his daughter."

"And you sold them to him for ten times what you paid for them."

"Only d - double this time."

"I do not believe this," Mesrine spoke to himself.

"It - it is true, m'sieur. I swear."

"This is simply impossible. These letters are more elusive than a virgin in Pigalle. *Alors, monsieur,* a simple request then you will never see me again."

A piece of paper was placed in front of Buisson.

"Name and address please."

Slowly, Buisson's trembling fingers picked up his pince-nez from the desk. He got them onto his nose at the second attempt. Carefully he stood up, all the while keeping an eye on the gun. A rivulet of blood was running slowly from his mouth and pooling on his chin.

Under Mesrine's close supervision he searched through his index. About halfway along he pulled out a card.

Mesrine reached over and grabbed his hand, holding it steady as he looked at the details on the card. Then he gave a soft, ironic laugh.

"*This* man?"

"*Oui.*"

"This *is* impossible. Someone up there is playing games with me. *This man?*" He stared at the card for a few more moments, shaking his head. "It is so ridiculous, I believe you. *Bien.* Now, please sit down, m'sieur - No, no, take the card with you." He stood behind him again. "Now, I want you to make a little phone call, do you think you can do that? To that gentleman there."

"Him?"

"Yes. Can you do it without sounding unnatural? I can always impersonate you, but it would be much better coming from the real thing."

"Im - impersonate me?"

"It is always easy to impersonate the dead."

Buisson wiped his mouth and sighed. "What do you want me

to say?"

"Make it chatty. Talk about the weather. Ask after his family. You know. Then I want you to ask him whether he still possesses the autographs. Ask him whether he still has them and, if so, would he sell them back to you? Haggle if they are for sale, complain if they are not, the usual thing. You know, what you are expert at."

"That is all, m'sieur?"

"Yes. Don't enter into any agreements with him. If it comes to it, say you will have to confer with your client and get back to him."

The shopkeeper nodded that he understood.

Mesrine squatted beside him, the gun pressed snugly into his ribs. "Hold the telephone between our ears so that I can hear."

It took the shaky fingers three false starts before they managed to dial the number fully. A switchboard answered and put him through to a secretary. After explaining who he was and that it was a call regarding investment, Buisson was put through to the gentleman himself.

Mesrine listened and was pleased. The man confirmed to Buisson that he still had the papers in question but no, they were not for sale, not at any price.

After some concluding platitudes, Buisson terminated the call. He turned to Mesrine as the criminal stood up from his crouching position, rubbing his right buttock. The stab wound still nagged.

Mesrine smiled. He was pleased with Buisson. He had performed well. He could not have asked for better.

Which made it even more of a shame to kill him.

Mesrine looked at Buisson.

Buisson looked at Mesrine.

Click.

‡

49. Voleur

Jeudi 2 Août

The Avenue Alphonse XIII is a small residential avenue off the Rue Raynouard, just to the north of the church of Notre Dame de Grace de Passy in the select 16th Arrondisement of Paris. The buildings in the avenue are typically Parisian, between six and eight storeys high, tall narrow windows, daunting three metre high double black front doors, some leading into courtyards beyond.

As with most of these elegant buildings in the capital, those in Alphonse XIII have been converted into apartments, nonetheless luxurious and spacious for that. The apartment in question on this day was at number 5.

The clean-shaven man with the large, square spectacles, hair short, almost cropped and pushed straight back from his forehead, dressed in T-shirt and jeans, ambled along the Avenue. A man with a purpose but in no hurry to complete it, blatantly unhappy with his surroundings. He would have been more at home in the 14th across the river.

Standing outside number 5, he looked up at the building as if making up his mind that this was indeed the place he wanted. The decision made, he walked inside.

Although his rubber-clad shoes made no sound on the tiled floor, he was spotted by the concièrge immediately.

"Yes? Where do you think you're going?" snapped the man

from his *loge*, adapting his tone to suit the person in front of him.

"Ah," the visitor turned as if he had only just noticed the kiosk. "*Bonjour m'sieur*, I am looking for - " He fumbled in his pocket and produced a scrap of paper, folded in half. "Er - " He passed it across.

The concièrge frowned at the rough, uneducated writing, and held the scrap of paper with the tips of his fingers. "What month is it?" he asked disdainfully.

The visitor was taken aback. "*Comment?*"

"The month. What is it?"

"Er," he fiddled nervously. "August?"

"*Exactement!*" The concièrge threw the piece of paper back, point made. It fell to the floor. "How do you expect such a man to be in Paris in August? He has gone away, dolt. Always does this time of year. Won't be back till the end of September at the earliest, maybe later. What did you want to see him about anyway? What would the likes of you want with him?"

"That, m'sieur, is my business."

The concièrge looked up, surprised at the sudden change in the man's tone. The man was staring at him. The concièrge felt angry but also, for some reason, very much afraid. Damn upstart working classes, didn't know their place nowadays. "Was there something else?" he asked.

"No."

"Then I think you'd better leave."

"Yes." The man turned and left.

The concièrge stared after him.

Only later, when he was leaving his *loge*, did he notice the piece of paper on the floor, lying where he had thrown it.

‡

50. Flics

Lundi 3 Septembre

This day in 1979 was noted for two reasons. Firstly, it was the fortieth anniversary of the outbreak of the Second World War. Secondly, and more importantly, it was the day Paul Richer made the mistake.

It had been such a fine summer as well, in all ways. Richer was deeply tanned after three weeks camping on the Côte d'Azur. In the two weeks since his return he had sorted out four major problems concerning diverse foreign interests and was well on his way to organising the deportation of a certain Middle Eastern religious leader who had only been admitted to France on the strict understanding that he would engage in no political activity and had then proceeded to do just that.

Richer felt good, both physically and professionally. And it was probably this that led him into the blunder.

It was 15:00. Richer, brown and open-necked, sat smoking in the office as he completed a report on the suspected bestial proclivities of the son of a German industrialist baron resident up north. Across the room Gerard, peeling pink from his annual week in Ostend, could just be seen through a haze of Disque Bleue, writing in a file.

Richer's telephone rang. Absentmindedly he stretched out a hand, still concentrating on the report in front of him.

"Richer."

"Bruno."

He said it. "Bruno who?"

Gerard's head shot up as if he had been hit in the back by an RER express train.

"Bruno."

"Oh! Yes!" Richer looked across the room. His colleague was fumbling in a drawer, coughing. He appeared not to have heard. "Sorry. It's been so long. Thought you'd given up."

"I've had other things to do."

"So I've read. Congratulations. A good job. But you know the numbers were noted?"

"So I have discovered. I have had to have them laundered. And that is expensive. I wanted to retire but now there must be one more job."

"Who?"

"Don't be silly. One more, then I can retire. But I never forget an agreement, *Capitaine*. I am very close now. Shortly the item will be yours."

"I have authority to end it. You can stop if you want to."

"An agreement is an agreement. I will contact you soon."

"D'accord."

The caller hung up.

Richer sat, his eyes on the report on the desk.

Mesrine had had to launder the six million franc ransom paid for Henri Lelièvre because the bank had recorded all the numbers before handing them over. At the most he would get forty per cent of the true value. So he was not as rich as he had hoped to be. Now he was tying up loose ends prior to his final job and his retirement. And Richer was a loose end.

Across the room Gerard calmly picked up the telephone and, with no pretence of stealth, keyed the British Embassy.

"Meester Becker if you please." He spoke in English. A few moments later he said, "Good afternoon, Gerard BaySayPay."

"'Afternoon Claude old son. How's things?"

Without even looking at his colleague, Gerard said "A matter has raised its head again."

"Oh yes? And which matter would that be?"

"A matter of some time ago."

"Can't you - ? Oh, I see. Is someone there?"

"Yes."

"Right, so what matter concerned us some time ago? Not our man and his fancy lady, the one in the photos with nipples like coathooks? The bit of stuff that disappeared?"

"No."

"No, he's back in the UK now. The secretary who kept taking fees off casual enquirers?"

"No."

"Some time back?"

"Yes. Serious. The man."

There was a long pause, then Becker said lowly "I think we should meet."

"So do I. Soon."

"Tomorrow morning? At ten?"

"At your place."

"Right."

"*D'accord.*"

Gerard replaced the phone and stretched. Arms behind his head, he looked over at Richer. He was writing.

"Hey!" Gerard smiled as he attracted the other man's attention. "Fancy a snifter?"

"Later," said Richer. "Fleury's just buzzed."

‡

51. Le Colonel

Commissaire Charles Fleury-Goujon looked out of his window at the mid-afternoon traffic moving smoothly along the Rue des Saussaies. Across the road and a block beyond, he could see the top of the Palais d'Elysée.

He turned as Richer knocked and entered, and he said without preamble "La Dame."

Richer was stone faced. "What about her?"

"I've decided. I want to know."

Richer's eyes travelled around the room. "Not here."

The Commissaire looked at his watch. "I have an appointment over in d'Orsay in half an hour. Travel with me."

The chauffeur-driven Citroen pulled out of the gates of the Interior Ministry, crossed the Place Beauvau and purred down the tree-lined Avenue Marigny. In the partitioned, sound-proofed back, Commissaire Fleury-Goujon lit a Gitanes and blew the smoke towards the ceiling. He turned to the man next to him.

"*Alors*, Captain Richer. I want to know. What is this secret that has been kept hidden all these years by the Duchess of Windsor?"

The vehicle pulled up in the courtyard of the imposing building on the Quai d'Orsay. Both men sat in silence.

At length, Fleury-Goujon said, "*D'accord*. I now understand.

Who would have thought? De Gaulle was worse than any of us imagined."

"He was only a minor part of it."

"Yes."

"Will you tell the others?"

"No. I agree with you. Not until we have the document. As your Commissaire I have not heard a word you said. As your Colonel I instruct you to carry on. Let Mesrine get the document. We have been waiting years for this opportunity."

"Yes sir."

"The car will take you back."

Without further word, the head of the OAS climbed out of the vehicle and walked into the building.

‡

52. Flic et les Anglais

Mardi 4 Septembre

"We are very grateful to you for contacting us."

Gerard shrugged with due diffidence and wondered for the umpteenth time if he had done the right thing. He was sitting in the chair in the small office at the back of the British Embassy. The thin, anonymous man with the sunken eyes, and the small, lively Ron Becker each sat on a corner of the desk facing him.

This time Gerard smoked with full permission, an old saucer for an ashtray balanced on his knees. Underneath his legs was a large, and obviously full, holdall at which Becker kept casting curious glances.

The man thanked him again. "Very grateful."

Gerard waved his cigarette and narrowed his eyes as he exhaled smoke. "Last time, monsieur, you indicated that I was being unco-operative. I told you then that you were wrong."

"You've always been a good lad, Claude," Becker sounded disgracefully insincere. "We've always had faith in you."

Gerard looked at him but said nothing.

The man pushed himself up from the desk and walked round to sit behind it. Becker quickly shoved himself off the corner and stood in proximity to Gerard.

The man joined his hands together in front of him. "After you rang yesterday I contacted Clarence House."

"Clarence who?"

"Clarence House."

"A place not a person, Claude," explained Becker.

"Oh." The reference to the residence of the matriarch of the British Royal Family meant nothing to the policeman.

"In London."

"Ah." He nodded, absolutely none the wiser.

"Had to disturb our lady as she was dressing for a film premiere. Wasn't very happy."

"Ah."

"Anyway, she has now told me more. It is not the jewellery that we are after. It is a *document*."

"A document, m'sieur?"

"A document."

"What sort of a document?"

"She is being cagey. Wouldn't amplify. A document, that is as far as she would say. A document containing a secret. And the short of it is she wants a point (d)."

"A point (d)?"

"Situation as before - but she would now like the document herself."

"*Quoi! Mais c'est -* " As Gerard straightened himself in the chair, his legs parted. The saucer of ash plummeted downwards, bounced off the side of his holdall and spilt its contents all over the thick carpet. All three men looked at the mess.

" *- impossible,*" said Gerard.

They all looked back up.

"*Impossible*, Claude?" queried Becker. "Surely not."

"Surely yes, m'sieur. I can keep an eye on things, advise you, as agreed. But to actually get it myself! How am I to know what it is when you don't? A document? Could be anything. A laundry bill? A theatre programme? There are millions of *documents*. That is an impossible task. There is no one that could find a document without knowing what it is!" He made a dismissive motion with his hand. *"Non."*

"In that case, how about point (e)?"

Gerard sighed, tired of this stupid Anglo-Saxon way of talking. "Point (e)?"

"If you cannot obtain it yourself, suppress it."

"Suppress it?"

"Our lady has instructed that at all costs the information in the document must not become public. The document can be returned to the Duchess if needs be, but even that would be inadvisable considering the state of her mind. But all information as to its contents must be suppressed."

"We are very discreet in the BCP, m'sieur."

"Of course, of course. But…" The outward movement of the man's hands said more than words.

Gerard pulled out a grubby handkerchief and loudly blew his nose. He mumbled, "I will do what I can do."

Surprisingly, the man accepted it. "All right, so be it. I appreciate we cannot ask the *impossible.*" (Gerard raised an eyebrow at the piss taking.) "But all points (a) to (e) are extant. Please keep us informed. And bear in mind point (d), won't you?"

"Certainement. Messieurs, may I ask? Do you have *any* idea what this secret is?"

The man snorted and shook his head.

Becker spoke. "We know no more than you. This document - and we're not even too sure exactly what it is - contains something important about or concerning the Duke and Duchess of Windsor. Other than that we know nothing. Perhaps it's not our place to know."

"Perhaps," put in the man, "it is better that we do not know."

"Whatever it is," continued Becker, "it is important enough to warrant the personal attention of our lady in London. And that means important with a capital 'I'."

Gerard picked up his holdall as he got to his feet. "I will keep you informed of anything I find out. And if I can do anything, I shall."

"Thank you," said the man, rising. "We are pleased with your help and co-operation, monsieur. It will not go unforgotten."

Gerard gave a formal little bow and turned away. Becker followed him out.

"If only we knew what this secret was," said Becker as they walked along the corridor.

"Does he know?" Gerard nodded backwards at the room.

"No, I think he's on the level."

"Will we ever find out what it is all about?"

Becker stopped at the top of the stairs as Gerard continued on down.

"Oh undoubtedly," he said. "Undoubtedly."

Back in the office, the thin man was sitting, fingers forming a pyramid. "Do you trust him?" he asked when Becker returned.

"That shifty-arsed frog? No way."

"But he did alert us to the renewed activity."

"He was duty bound."

"Ron, I have to tell you that Her Majesty has instructed us to take an active interest. No more back seats."

"Are you sure that's wise? Activity in a foreign country?"

"We no longer have any alternative. She thought that the document had gone and the secret was safe forever. H M has issued strict orders. It must not get out. The only way she can be certain is if she has the document. No suppression like I told him. She wants the document. And if anyone knows the secret they are to be *persuaded* to remain silent."

"I see."

"She has said that *whatever* needs to be done must be done."

"I understand."

"Do what needs to be done, Ron."

"Yes, sir."

‡

53. Flics

The door to the Chief Inspectors' office opened with a thumping crash. Claude Gerard came in lugging a heavy-looking holdall. Richer looked at him absentmindedly and then looked at his watch. "Claude? Thought you weren't on till later."

Wordlessly, Gerard nodded at the bag. Richer glanced at it and then looked up into the other man's face. For a moment he did not comprehend. Then realisation hit him. "You're joking!"

Still not saying a word, Gerard went across and hefted the bag onto his desk.

"You *are* joking," repeated Richer.

Gerard stood there with his hands on his hips.

"You have *got* to be joking!" insisted Richer. "Tell me you are!" Thoughts of Mesrine had temporarily taken a back seat to the horror that now confronted him. "I *cannot* believe it."

"You'd better, *mon ami*."

"Come on! It's one of your little comedies, right?"

"No."

"Permanent?"

"Who knows?"

"*I* don't. Tell me. Spell it out."

Gerard spelt it out. "Mathilde's thrown me out."

"Don't tell me! Christ! But I thought you were talking again?"

"We talked too much. Sharp words."

"What're you going to do?"

Gerard shrugged, a lost orphan.

Richer groaned at the creeping realisation. He rubbed his right hand down his face. "No way. No fucking way. It won't work. Look, I don't… You *are* serious, right?"

Big puppy dog eyes.

"Oh, damn*nation* Claude…" He stood up, shaking his head. "Shit. Okay, okay. But only temporarily. A week at the most. Then you'll either have to effect a reconciliation or find a place of your own."

His rotund, overweight colleague grinned like a simpleton. *"Tu es un vrai copain."*

"Un vrai idiot! I'll do the cooking, but don't expect extravaganzas every night. Some days it'll be Burger King."

"Of course."

"You can do the housework. And you can damn well give me some money for the grub."

"Whatever you say."

"And the bed is mine. You get the couch."

"Naturellement… et merci. I'll buy you a drink later."

"You'll buy me a bottle. And why not now?"

"Got to see the old man. Is he in?"

"You might catch him. He's going to lunch somewhere. Important?"

"Just something that's come up. Need some guidance."

"Anything I can do?"

"Get me the document you've got Mesrine looking for," thought Gerard. He said, "Just an embarrassment the *rosbeefs* want hushed up. You know, if fucking hadn't been invented the world would be a much happier place."

"It would be full of bloody wankers. Like the Brits," said Richer.

‡

54. Voleur et le pouvoir

Mesrine spent the remainder of September planning his last crime: the kidnapping of broadcaster and journalist Philippe Bouvard, a man with many political connections and one of the most famous figures in France.

Mesrine found it difficult to plan the operation with the detail he required. He knew that he was on his own. Apart from Sylvie, he could trust no one. He could not even visit Janou, the hunt for him now was too intense.

Mesrine knew that the underworld would not deliberately betray him, but with the Press and the police now totally obsessed with him to the virtual exclusion of everything else, slips could occur. One wrong word by someone somewhere could do it. He had to work alone.

Commissaire Devos and his Brigade de Répression de Banditisme and Commissaire Broussard and his Brigade de Recherche et d'Intervention had conducted the biggest criminal manhunt Europe had ever known – but without success.

All three police forces of France had been looking for Mesrine. The Paris Préfecture of Broussard and Devos. The Sûreté and its own Office Centrale de Répression de Banditisme under Lucien Aimé-Blanc and Charles Pellegrini. And the provincial police forces, the gendarmerie.

And Mesrine had not been found.

The President of France, Valéry Giscard d'Estaing, had indicated that he wanted l'affaire Mesrine ended once and for all. In private (which meant that it was reported in Le Figaro) he had confided that *he did not even want Mesrine brought to trial. He issued an ultimatum. Either Mesrine was found or Christian Bonnet, the Minister of the Interior, would be replaced.*

It was time for innovation. For a fresh initiative. A new man was called in to take overall charge of the national hunt for Mesrine: Maurice Bouvier, one of France's most eminent and successful career policemen. Bouvier's notable triumphs included the breaking of the OAS campaign of terror in France in the early 1960s, and the arrest of Lieutenant-Colonel Jean-Marie Bastien-Thiry and the others responsible for the assassination attempt on President de Gaulle at Petit-Clamart on 22 August 1962.

It was hoped that a combined national unit under Bouvier could succeed where the fragmented efforts of the others had failed.

Mesrine had moved again, now ensconced with Sylvie in a third floor apartment at 35-37 Rue Belliard in the 18th Arrondisement. Some of the proceeds of the Lelièvre kidnapping had bought an unfurnished apartment in a luxury block in Marly-le-Roi near Versailles, to which he intended to take his bride. Unbeknown to Sylvie, he had spent a lot of time decorating and furnishing it, hopefully to her taste.

By October he was ready on all fronts. Ready for Marly-le-Roi, ready for Philippe Bouvard. And ready for a certain Monsieur Lensens.

‡

55. Voleur

Vendredi 12 Octobre

This time the concièrge at 5 Avenue Alphonse XIII was charming. He knew class when he saw it. The caller was a tall man with spectacles and a three-piece suit, hair parted in the centre, too prominent chin and with a hint of an effeminate manner. He reeked of money.

Yes, there was someone in the Lensens apartment, please go on up, fifth floor.

The doorbell of the apartment *ding-dong*ed in expectation. After a moment the door was opened by a distinguished, late middle-aged lady.

"Madame Lensens?"

"*Ah non, monsieur*, she is away. I am just the maid."

"*Oh, pardon*. Actually it was *Monsieur* Lensens I wanted. I'd best explain. My name is de Guy, Guillaume de Guy, from de Guy Rare Books and Prints. Monsieur Lensens ordered some special manuscripts from us. I just wanted to advise him of the state of his order. Is he in?"

"*Je regrette, monsieur*, nobody is here. The family always goes to the house in the country on a Friday for the weekend."

"*Ah, quel domage!* Never mind, madame, my own fault. I should have telephoned, but the order just came in as I was leaving the office. No problem. In fact, Monsieur did mention about his country house, now I reflect. Out near Versailles, is it not?"

She smiled. "Wrong château! Fontainbleau. La Ferté-Alais."

Monsieur de Guy slapped himself on the forehead. "Of course! I knew it was one of them! Well, I hope he has a pleasant weekend. I'll see him next week. Oh - I wonder… Should I deliver the order to the house or here? Does he keep his books and papers here?"

"*Non, monsieur,* the house is the true family home. None of his collection is here."

"Do you have the exact address, madame?"

"Of course. *Un moment, m'sieur.*"

She returned momentarily and handed him a slip of paper.

"*Alors,* you have been very helpful. I am sorry for having disturbed you, madame."

"*Pas de probleme, monsieur. Bonsoir.*"

"*Bonsoir madame, et merci!*"

Guillaume de Guy knocked politely on the door of the apartment in Rue Belliard. It was opened by the demure, plainly-dressed Madame Mercier.

"Madame Mercier?" enquired the caller.

"*Oui?*"

"de Guy - Rare Books and Prints. About your husband's order?"

"*Ah oui, entrez, monsieur, entrez…*"

No sooner was the door closed than de Guy's hand was grasping Madame Mercier's left buttock brutally as she forced her tongue against his tonsils. When they broke for air, they were laughing.

"It's funny, this play acting," said Sylvie.

Mesrine pulled off the glasses. "One can never be too careful. There didn't seem to be anybody out there, but one never knows nowadays. The casual, moustachioed Monsieur Mercier lives here. Questions would be asked if the smart, bespectacled, clean-shaven Guillaume de Guy marched straight up with a key to the door."

"You are right, of course." Sylvie pressed herself against him and mussed up the slick hair. "I missed you."

"My child, I have been gone but two hours!"

"Seemed like two years. And I am hungry."

"But we ate before I went out!"

"Not that sort of hunger."

"You are insatiable!"

"I have never denied it."

He swept her off her feet with one movement of his mighty arm, tossing her over his shoulder, her bottom next to his right ear. He smacked it with his free left hand. The cheek wobbled.

She squealed and playfully kicked and punched as he carried her to the bedroom. He was pleased to feel that underneath the plain dress Madame Mercier wore suspenders and stockings and - he moved his hand in verification - no panties.

"My darling," he mumbled into her right butt cheek. "How would you like to spend next weekend in the country, near Fontainbleau?"

Very late that night, the body of a man was found at the foot of a staircase at 5 Rue Alphonse XIII. It was the concièrge of the block, the one who had been so rude to the *parvenu* in August. Apparently he had slipped on the top step, broken his neck with the backward whiplash as he fell, and was dead before he hit the bottom.

‡

56. L'opération

Dimanche 21 Octobre

La Ferté-Alais is some forty kilometres south of Paris in the *départment* of Essonne. It is a small, peaceful town living contentedly in the shadow of the nearby larger town of Milly-la-Fôret and the sprawling forest known as Fontainbleau.

At 18:30 on Friday 19 October, Monsieur and Madame François had checked into the hotel in the town square, fulfilling their reservation made earlier that week by telephone.

The staff of the hotel remember Monsieur François as a big, charming man, close cut receding hair greying at the temples, with a neatly trimmed moustache. Every inch the businessman. His wife was a petite woman with huge breasts, long black hair and minimal make-up, who looked exceedingly young. Common opinion agreed that *le monsieur* was in fact having a weekend of naughties with some waif from the typing pool. The staff sniggered knowingly and left them to it.

Jacques and Sylvie enjoyed their weekend. The weather stayed clement and, once they forced themselves from bed in the morning, they roamed the surrounding countryside, more than once laying together in some quiet, sunny field.

They had been booked in for two nights, the Friday and the Saturday, so after a superb meal in the hotel's small restaurant at Sunday lunchtime, *les François* bade a bashful farewell and drove off in their hired car along the N191, heading for Paris.

However, at Baulne just outside la Ferté-Alais they made an

abrupt right onto the D87 and, five kilometres further along, turned right again onto the D83, facing La Ferté-Alais from the east. It was now evening and they pulled off the country road near the crossroads at Chêne-Bécart.

Mesrine switched off the car's lights and they sat in the penumbra of dusk, watching the remarkably quick nightfall. Now and again they kissed, occasionally they whispered something. They were far enough off the road not to be seen, but Mesrine had already explained that they would not tempt fate by playing the radio to pass the time.

When it was dark enough, Sylvie removed the black wig, scratching and fluffing her blonde hair. In the close confinement of the vehicle, Jacques could smell her perfume as she moved her body.

"How romantic," she whispered. "Just you and me and the starlight."

"And a job to do." Mesrine ran his finger gently down the centre of her face, from hairline to chin. "Shortly." Again they kissed and his hand crept up the softness of her left thigh to the warmth above. She was damp.

For a while he let his fingers play with her. Soon her deep, quiet sigh indicated at least partial satisfaction.

Two minutes later he reached over the back seat for a holdall. "Time to say *au revoir* to Monsieur François." He stepped out of the vehicle.

Quickly he changed from François' formal suit into black slacks and runners, shirt and black windcheater. With one rip he pulled off the false moustache and discarded it in the grass, a petrified caterpillar. Before packing away the suit, he took one last item from the holdall: a hood.

Opening the trunk, he placed the holdall inside and removed a shotgun. He came back round, leant in the side window and kissed Sylvie firmly on her half open lips.

"Now then, my love, you have food in the *sac* there, yes? You may play the radio now, but if you do, play it *softly*. No one will disturb you, absolutely no possibility. I hope to be back within the hour, but give me until midnight. If I am not back by then, return home - and listen to the radio in the morning."

"Jacques, I am worried for you. Please won't you tell me what you're going to do?"

"*Non*. What little girls don't know, won't hurt them."

She pouted. "You wouldn't hurt me, would you?"

He grinned and flicked her chin. "Only in lust, my darling, only in lust. Remember, one minute past midnight you leave. But I will be back long before then."

With one final kiss he disappeared soundlessly into the darkness.

Sylvie wound up the window, turned out the light, checked that all the doors were locked, and sat there in the silent starlight.

A couple of minutes later, she reopened the door, got out, had a pee, then got back in. Rummaging in the *sac*, she pulled out a litre of *Perrier* and a roast leg of chicken and began to tuck in.

The house had a gravelled driveway curving up the front and disappearing around one side. It was a big place, probably with at least six bedrooms, but the land had obviously been sold off over the years and it seemed an incongruous giant in relation to the small gardens.

Mesrine made no pretence of stealth, walking up the pathway, feet crunching on the gravel, hood on with just eyes, nose and lips protruding, shotgun held casually under his right arm.

Lights shone from various windows. He reckoned on there being two servants, Monsieur et Madame and, perhaps, an *enfant* or two. That was why he had decided on the direct approach. Stealth and deception were too dangerous when there were many people about. Fear was the key, as somebody had once said.

He walked around the building, looking in each window, whether it was illuminated or not. In one room to the side, a maid was putting the finishing touches to a cold collation, spread out attractively on a long table.

Mesrine frowned. There was more food there than for the number of people he had estimated.

Turning the corner to the rear, his suspicions were confirmed. There were about ten vehicles parked in a neat row, and from here he could hear the muffled sounds of merriment from within. There was a party going on!

The sounds were coming from an open window a little way along. Inside about twenty people were standing in a circle around a young couple, glasses raised in a toast.

He pulled himself back quickly as the girl in the centre seemed to look straight at him. There was no change in the sound from within, no shout or scream.

A distinct voice was raised. *"Michel et Veronique.* May their marriage be long and happy!" The other voices were as one in salutation.

Mesrine nodded grimly. *Merci, Michel et Veronique.* You have made the job that much harder.

There was movement and he pressed himself into the wall. Someone opened the windows as music started playing. The party was getting under way now, formalities over.

Up above, a balcony stretched the width of the house, connecting the four rooms on this side.

Holding the shotgun in his left hand, Mesrine leapt, grabbing the iron trellis with his free hand.

For a moment the huge, hooded figure swung in the air, then he eased the shotgun through the ironwork and swung himself up and over.

He looked through the windows at each room in turn. As he

had guessed, they were four bedrooms. And each full-length window was fractionally open, letting in air. And letting in Jacques Mesrine.

He squatted at the far end of the balcony and waited. Whatever room was entered first would be the one he would choose. Fate would decide. He rested the shotgun on his lap. He hoped fate would not keep him waiting long.

Half an hour.

And that was too long. He was becoming stiff and irritable. But at last there came the sound of muffled conversation from the second room along.

Before rising, he checked over the railings. Noise and music still came in equal volumes from downstairs. Nobody was outside.

He stood up, stretched, and then walked to the window as silent as death. He smiled. There were no lights on in the room but he could now hear the familiar grunting, groaning, giggling and sighing of copulation.

The window opened outwards noiselessly.

Mesrine walked across the room in the dark. The couple on the bed were oblivious, the body on top giving the body underneath a massive pounding.

Mesrine flicked on the light switch, and in one stride was across to the bed.

The female's scream was blocked as both barrels of the shotgun were thrust into her open mouth.

Apart from their genitals, both of them were fully dressed. Mesrine looked down the barrels of his gun into the bewildered, terrified face of Veronique, the girl whose engagement they had been saluting downstairs.

The man on top of her, face awash with perspiration blended in equal amounts from fear and carnality, was not Michel.

Mesrine gave them a full minute to appreciate the situation.

Then he said politely, "Mademoiselle Lensens?"

"Gng." Her head moved up and down as much as the obscene phallus in her mouth would allow.

"Get off please," said Mesrine to the male. "And lay down beside the lady."

The male obliged.

"And please adjust your clothing. Your winkle is wet, it will catch cold."

The male flopped his now shrunken penis back into his fly.

"Thank you. And my condolences - but I'm told size doesn't matter. Mam'selle Lensens, I am sorry for this unpleasantness, but I wish to speak with your father. You are my instrument. I am going to move this weapon from your mouth. Please do not emit one sound, for you must rest assured that I will have no hesitation in blowing your pretty little brains out if you do. You understand?"

"Gng."

"All right."

Slowly, the barrel withdrew. She lay there without moving, eyes wide, mouth still open, gaping at the hooded man in front of her.

"Put your legs together."

She did as she was told.

"Close your mouth."

She did as she was told.

Mesrine stepped backwards. "Now off the bed please."

Hesitantly she rose.

The man moved to rise also. Without the flicker of an eyelid, Mesrine hit him in the face with the butt of the gun. As the girl gasped, her lover fell back onto the bed unconscious, flat as a deadweight. His front teeth had disappeared in a welter of blood and horrible white pieces.

"I will pay his dental bill," said Mesrine. "Now, we will go outside together. You will go to the top of the stairway. The first person you see, tell them you want your father. Say you do not feel well - you certainly don't look it. But insist it must be your father. If anyone else comes, I will kill you. If you say anything to alert your father or anyone, I will kill you. Look at your friend on the bed. LOOK AT HIM!" He grabbed her by the hair and wrenched her head round. She cried out. "Believe I mean it! He is alive. You will not be. Now, if you please."

Standing in the lee of the doorway as he opened it, he motioned Veronique outside. She moved out, walking stiffly as if her legs were about to give way.

Mesrine nodded for her to go to the top of the stairs while he stood forward and to the left of her, out of sight from below. He raised the gun and aimed it at her head.

Considering the circumstances, she performed well. Yes, whoever it was would get Papa, *vitement*. Too much Beaujolais, eh? Yes, something like that. Did she want Michel? No, no, just Papa.

Mesrine indicated for her to come back to him. "Is that your room?" He nodded at the one they had come from.

"*Ou - oui.*"

"Which is your father's room?"

"*Là*," she nodded at a door further down.

"*Venez.*"

Mesrine positioned her in the doorway of her father's room and stood behind her out of sight, the shotgun firmly at the base of her spine.

It took five minutes before he heard the reassuring *thump-thump* on the stairs.

When Monsieur Lensens turned onto the landing, Veronique could not contain herself. "Papa," she cried. "Oh, Papa!"

Mesrine held her roughly by the back of the dress so she could not run out.

She began sobbing uncontrollably, certain in her own mind that she was signing her father's death warrant.

"My darling, what is the matter?" Lensens hurried along the corridor, puzzled at why his daughter was standing there, arms loosely by her side, apparently unable to move.

He was but two metres from her when she fell backwards through the doorway, out of sight. "Veronique?" He rushed into the room and then found himself going sideways involuntarily. Something was pressing against his head and forcing him to the wall.

He heard the door slam behind him. Veronique was on her knees on the floor in total distress.

Lensens turned slowly, realising the inevitable. His grey eyebrows rose just slightly as he saw the gun and the hooded figure holding it.

"*Bonjour* Monsieur Chief Prosecutor," greeted the hooded Mesrine.

"*Bonjour* Mesrine," nodded Lensens. "I have been expecting you. But not tonight. Only *you* could have picked a night when I would be surrounded by people."

"Although good for the image, a pure coincidence I assure you. As is this whole affair."

"Get it over with then. But don't let my daughter see it."

"You were the man who was instrumental in having me sentenced to twenty years. At the time I swore vengeance. And I still might have it. But not now, not tonight. Tonight I am on different business."

"Really? Why don't you just shoot me and get it over with? Why should I believe a convicted murderer?" He looked at his daughter on the floor. "What did he do to you, Veronique? Or need I ask? Tell me, so I can damn him in hell."

She looked at her father, her bottom lip quivering.

"Tell him," urged Mesrine. "Go on. I simply disturbed her with a friend." The eyes beneath the hood looked coldly at Lensens.

"Is it true?"

"Y - yes, Papa."

"He didn't touch you?"

"N - no."

"A sign of my good faith." The hood lifted in a smile. "The friend, alas, is having a good sleep. But your daughter is unharmed."

"What is it that you want? Kidnap? A ransom? Not me, they'll never pay. I'm no Lelièvre."

"You delude yourself, monsieur. You are not even worthy of it. No, you have something which does not belong to you. I want it."

Lensens was perplexed. "I have not the faintest idea what you are talking about."

Mesrine thrust the gun into Lensen's neck. "You recently bought something. From Buisson, the bookdealer ."

Fear shot through Lensens' eyes. "So his death *was* connected. I couldn't believe it when I heard he'd been killed. You were after the document?"

"Yes."

"And you killed him. Tortured him first, I suppose."

"I will kill *you* if you are silly - and I will shoot the whore-hole of your charmingly promiscuous little girl here. Give me the document and I shall go. And you can call the police and the Press and tell them what a brave man you've been, fighting off the infamous Mesrine, who came to kill you. Naturally, you would not mention the document, for your own sake."

"Naturally. But do you think you can get away - "

"ENOUGH!" The shout made both father and daughter jump. "Enough talking, monsieur. Where is the document?"

"It is in my safe."

"And the safe is downstairs, I suppose?"

"No, it is here in this room."

Mesrine's eyes roved. He frowned. There were no pictures on the elegantly-papered walls for it to hide behind, nothing else obvious that could conceal a safe. "Mam'selle Lensens," he said. "If you would be so kind. Please lay on the bed."

Veronique looked at her father, who nodded. She did as bidden.

"Good. Now raise your hands above your head… *Bon*… please stay in that position. Now monsieur, if you please. The document."

"It is not worth that much now, you know. I bought it as a long-term investment for Veronique and Michel - "

"*Please.*"

With the gun pressed into the back of his skull, Lensens led the way over to the wardrobe. Watched every centimetre of the way by Mesrine, he unlocked the double doors and pulled them open. Inside there was still no indication of a safe, simply clothing and, down one side, a set of open shelves holding such items as handkerchiefs, underwear and socks.

Lensens put his hand under the middle shelf and pulled. The entire top half of the shelving unit swung outwards to reveal the safe in the wall behind. It was a small affair, no more than thirty centimetres square, and was controlled by one of the modern press-button combination devices rather than the standard dial.

Lensens pressed an activation switch and then keyed five numbers. The steel door clicked open.

"Hold it!" snapped Mesrine, prodding the gun into Lensens' head. "Just don't move."

"Oh for goodness sake!" sighed Lensens, but he obeyed.

Swiftly, Mesrine transferred the gun from the father's head to the daughter's groin. He ordered the Chief Prosecutor to observe what he had done. "Just in case you feel brave."

"You are a pig, Mesrine."

"I have never denied it. Now, if you please…"

Lensens took a buff envelope from the safe and held it out.

Still with the gun pointing at the girl, Mesrine stepped back a couple of paces. "Now do exactly as I say. Keep the envelope where I can see it and come to the bed... Lay on top of your daughter. Face down."

"*What?*"

"DO IT!"

The grotesque incest took place, the father laying gently on his daughter, trying to take his weight on his elbows.

"Now both of you. Roll over so Mademoiselle is on top."

It took an effort but it was accomplished, Veronique's dress rising in the manoeuvre to reveal two petite, but far from modest, cheeks.

"Forgive the indelicate position," apologised Mesrine. "But I am sure you understand." He snatched the envelope from Lensens' fingers. Sitting on the far edge of the bed, away from any lashing feet but with an enviable panorama of the delights of Veronique, he cradled the gun and carefully opened the envelope.

The paper had yellowed at the edges, but it was good quality stuff and far from brittle. He read it slowly, eyebrows rising beneath the mask.

He understood the implications immediately. It was unbelievable. There it was. About de Gaulle, about the agreement. About Elizabeth.

He read it again, shook his head in amazement, and then popped it back into the envelope, satisfied. "At last," he said softly. "At last. Debt paid, Captain." The envelope disappeared into an inside pocket of his windcheater.

He was pleased. In an effortless movement he leant to his left, slowly French-kissed the join of Veronique's cheeks through the mouth gap in his hood, his tongue intimate and probing. Then he stood up from the bed. Her father was not witness to the violation, as from his prostrate position with his daughter on top of him, all he could see was the ceiling. And Veronique never told him, but she was later to confide to a friend that it was the most erotic experience of her life.

Mesrine helped himself to some wads of diverse currencies from the safe and a handful of what appeared to be gold coins. "Monsieur Chief Prosecutor," he announced. "You have pleased me. Because of your co-operation, I will consider the matter of the twenty years cancelled. I will not bother you again. But please be sure to cry from the rooftops that the great Mesrine was here. Say I stole all your cash and jewellery - you can even claim on your insurance, no one will know.

"Now, one final favour if you would. Both of you, please. Into the wardrobe."

They moved hesitantly. Stiffly. The man with a defiant expression he patently did not feel, the girl with a look in her eyes a mixture of fear, admiration and downright animal lust.

"Your party is still in full swing," chatted Mesrine. "But someone will miss you soon. And your knocking might even attract someone passing by. Monsieur, I thank you. We will never meet again. Mademoiselle," the eyes beneath the mask smiled, "it has been a pleasure." He closed the doors and turned the key.

Over to the window, out onto the balcony.

From inside the bedroom, the banging started on the wardrobe door.

Effortlessly, he swung out over the railings.

He landed perfectly on the gravel. Straightening up, he pulled off the hood and stuffed it into a pocket. The shotgun was covered by his jacket and held there by his left arm.

Smoothing his hair, he walked leisurely away, calling *"Au revoir!"* to a small group of people outside the front door.

They shouted goodnight and waved goodbye, not one of them querying the fact that he left on foot instead of by car...

4ᴵᴱᴹᴱ PARTIE

‡

LA CONCLUSION

‡

57. La suite

Mardi 23 Octobre

Monsieur Lensens did it well.

Unfortunately for the destiny of Jacques Mesrine, too well.

It was reported in the newspapers as the kidnapping that had been foiled. Each publication had its own version of the events, but the general story was that Mesrine had gone to the house to kidnap the only and beloved daughter of the Chief Prosecutor upon whom he had publicly sworn vengeance. The Chief Prosecutor himself had caught the supercriminal in the act of abduction and, although he had been overcome by the raider, he had caused enough of a diversion to thwart the kidnapping. Instead, the criminal had settled for jewellery worth half a million francs. *[Mesrine's experienced eye reckoned the value at nearer fifty thousand francs – but the insurance companies could afford it.]*

Had the story stayed at that, Mesrine could yet again have come out of it with his Robin Hood image intact. But there was one distasteful codicil. It was claimed by the Chief Prosecutor that Mesrine had been caught in the act of sexually assaulting Mademoiselle Lensens.

Although any true student of the exploits of Jacques Mesrine would have realised that this was out of character, indeed downright untrue, the casual follower - as most of the public were - was stunned. In the two-faced, hypocritical world of the late nineteen seventies murder, robbery, extortion and kidnapping were acceptable; *un morceau* of unilaterally consented sex was not.

Public opinion does not change over night, but the initial outrage when the story broke that Tuesday was encouraged by the Press whose diverse leaders were as one in their opinion: the time had come, Mesrine *must* be caught.

In Montmartre, Paul Richer read of the incident in *Le Figaro*, and he thought it was just another Mesrine attempt at revenge not connected to La Dame's document.

In a cubicle of the *WC* on the sixth floor of 11 Rue des Saussaies, Claude Gerard read about it in *Le Matin*. *Le Matin* was the only paper that included in its biographical details of Chief Prosecutor Lensens that he was a collector of rare books and manuscripts.

On Tuesday 23 October, Claude Gerard put two and two together. With perverse accuracy it made four. Now he knew something Richer did not yet know.

Mesrine had the secret.

‡

58. Flic et l'Anglais

It was noisy on the southern side of La Madelaine, cars roaring down on the right, up on the left, and meeting in mayhem in front at the top of Rue Royale. Down the rue, above the traffic, Claude Gerard could see the *obélisque* in the Place de la Concorde.

A cloudy sky was fulfilling the forecast of overnight rain. He shivered. It was chilly.

He farted softly. A moment later a voice said, "Doesn't get any better, does it Claude?"

He turned around to face Becker. "What doesn't?"

"The smell of Paris. You French are so fastidious in some things. You wash your gutters every day and yet the smell of your sewers still rises above the ground. You should have watched where you were digging your metro tunnels."

"And you need to watch your mouth, you insolent fucking *rosbeef*," thought Gerard. Aloud he said, "I have a story to tell you."

"A story? A story is no good to me, old son."

"A true story. About a cop, about the most wanted man in Europe - and about a document containing a secret."

"I think," said Becker, "we should walk."

"No, Englishman, I have a better idea. I am hungry. That little red-fronted *café* down there serves good food. If you want to hear what I've got to tell you, you will buy me the most expensive meal on the menu."

That day, for the first time in his life, Claude Gerard dined in Maxim's.

‡

59. Flic

Mercredi 24 Octobre

It could have been worse, concede Paul Richer. Much worse. On the other hand, it could have been better. Much better.

The man who, last year, had goaded him to the point of violence and even resignation was now his lodger! It had lasted more than a week, of course, as both of them had known it would. Claude had attempted a reconciliation with Mathilde but had been rebuffed, and apparently she had now taken the brats from their place in Levallois and had gone off to relatives on the west coast. Regrettably, before going she had changed all the locks in the apartment so Claude could not make a furtive trip back to claim any meagre rights he may have left.

It had to be admitted that Claude was more than generous with his rent contribution, and his nocturnal snoring did not penetrate through to the bedroom. So Richer had little to complain about - apart from the fact that he wanted his privacy.

That evening Claude was due in late (with instructions to pick up a fried delight from *Au Petit Comptoir* in the Place du Tertre on the way), so Richer relaxed listening to music and stroking Chivas, grateful there was no cooking to do.

Only after one side of Jean-Michel Jarre, two of Sylvie Vartan, and three cognacs, did he realise that time was getting on. Claude was late. Wonder what crisis there was tonight?

He went into the kitchen and began to prepare himself an

omelette, beating out the tensions of the day as he whipped the three eggs in the bowl.

The telephone rang.

Turning the music down, he picked up the receiver. "Richer."

The voice was muffled and distant, the line poor and cracking. "Bruno."

"Well, have you been getting yourself talked about! Greetings *mon brave*. Any news?"

"We must meet. I have something for you."

"You have? Where? When?"

He told him.

"Come alone."

"Of course."

The connection was cut.

In a vehicle down on Rue Caulaincourt, someone removed headphones, thought for a moment and then spoke into a radio. Instructions received, the car started up and pulled away.

‡

60. Flic et...

The Arc de Triomphe is a curious, almost unfriendly, place at night. Tourists are not allowed up to the top of the Arc come dusk (on the assumption that they would not be able to see anything anyway once the powerful floodlights were turned onto the monolith), but the island in the middle of the Etoile, the Place Charles de Gaulle, still attracts people in the darkness to admire Chalgrin's illuminated masterpiece and the tomb of the unknown soldier underneath.

Having left a note for Claude to say he was going out, Richer took the metro, changing at Pigalle to Ligne 2 Diréction Porte Dauphin, and alighting at Charles de Gaulle Etoile. He crossed the island by the ornate subway, throwing a couple of francs to the busker in the tunnel (love was still such an easy game to play, yesterday).

There were upwards of fifty people on the island, walking round Napoleon's magnificent arch, mostly couples arm in arm, huddled against the fine drizzle that had taken a day to drift west from Luxembourg. As always, two uniformed *agents* patrolled the place, their sole duty on this shift.

Standing on the island of the Etoile, one experiences a strange auditory effect. Traffic moves in frantic disarray round the Place well into the night, yet from the island itself the traffic noises are muted, almost distant, not really there, as if the island at the top of the Champs Elysée is removed from reality.

The meet was a typical piece of Mesrine stage-management,

reflected Richer. In the middle of Paris, right under the noses of two *flics* who patrolled with nothing to do except survey the passers-by, and at night when there were fewer people around and more chance of being noticed.

He looked around. So, this was where it would end, where his association with Mesrine would conclude. He couldn't say he was sorry. Like the old man of the sea, Mesrine had been on his back for a long time.

Richer turned up the collar of his raincoat as he walked round the Arc, passing a hopeful tourist trying to take pictures in the dark with his box camera, passing the young couple kissing, passing the more mature couple admiring Etex's reliefs of Peace and Resistance on the western side.

Richer stood in front of the tomb of the unknown soldier and lit a cigarette, cupping the flame of his lighter against the cool breeze. As he smoked he stared down the Champs Elysée, the red rain-washed rear lights of the vehicles descending on the right, the yellow beams of the headlights approaching on the left. Far down at the other end of the avenue were the diffused lights of the Place de La Concorde.

Come on, Jacques, come on. Hurry. Hand over the document and we need never meet again.

A gust of wind blew into his face, the weather turning worse by the minute.

He stood looking at the vehicles, even at this hour still streaming round the Place, but because of the peculiar numbing of the noise they seemed far away.

After a while one of the *agents* approached, rubber cape blowing in the increasing wind.

At the same time a car started to come round on the inside next to the island.

"Monsieur, you are waiting for someone, yes?" The agent asked it politely, respectfully, but with the smack of authority.

The car slowed down. Richer saw it over the *agent*'s shoulder.

Richer pulled out his identity card. The young *agent* frowned at it and then saluted casually. *"Excusez-moi, Monsieur l'Inspecteur."* As he saluted he stepped in front of Richer and simultaneously his *kepi* flew off his head. He tried to grab it. *"Merde alors!"*

"Don't worry!" A few quick strides and Richer had the rolling hat in his hands. As he turned back he noticed the vehicle speeding away into the traffic heading south on the Champs.

"Bloody wind," he commented to the young *agent*. "Here - " He went to hand over the *kepi* and then stopped, puzzled. His finger on the inside of the hat was not where it should be. He looked down. His finger was poking through a hole in the back of the hat. There was a similar one in the front.

A bullet had passed clean through the *kepi*.

Christ, Christ, Christ, *Christ*. It was not possible. The car. The bullet was meant for *him*. If the *agent* had not got in the way and spoilt the aim. But why? Who would want to kill him?

The gun had probably been silenced, but it would not have been heard anyway due to that strange effect of the island. The *agent* had not noticed anything untoward, merely thanking his superior for retrieving his *kepi* and hurriedly placing it back on his head. He would notice it later, of course, and the roof would fall in, but he would not remember the Chief Inspector's name or what he looked like, and he might not even link the two things together.

Richer rushed along the subway. He did not notice the busker rising and he cannoned right into him, knocking his collecting cap from his hands, coins scattering noisily.

"Pardon - " Richer stared at the busker's face.

The busker smiled. He reached into an inside pocket.

Instantly Richer slammed him against the wall, pinning his hand in his coat. "No," Richer whispered urgently. "Not here.

It's blown. Some other way, Jacques." Aloud he shouted, "Get out of the fucking way!" and hurried on.

He took the outside escalator of the Champs Elysée entrance to the metro.

Leaping over the waist-high ticket barrier, he headed for Ligne 2 Diréction Nation. From near the ticket booth, somebody watched him.

The smell of the metro system rose to meet Richer as he jogged nimbly down the escalator. A few people waited on the opposite platform, none taking more than a natural casual interest in him. Behind him, a *clochard* was stretched out on a bench, snoring noisily.

For something to do, he put two francs into a confectionery machine and pulled the first drawer to hand. A packet of scented *cachoux* was delivered. He put them into his pocket.

There came the high-pitched whine of an approaching train. *Bon.*

The train came from the right, on the opposite platform. *Merde.*

Illuminated faces looked out of the carriage windows. In the yellow first class compartment he could see a busking puppeteer.

Almost at once the sudden cool draught preceded his own train, thundering in from the left. His carriage was half empty, but he stood by the doors, scrutinising the handful of others who entered: a pair of lovers, a youth, an old veteran, a dubious-looking eastern European from over Belleville.

After changing at Pigalle, he eventually arrived at Lamarck-Caulaincourt. There was no lift waiting at platform level so he ran up the stairs, the run reducing to a breathless trot after five flights.

He emerged into the now heavy rain, feet splashing up the steep stone steps from the station into Rue Caulaincourt. He turned immediately left past the Hotel Roma. The street was deserted save for a cruising cab which accelerated once it saw he had no interest.

Bearing right past the shuttered Co-Op, he entered Rue Lamarck and began the ascent up the *butte de Montmartre*.

‡

61. Flics

Claude was in, feet up, watching some foreign American film on the television. The smell of smoke and fried food enveloped Richer as he entered.

Claude looked around. "Bloody hell, you look a state. Blowing up out there?"

"And then some." Richer pulled off the raincoat. His pants were wet from the knees down, clinging.

"Chicken and chips in the oven," Claude swilled from a can. "And a few beers in the *frigo*. You look as if you could do with them."

"I'll make it a cognac first." Richer slid out of his shoes and went over to the cabinet. "Want one?"

"Sure, why not? Successful meet?" It was half-asked, Claude more interested in the goings-on on the television.

"Meet?"

"You said in your note."

"*Ah oui*. Like shit. Bastard snout didn't turn up."

"Huh! Thought it was a strange time of day."

"You been in long?"

"An hour. Must have just missed you on your way out."

Richer stood Claude's cognac on the arm of his chair and went into the kitchen. Chivas looked up from a bowlfull of food, mewed and carried on eating. Richer's food smelt good as he pulled it out of the oven with the aid of a glove. "Why were you late?" he called. "Something new on?"

"Eh?"

"Something new on?"

"Had to see the British Ambassador. Informally. Could only fit me in this evening, while he was dressing for some bloody ball or something. Been receiving less than kind letters from some farming co-operative up north, about our turkeys. And my car broke down earlier so I had to use the metro. I'm getting like you."

"Cars are no good in Paris for our work, I've told you." Richer knocked back his cognac and put the glass in the sink. He transferred his food to a plate and went back into the *salle*. "Any calls while I was out?"

"Mm?" Two men were shooting at each other on the television.

"Any calls while I was out?"

"No. Expecting any?"

"No, no. Just wondered." He forked a piece of chicken into his mouth. It was hot.

He went back to the kitchen for a beer and stopped in the doorway, staring at the cat still eating his food. He looked down at his own food. He looked back at Claude Gerard. He frowned.

The cat's bowl was full. Why would Claude, who had really taken to the animal, settle down for an hour before feeding him?

He touched the oven. It was luke warm, as if it had only just been turned on. Yet his food was hot, as if it had just been bought.

"Paul," called Claude, eyes fixed on the television. "What's the English for arsehole?"

Richer turned in the doorway. *"Trou du cul."* His eyes were burning into the back of Gerard's head. *"Trou du cul."*

‡

62. L'exécution

Jeudi 25 Octobre

At 23:00 that night, Veronique Lensens and her fiancé Michel pulled into the driveway of the Lensens' home near Fontainbleau. Because of the wind and the rain, Michel drove as close to the front door as he could so that Veronique could be in the house in two quick steps.

They had already had sex that evening, so they just kissed goodbye and Veronique nipped smartly out of the car, waving as she closed the front door behind her.

Michel reversed the car then drove off back down the driveway. It was as he was pulling out onto the road that he looked in his rear view mirror. He slammed on the brakes.

Veronique was running back down the driveway waving frantically. Had she left something in the car?

She was running strangely, as if she had one shoe off and one on. She would catch her death in that flimsy dress in the rain, silly girl. What had she left behind? He looked on the floor of the car and on the back seat but could see nothing.

Only when he wound down the window did he hear her mad, hysterical screaming.

‡

63. Flics

Vendredi 26 Octobre

The story caught the late editions of that morning's papers.

MESRINE'S REVENGE

Chief Prosecutor and wife die in hail of bullets

"We have been asked to assist in the hunt for Mesrine."

Commissaire Fleury-Goujon threw down the paper and watched the faces of the men seated in front of him. Claude Gerard's showed surprise. Paul Richer's was blank.

"*We* have?" asked Gerard.

"Giscard is positively doing his pieces after the Lensens murder. He has repeated that it is Minister Bonet or Mesrine – and it's no idle threat. One of them will have to go. Rumour has it that he just favours Mesrine. But only just. Paris is being saturated. Every known associate of Mesrine is now being watched and tailed twenty-four hours a day. Every known haunt is staked out. His family can't have a crap without somebody counting the number of turds. Bouvier has taken overall control, as you know. He says he is getting close, that it is only a matter of time."

"If Bouvier thinks that's all there is to catching Mesrine, then he's an optimist," said Richer lowly. "Mesrine's made mistakes recently. But he is a professional. While the entire force is watching his family and friends, he could be up to all manner of things free of police interference. Remember, he is always one thought ahead of his pursuers. He will not let himself be caught. But then the combined mights of the BRB, BRI and OCRB are not out to *catch* him, are they?"

The Commissaire did not respond to the question. "Our involvement is to warn all embassies and other foreign interests. Security is to be trebled. If, for any reason, Mesrine or anyone who looks like him or anyone who even looks suspicious sets foot in any area under BCP control we are to be informed immediately. For example, he might go to a South American embassy for a visa. Naturally he is not to be detained by them but if they can delay him until Bouvier gets there, all the better. But *no* chances are to be taken. The man is a killer, remember that."

"They should have shot him when they had him in La Santé," said Gerard. "Liaising with every one of our clients is going to take time."

"Which we don't have. Phone them all. Speak to your usual contacts. *Allez, messieurs.*"

When they were at the door, the Commissaire called Richer back. "Paul, one more thing if you please."

"See you back there," Richer said to Gerard, who nodded and walked quickly away.

Richer closed the door and came back in. He said, "It wasn't Mesrine."

The head of the OAS raised an eyebrow. "You don't think so? He always swore revenge on the man who put him away for twenty years."

"I know it wasn't him. Mesrine was with me last night."

"Ah. I see. So you have the document?"

"No. We were interrupted. And I know who by."

"Who?" asked the Colonel.

"The same people who murdered Lensens. The people who do not want the secret to come out. The people who, it seems, want to get the document and silence anyone who has read it."

"Or who knows the secret."

"Yes."

"Which means we are in danger."

"*I* am. You should be safe. No one knows you know."

"How did the British find out? Or need I ask?"

"Most organisations have a mole," said Richer. "We have a rat in ours."

"What are you going to do? I can have him moved."

"No, it's too late for that."

"More drastic action?"

"That shit is not worth it. The damage has been done now. The savages from the northern island are on the warpath. No, let me play this my way. Mesrine has the document. We are only one step away from having it in our hands. And when we do, *mon Colonel*, the British won't dare come anywhere near us."

Back in the office, Gerard was tucking-in to a mid morning *pain au chocolat*. A greasy bag containing its brother sat on Richer's desk.

"*Merci.*" Richer nodded at the bag as he came back in.

"What did Fleury want you to stay on for?" A piece of *pain* fell off the end of Gerard's snack straight into his ashtray.

"Just one of my cases. The Irish in Vincennes."

"The one Bauer's been handling?" Gerard picked up the fallen morsel, blew on it and popped it into his mouth.

"Have you seen the report? He's done a good job."

"That's because he's got two good superiors to teach him."

"Right."

"Do we really have to phone *all* our contacts?"

"That's what the chief say. Better. Sod's law says the one place you don't phone is the place he'll turn up."

"Bloody Mesrine. There must be a quicker way to catch him. Are there no grasses? Does nobody know nothing? Somebody somewhere must have contact with him."

Richer shrugged and tore open his bag. The phone rang.

"Coffee?" Gerard helped himself to one of Richer's Gitanes.

"Just had some."

Gerard went out, closing the door behind him.

Richer picked up the phone. "Richer." His voice echoed hollowly down the line.

"Bruno. *Printemps*. One-thirty. Walk about. I'll find you."

The phone buzzed and he was gone.

Richer was gone when Gerard returned with his coffee. Gerard sat down and unlocked his right hand desk drawer. Inside a red light flashed on top of a small tape recorder. He rewound the cassette and pressed *Play*.

He heard his own voice saying, "Coffee?"

The rest of the tape did not take one minute.

At the end he grinned, went over to Richer's desk and began to eat the abandoned *pain*.

Back at his own desk, he rewound the tape and once more listened.

He looked at his watch. It was midday. That gave him ninety minutes. Plenty of time.

He picked up the phone.

Fifteen minutes later, Gerard poked his head round the door of the Inspectors' office.

"Bauer, can I have a word?"

Out in the corridor, Gerard took the young inspector by the arm and asked, "How would you like to be the most famous *flic* in the whole of France?"

‡

64. Flics

Au Printemps is one of the three large department stores in Paris, at that time sharing the market with Galeries Lafayette and Samaritaine. It was the equivalent of Selfridge's in London, Macy's in New York and Penney's in LA.

At this time there were three Printemps in Paris. One was in Place d'Italie and another was at Nation. But whenever anyone simply referred to 'Printemps', it was the one in Boulevard Haussmann they meant.

Printemps, like the Galeries Lafayette (its immediate neighbour and rival on the boulevard), is a complex of more than one building, each with a varying number of floors stretching over a wide area. It was a ridiculous place for a meet. But, like the Arc de Triomphe, well in keeping with Mesrine's unpredictability and cunning.

A gusty breeze was blowing from the west as Richer crossed the road from the Opéra and walked up Haussmann. As always, the Boulevard was crowded. He passed the kerbside stalls, the suitcase men selling dolls that swam in a basin of water and those damn mechanical birds that you wound up and threw and which were supposed to fly but never did when you got them home. Past a morose-looking donkey holding two panniers of lavender across its back, past the pathetic sight of an Algerian mother sitting on the ground with a sleeping child in her arms (mouth open, teeth rotted to stumps) and a begging message written on the paving in front of her. Past the *bona fide* sellers of curtaining or food or the latest product from *Ronco* you could not possibly do without, in front of the shop's windows.

It was as Richer passed the woman selling hot, gooey *crèpes* that he became aware of the commotion outside Au Printemps. Almost at the same time, he heard the sirens as the black police vehicles appeared from everywhere. Whistles blew. People either fled in panic or stayed to gawp.

He ran, pushing his way through the milling crowd, shoving aside fur-clad madames with their green and white Printemps carriers. *"Pardon, pardon, pardon,"* he mumbled. *"Police."*

He stumbled off the kerb opposite the side entrance to the store in Rue Caumartin, and a uniformed *agent* shouted "Hey, get back! You!"

He thrust his ID in the air as the *agent* came towards him.

"Oh, pardon monsieur!"

Keeping the identification held high, Richer passed the two men now guarding the entrance and went through the double doorway into the store.

There was not much pandemonium, simply sheer confusion. People tried to leave but were restrained, in some cases forcibly, by the officers on the inside of the doors. By the souvenir counter on the left, a woman had fainted and was being tended to by a member of the staff.

"What's up?" Richer held his card in front of the nose of a young officer. "I was just passing."

"Mesrine. Tip-off - *Non, non, monsieur,* you must wait - " He blocked the exit of a grumbling customer. "Upstairs on the second floor, record department."

Richer ran up the escalators. There were fewer people on the *premier étage*, mostly queuing to give details to notebook-loaded *agents*.

Up another flight. A burly plainclothes officer guarded the top of the escalator on the second floor. He nodded at Richer's card.

"*Où?*"

"*Là-bas.*"

He dashed down to the other end of the floor, through the book department and into the record section. A rack of budget-label discs was lying sideways on the floor and, just beyond, a pair of feet jutted out from behind the counter. By the way nobody was taking any notice of the prostrate figure, its condition was obvious.

Richer rounded the edge of the counter. It was not a pretty sight. The chest had been blown away to leave a bloody red puddle, and there was something maroon caked onto the carpeted floor. He looked at the staring face. It took a few moments to register.

It was Inspector Bauer.

Back on the *rez de chausée*, Richer moved through the throng of people, past the perfumiers' islets. At the door at the far end where he had come in, he asked the *agent* "What happened to the woman who fainted?"

"Ambulance."

"And the salesman who was treating her?"

"Went with her."

"*D'accord.*"

‡

65. Voleur

The ambulance pulled into the square in front of the Hôpital Saint Lazare and stopped in front of the entrance. The driver alighted, curious as to why Eric, his colleague inside, did not open the rear doors. Lazy shitehawk.

The driver did it himself. He supposed *he'd* have to carry the patient in as well -

But the patient was not there. Neither was the man from Printemps who had insisted on accompanying her ("The good name of the store, sir."). But Eric was. Laid out. Fast asleep. Peaceful as a lamb…

‡

66. Flics

Richer hurried up Rue Lamarck.

Nodding at the *concièrge*, he took the steps two at a time, knowing that the twelve flights up to his apartment could be walked in quicker time than the old lift would take.

He stopped at the top floor, fighting to control his breath. God, he was getting old. Still, if this went wrong now, age was the last thing he had to worry about.

He listened at his own front door. There was no sound from inside.

Gun in his right hand, he turned the key with his left.

He crashed in, gun in the firing position. In a rush, he kicked open the doors to each room, making a hell of a racket. There was a screech as Chivas fled behind the washing machine.

No one was there.

He relaxed. He went to pick up the telephone, then thought better of it. He'd been caught like that just a couple of hours ago.

The bar by the Lamarck-Caulaincourt metro station had a few clients at the *zinc* and three sitting down. Richer ordered a *café cognac* and some *jetons* for the telephone, and took his drink with him over to the instrument.

The first call was Claude Gerard's last chance. Richer was giving fate a final opportunity to prove he was wrong

A meek, mild sounding woman answered the Levallois number. She was surprised at Richer's guarded enquiry as to the whereabouts of her husband. But surely he was on detached duty in Lyons for two or three months? Richer cluck-clucked, what a fool he was, hadn't been thinking, and terminated the call.

So Gerard had lied about everything. Madame Mathilde Gerard had just confirmed it. There was no family split. Gerard had moved in to keep a closer eye on him.

The second call was to Saussaies. "Chief Inspector Richer direct for Commissaire Fleury-Goujon."

It took a few moments then the Commissaire's voice said, "Hello?"

"Is someone there, sir?"

"Yes. A few."

"Tonight. The butcher's."

"Thank you."

The head of the OAS was on his own in the room above the butcher's shop in Belleville.

"Gerard came clean," he said as soon as Richer entered. "Admitted tapping your phone, admitted sending Bauer to intercept you and Mesrine. Implicated you to the hilt. Said you were a crook, an accomplice, Mesrine's mole. It is because of you that Mesrine is always able to be one step ahead of the police."

"The man is a *con*. He's dead meat."

"Oh, most certainly," agreed the Colonel. "But not yet he isn't. When you rang I had Bouvier, Devos and Broussard in the room with me and Gerard. Gerard had carefully planned it with witnesses. He's basking in the glory."

"Even though one of his inspectors was killed?"

"Honourably. In the line of duty."

Richer's nostrils flared and he punched his right fist into his left palm as he walked slowly across the room.

"So where does that leave me?"

The Colonel shivered. It was colder inside this room than outside. "You can come in and clear yourself."

"Or I can finish this assignment."

The Colonel paused, turning up his collar. "And how will you do that?"

Richer stopped pacing up and down and turned. "Mesrine is the most wanted man in Europe. The British are on the rampage and they don't care who they kill. Anyone who even comes near the document - and that means near Mesrine - is marked."

"Yes?"

"I am going to find Mesrine before either the police or the British do."

‡

67. Voleur

Jacques Mesrine gave Sylvie a final kiss, slipped out of her saturated sex, and rolled off of her. He lay back, a thin film of sweat on his brow. Sylvie snuggled up under his arm, one breast resting softly on the edge of his stomach, the nipple still hard.

Mesrine was not so much puzzled as resigned. Resigned to the fact that he had been right all along. The Captain's phones were monitored. Either that or the Captain had betrayed him, and that was an idea that was simply unentertainable.

He had the document. He had read it a hundred times. The secret it contained was explosive. Too explosive, perhaps, even for the OAS. In his opinion it should be left undisturbed and the document itself should be destroyed. But that was not his to decide, the Captain knew what he was doing.

But how to get the document to him? This had been the potential thorn all along. But now, with any arranged meet the subject of a barnstorming by Bouvier and his crew, it was going to be an impossibility.

Telephones were out. He would have to find some other way of contacting the Captain.

‡

68. Flic

"You have no knowledge of Mesrine's whereabouts? Or is it just that you don't want to tell the BCP?"

"Inspector Gerard, if we knew we would tell our fellow enforcement officers, common cause and all that." The voice on the other end of the telephone belonged to Sergeant Maurice Goise of the BRB.

"Of course you would. What is your last trace?"

"Printemps today. We *think* he is holed up somewhere in the eighteenth. But we can't be sure. We have checked everywhere. He must live in the sewers."

"Or right under your noses."

"*Monsieur l'Inspecteur!* It is nearly midnight. Why don't you phone back in the morning and speak to my Inspector? You never know, we might have something by then."

"You know something Sergeant?"

"*Monsieur?*"

"You lot are about as useful as a cunt to a eunuch." Richer slammed down the phone and left the booth.

‡

69. Le motard

Samedi 27 Octobre

Gilbert Pascal had been a government outdoor messenger, a *motard*, on the d'Orsay-Elysée-Saussaies route for a number of years. As with all government jobs it was not well-paid, but he enjoyed it; it was a responsible position to have to carry important documents between the three most powerful buildings in France. And besides, since his retirement from the police, it was either that or the dole queue.

That day, as every day except Sunday, he set out from the Quai d'Orsay on the first of his two morning runs. Turning his motorbike right onto the Pont d'Alexandre III, he crossed the Seine, sparkling in the autumn sun, and drove into the Avenue Winston Churchill.

The first thing he noticed was the girl's panties.

She was bent over the engine in the rear of her Volkswagen, orange mini-dress risen high to reveal her white panties pressed tightly into her crack. His immediate thought was that she must be a very, very cold young lady; the waist-length, armless white fur jacket she was wearing would not even keep her titties warm. Even he felt a chill and he was dressed in his usual black leather outfit.

She turned at that moment, seemed to pick him at random, and waved at him to stop.

It was against regulations, of course. It was written down that he was to stop for nothing but normal traffic signals. But she looked hopelessly at him like a lost kitten and it was obvious she needed help. And she did have lovely thighs.

Pascal pulled up behind her. *"Bonjour mam'selle.* You are in need of assistance?" He parked the bike and climbed off, adopting the firm, authoritative attitude of his police days.

She was wide-eyed and innocent with the prettiest of smiles. *"Oh monsieur, s'il vous plait,* it just stopped! I do not know what is wrong. I do not understand these things."

"It might be your big end," said Gilbert Pascal with a leer. "May I look at it for you?"

He did not notice that further up the road, from the Avenue Charles-Girault by the side of the Petit Palais, a motorbike identical to his own, with an identically leather-clad rider, pulled out into the Place Clemenceau and manoeuvred through the traffic into the Avenue de Marigny at exactly the same moment that he should have done...

The substitute rider passed beneath the golden trees by the side of the Palais d'Elysée and moved quickly across the small Place Beauvau and through the ornate gates of the Ministère de l'Interieur. The guard on the gate let him through without so much as a nod. He was right on time.

The rider parked in front of the entrance and skipped lightly up the steps. He did not remove his helmet, but he did raise the visor to reveal the dark, deep-set eyes. In his hand he held an envelope and a bulky package.

"Bonjour," said the clerk on duty without actually looking up from the paperback hidden under the desk.

"'Jour," said the rider. "Can't leave it. Special Personal for Chief Inspector Richer."

The clerk looked up, bored, irritated at being disturbed. "Who?"

"Richer. Chief Inspector."

With a sigh, the clerk pulled over a large black book and began to thumb through the pages. "He's in Saussaies. Room four hundred and forty-two. Know the way?"

"Sure. Thanks."

He did not know the way, never having been in the complex before in his life, but it was common sense to presume that if one kept turning right one would come out at Saussaies eventually. The first priority was to get away from the duty clerk. The next was to get to the fourth floor where Room 442 would be located.

Out on the Avenue Winston Churchill, the hapless young lady moved closer to Gilbert Pascal until her body was actually touching his.

"You can see what it is?"

Pascal sniffed, casting a sideways glance at the huge breasts which were within stroking distance of his right hand. "I'm not used to these foreign cars. Nevertheless, I think I might be able to help you."

She sneaked a look at her watch. Five minutes. She had been told to give it fifteen.

Bending with him into the engine, she manoeuvred her face close to his, knowing he would get the full blast of her *Rive Gauche* perfume and *cachou*-scented breath.

"Is there anything you can do for me?" she asked innocently. "What's this hole for? It's all wet…"

The substitute Pascal could not hurry overtly. But years of practice in deception and disguise had given him the ability to walk at speed while giving the appearance of partaking in a leisurely stroll.

He went wrong twice but eventually made his way through the maze of interconnecting corridors to the Saussaies building. He now carried his helmet in his hand. He would be conspicuous with it on, and nobody would recognise him, this being the last place anyone would expect to see him.

Several people passed him by, no one taking even minor interest in him.

He found Room 442, knocked and entered.

Jacques Mesrine came face to face with Claude Gerard.

"It is the petrol," concluded Pascal. "After all that, you are out of petrol!" He scowled but then softened as Sylvie pouted in regret, a schoolgirl awaiting her spanking.

"Petrol? But I never thought! So I just need a little something put in?"

"You could say that." Pascal could not keep his eyes from the mammoth bust straining against the confines of the dress. Her bare arms were goose-pimpled.

"Look," he said. "I've got to go, I'm on business. But wait here and I'll bring a couple of litres with me on my way back. That should see you okay. I'll be about half an hour."

"And you will put it in for me?"

"You bet."

"Monsieur, you are too kind…"

"Chief Inspector Richer?" asked Mesrine, emphasising his nervousness, a humble messenger where he had never been before.

"Gerard." He remained seated, hardly giving the messenger a second look. "Richer is on sick leave. You can leave it with me."

"Yes, sir." He handed over the bulky package, keeping the envelope. "I hope it is nothing serious, sir. The Chief Inspector, I mean."

"Why?" Gerard put the package down on his desk.

"Oh, nothing sir, nothing. *Merci monsieur, au revoir.*"

As he turned to the door, Gerard's voice said "Hey!"

Mesrine turned slowly.

"Haven't I seen you before?"

"Probably sir, I deliver every day."

"Ah." Gerard nodded then ignored him.

Mesrine headed for the nearest exit, being careful not to rush. He was pleased. Not only had he found out that Richer was not around, but his incursion into the very heart of the Interior Ministry and the *Sûreté* would go down in the annals, a further addition to his remarkable legend.

The bike, which he had stolen earlier that morning, could be left in the yard. It would not start attracting attention for at least half an hour.

Helmet on, he nodded at the *agent* on duty at the Cambacérès exit and strolled out into the crisp October sunshine. He removed the helmet as he doublebacked down Rue Penthièvre. Turning right into Avenue Delcasse, he descended into the Miromesnil metro station.

Pascal arrived in the courtyard of the Interior Ministry just as Mesrine left via the Cambacérès exit. He frowned at the bike parked in his usual spot, and went inside.

Gerard had a telephone call, so he did not get round to considering Richer's package until the messenger had been gone ten minutes.

After terminating the call, Gerard picked up the package and felt it. Then without hesitation he ripped it open.

It was a book.

It was *Instinct de Mort* by Jacques Mesrine.

Gerard stared at the picture of the author on the cover. It took five seconds for him to realise he was looking at the face of the messenger who had delivered it.

Then all hell broke loose.

‡

70. Flic

Richer crushed out his twentieth cigarette of the day and immediately lit another. Room 55 of the Hotel Roma stank like a crematorium on overdrive.

He had checked into the hotel on Rue Caulaincourt, just five minutes from his apartment, late yesterday evening. Provisionally booked in for three nights, he had the option of a longer period if required.

Unaware of the adventure happening at Saussaies, he had spent the best part of Saturday getting nowhere with his telephonic enquiries of various police sources as to the whereabouts of Mesrine. As he was a marked man and could not reveal his true identity, he had continued to take a leaf out of the Duchess of Windsor's book and refer to himself as Gerard.

There was a lot of hot air, but he had come to the certain conclusion that the police - even under Bouvier - were running round in circles and barking up their own *trou du cul*.

He was booked into the hotel under the name of Gerard also. He could not risk being identified now and hauled in - however innocent (or not) he may be. His ID and anything identifying him as Paul Richer had been left in the apartment. All he had were the clothes he stood up in and his gun.

From late afternoon he had been closeted in the room, thinking of the past. Remembering back fifteen years to the old days, recalled with fondness if not affection. Occasionally he interrupted his musing to write a name on a piece of paper. In the end he had four of them.

Four names that might be able to help him achieve what the entire combined might of the French police forces had failed to do.

Four names to help him find Jacques Mesrine.

‡

71. Flics

Dimanche 28 Octobre

"And Bouvier has given me full authority to pursue this angle," concluded Inspector Cordelier of the BRB. "Officially we do not see anything coming of it. Unofficially we hope to God it works. Mesrine *must* be found this time. No near-misses, no might-have-beens, no cock-ups. Or *all* heads will be on the block, even at our level."

The men he was addressing murmured un-nice words.

"So, if there are no questions?" Cordelier waited all of three seconds. "We'll get on with the job. Here is a picture, although I'm sure you don't really need one." He handed four copies to the nearest man of the quartet, who took one and passed them on. "Have them copied to all of your men."

There was a general nodding of heads.

"He must be located. But it must be stressed that under no circumstances is he to be intercepted. Report back. Don't try to be brave, don't do anything stupid. And above all *don't* lose him. Any questions?" Four seconds this time. "Then find him."

With a clatter of chairs, three of the group rose and left the office. The fourth man remained seated.

"Think it'll work?" asked Cordelier when they were alone.

The other man shrugged. "We've nothing to lose. If it doesn't work, it doesn't work. If it *does* work, we'll be heroes. We'll get Mesrine. Commissaire next stop."

"I hope you're right."

Claude Gerard smiled and looked at the picture that had been handed out.

It was a photograph of Paul Richer.

‡

72. Flic et belette

Mardi 30 Octobre

Richer played pinball in a bar in Rue Clichy, just ten metres to the south of Place Clichy, his third beer resting on the glass top of the machine. His face gave the impression of intense concentration on the game, but in fact he observed everybody who went in and out of the place. He was waiting for that one person he knew, hoped, *prayed*, would come in sooner or later.

He was desperate. The man he was waiting for was his last hope. Of the other men he had tried to trace yesterday, one was in jail, one was dead and the other was nowhere to be found. At least he knew that this time his man was alive.

He waited, playing the damn machine until he was sick of the infernal *ping-ping*ing. Three more beers and two crusty rolls were consumed, and the beer reappeared five times in the *cabinet*.

It was nearing 22:00 when he came in. Small and weaselly in a dapper fawn suit and undone sheepskin overcoat. On his right arm was a black girl, beads in her hair, dressed in a tight-fitting gold one-piece lurex suit, open to the waist. A *maquereau* with his lady come in for a drink before the night's work. They walked over to a table and sat down. Unasked, the barman began preparing two drinks.

Richer wasted no time, enough had flown past already. He came across smartly and sat down in front of them.

The weasel looked at him stonily. "This is a private table, friend," he hissed. "Piss off."

"Hello Lenny," said Richer.

The other man frowned. "Do I know you?"

Richer leant forward and said lowly, "You bet your sweet arse you do, Corporal."

"Eh?"

"The Army. Algeria. Constantine 58."

The weasel stared long and hard.

"The Army...?" Slowly, uncertainly, realisation, disbelief then acceptance crept across his face.

"C'mon Lenny, you know me."

"I *don't* believe it. Captain, wasn't it? Captain...?"

"Richer."

"Captain Richer. My godfathers! Yeh, I remember you. God almighty, rumour had it you were shot down an alley one dark night - "

"You know rumours, Lenny."

"Jesus! It's been twenty years!"

"And you're still as beautiful as ever."

"What you been doing with yourself?"

"Oh, this and that... business, you know how it is."

The barman delivered the drinks for Lenny and his girl, looked at Richer's half-full glass and slouched away.

"Oh, I haven't introduced you," Lenny smiled, showing a set of perfectly, and expensively, capped teeth. "This is my old Captain from the army. Captain, this is Lettice, my number one lady."

"Hello." Her voice was deep and more than a little inviting.

"*Enchanté mademoiselle*," said Richer.

"Very nice girl," Lenny tapped her knee as her thick red lips fellated the straw in her Campari and orange. "You, er, interested?" He indicated the girl.

"I'd like to Lenny, but I need to talk to you. On business."

"Of course, Captain, of course. Lettice go and powder your bum, love."

"What?"

"Vamoose, make yourself scarce. But wait for me. It's not opening time yet. Go on, be a good girl." He handed over a handful of coins. "Go and put some music on, then play with the balls on the machine. Metal ones will make a change for you."

She pouted but obeyed.

"Now, Captain," Lenny leant forward, all unctuous ears. "Business?"

"Extremely important and extremely urgent business. For the army."

"The army?"

"The Organisation."

"Ah!" Lenny nodded conspiratorially as Lettice's first choice, Bob Marley, reggaed from the juke box.

"Now, I trust you Lenny. The Organisation has been following your career closely."

"It has?"

"Believe it. Lenny Le Coq, one of - no, *the* - top pimp in Paris, receiver of stolen goods, angel in many a job, owner of a string of sex shops, producer of the filthiest porno movies on the market today - and many other talents besides."

Lenny looked pleased with the list of his accomplishments.

"We need you, Lenny. We want you to do something for us right now. For old time's sake. And for fifty grand."

Lenny smiled and shook his head as he said, "Captain, Captain. One of my shops takes that in a day. I don't want money. If I can help the Organisation, it will be a pleasure. *Gratis.*"

"You're a brick Lenny, always have been. I'll give it to you straight. We need to contact Mesrine."

"Christ!" Richer was sprayed with *crème de menthe* as Le Coq began to choke. His subsequent swearing caused many a head to turn. His consequent murderous glare caused them to turn back again.

"I know, Lenny, I know," soothed Richer as he wiped his face. "But he's working for us and we need to contact him quickly. Our usual lines have failed."

"Can't be done," Le Coq's voice was raspy and two octaves higher. He coughed.

"We *must* contact him. We don't want any address. He can come to us. Me."

"But Captain," he looked about to check that all heads were turned away and said softly, *"Mesrine!"*

"You can do it, Lenny. We have faith in you. And Mesrine will thank you too. I told you, he's working for us."

Le Coq rubbed his hands over his face, ending with a slow downward drag on his cheeks. He said, "You ask a lot, Captain."

"We wouldn't ask just anybody, Lenny."

Le Coq pulled an outsize cigar from his pocket, ripped off the end, lit up and started coughing again. He put the thing down. "Look, if - and only 'if' mind - I could even remotely contact your man, I *couldn't* ask him to meet. Supposing something went wrong? Suppose the *flics* were there? He's a marked man. Too hot to handle. I couldn't take the responsibility."

"Just get a message to him, Lenny, that's all. Say Captain Richer is desperate. Ask him if *he* has a message for *me*. That's all."

Le Coq tried the cigar again, blew out a cloud of smoke and became mysterious behind it. "Can't promise, Captain, can't promise. But, for the sake of the Organisation, I'll try. It might take some time."

"That's the one thing we haven't got. Tomorrow at the latest. Now, preferably."

"Merde alors. Look, I'll see."

"Thanks Lenny. The Organisation will be grateful. Meantime," Richer sat back, "the least I can do is buy you a drink."

Le Coq laughed. "Captain, that's the one thing you can't do. I *own* this place."

"This bar is yours?"

"This block is mine."

"Ah."

Le Coq swilled back the remainder of the *crème de menthe*. "I've got some calls to make. No point you hanging around, I might not have any news for you tonight. But in case I have... why don't you entertain Lettice for a few hours?"

Richer looked over at the tightly-clad golden rump, lightly trembling as she played the machine.

"For old time's sake," explained the pimp. "On the house. She'll know where to go. And what to do." He stood up and sauntered over, slapping the inviting bottom.

Richer could not hear above the din, but Le Coq appeared to be giving the black girl her instructions.

She turned to Richer and gave a bright, toothy smile.

Le Coq waved and went out.

Lettice came across. "Hello again." Her accent was thick West Indian. "My man tells me you and he go back long way." She ran a soft finger across Richer's lips. "He say you old frens. Any fren of my man is a fren of mine." She pulled the chair over and sat close to him. He had an uninhibited view of her dark cleavage. "What would you like to do?"

As Lettice stroked the back of his hand, Richer said "Know how to find a fox?"

She raised an eyebrow. "Foxes are hard to find. How about a pussy?"

‡

73. Flics

Inspector Cordelier of the BRB drove as slowly as he could in the maelstrom of traffic that occupies the Champs Elysée at night.

"Not a trace," he was saying. "Not a trace. Not only has Mesrine gone missing, he's take Richer with him. Where *is* the bugger?"

Next to him, Claude Gerard wound down the window and deliberately chucked his cigarette-end at a passing motorcyclist.

"He'll turn up." He spoke with a confidence he did not feel. "Just a matter of time."

"Which we do not have."

"Hmm." Gerard wound the window back up. "That's the whole problem with you lot. No patience. If you're patient and don't rush into things, things have a strange habit of falling into place." He unwrapped a chocolate bar and began to munch.

Cordelier cast him a sideways glance. "You never have told me exactly what Richer's interest in Mesrine is. Only 'unfinished business' you said."

"Right." A brown drool rolled down Gerard's chin and was smeared against his collar as he turned his head, grinning.

Cordelier negotiated the intersection of Avenue George V. "Going to tell me?"

"Best that I don't, state security and all that. You just find Mesrine, don't worry about our side."

"What's going to happen to Richer?"

"Depends. There's others involved. He might go down for a few years, or he might be quietly retired. You concerned?"

"No, just that he's a cop."

"Don't start giving me any of that comrades-in-arms crap. That's how this whole thing got started."

Cordelier blew his horn at the same motorcyclist who had received Gerard's unsolicited gift. Gerard said, "Fancy a drink? Before you go home?"

"Best make it a quick one."

"There's a bar I know in Châtelet. I have something on the owner. We won't have to pay."

"Suits me. It was on you, anyway."

"And he's got this lovely young daughter. Only fifteen but she's got tits like pumpkins."

"Sweet fifteen and never been kissed?"

"Hardly. But not by me. Jail bait. Although sometimes when I look at her arse…"

"Makes you sorry you're a *flic*?"

"Makes me sorry I'm fifty years old."

They moved into the Place de la Concorde.

‡

74. Flic et poule

Mercredi 31 Octobre

His first thought when he awoke was that he must get up to get Claude's breakfast. His second was that he didn't have to, Claude didn't live there anymore. His third thought was that neither did he.

He opened his eyes to see the black girl standing in front of him, beaded hair falling over her shoulders. She wore nothing but a wicked smile.

As he stared at the hairless black body, he tried to remember everything that had happened, everything they had done together during the night. He couldn't. Only the highlights remained in his memory, and even of those there were too many for permanent retention. He still had her taste in his mouth.

"Good mornin'." She knelt beside him on the floor-level bed.

"Good… morning?" He raised his left wrist. It was bare.

She held his *Seiko* in the air. "Here, you left it on the edge of the bath. Remember? You didn't wan' to get water in it."

"Ah, oui." He did not remember. It must have been those cigarettes.

"You didn't worry bout gettin' water in other things tho," she grinned.

As he put the watch on he looked at the face, then looked again. *"Midi moins quinze?"*

"Sho' is. What's wrong with that? You didn't get to sleep till gone five."

"Where's Lenny?" He made to get up but she pushed him back down and kissed his forehead.

"Said he would take a while, didn't he? He'll come when he's ready... He always does." She threw her legs across his arms and sat down on his chest. His view of her full brown-pink lips was uninterrupted. "Brudder, when Lenny tells Lettice to look after a fren till he comes back, Lettice does jus' that. *Relax, baby.*"

She laughed as she moved herself down his body until she was atop his stomach. She bent forward. "So, how about breakfast?" The pearl white teeth flashed. "I feel hungry."

She bit into his neck as her other end opened and swallowed him whole.

‡

75. Flic et belette

They were both washed, dressed and drinking coffee when Le Coq hurried in. He was pale, harassed, sweating and he had obviously not slept all night. His tie was askew and his fawn suit would need to visit the dry cleaners *vitement*.

He stared at Richer from the doorway, just a suggestion of fear in his eyes. "You didn't tell me, did you Captain?"

Richer looked over. "Tell you what, Lenny?"

"You're a *flic*."

"What?" Lettice gasped, nearly dropping her cup.

"Lenny, you didn't ask. And you didn't need to know. Remember the army days? 'Need to know' is everything. It was irrelevant. I am working for the Organisation, like I said."

"It might be b - bloody irrevalent to you, but *Christ*! If it ever got out - "

"A *flic*?" mumbled Lettice.

" - that I had let my best lady entertain a *flic* for the night *and* in my own pad… my God, I'd never live it down."

"I fucked a *flic*?" Lettice seemed on the verge of collapsing.

"You entertained a Captain of your regiment, Corporal Le Coq. You got a message for me?"

Le Coq still stood with his back pressed against the door, as if Richer was some evil spirit to be kept at arms length. "Have I! It took a lot of meetings, a lot of calls… a lot of money - "

"My original offer stands."

"Forget it. But I got a message. He seems to want you as

badly as you want him."

"Where is he?"

"Nobody knows. At least, somebody must, but it's all done by contacts and dead points."

"What's the message then?"

"What the hell does Mesrine want with a *flic*? There's rumour you've turned - "

"Lenny!"

"Tomorrow. Flea market at Clignancourt. *Midi*."

Richer returned to the Hotel Roma in Rue Cauliancourt. He resisted the urge to go back to his apartment. The bastard Gerard would be long gone, but someone might be watching. The murdering Brits perhaps? He hoped Chivas was looking after himself.

In his room on the fifth floor of the hotel, he spent the night. Not with an insatiable black *poule*, but with a bottle of *Napoléon* and fifty Gitanes.

At 01:30, the empty cognac bottle rolled across the floor and Richer began to snore heavily.

‡

76. Flic

Jeudi 1 Novembre

He awoke with the enforced subconscious delicacy and abbreviation of movement that afflicts most human beings who know they drank too much the night before. It was two minutes before he realised, much to his surprise, that he did not have a hangover. It was a further thirty minutes before the pressure on his bladder forced him out of the bed.

Claude Gerard stumbled into the bathroom, did what he had to do, and went into the kitchen without washing his hands. Chivas mewed and rubbed himself against the naked human legs.

Gerard opened a packet of something and emitted a volcanic fart as he bent to empty it into the cat's bowl. It was three minutes before Chivas re-emerged from behind the washing machine.

With two three-day-old croissants and a bowl of *Bonjour* instant coffee and chicory, Gerard shuffled into the *salle de jour* and sat by the window to eat, looking out onto a cloudy autumn day.

Richer had obviously not been located during the night, he mused, otherwise Cordelier would have called him. But it was only a matter of time. Richer certainly wouldn't be so stupid as to come back to his apartment.

Gerard left the apartment at 11:00 and, seeing as his car was still out of service, strolled at an easy pace towards the Lamarck-Caulaincourt metro station.

He popped into the small Co-Op in Rue Caulaincourt to pick up a boxed cake and a half-litre of red wine for his lunch, then continued on over the road and walked down the steps to the station by the side of the Hotel Roma.

He mumbled banal pleasantries as he bought *Le Matin* from the newspaper seller, then walked into the station, used the last of his *carnet* in the ticket gates, and waited for the lift. A couple of young female tourists, packs on their backs, travelled down with him, studiously avoiding his vacuous, lecherous grin.

As he left the lift and headed for the Diréction Mairie D'Issy platform, he started to read the front of *Le Matin*. Then he heard a train arriving, popped the paper under his arm and ran.

The train was at the platform and the tone signifying closure of the doors was blaring. Gerard wobbled frantically down the flight of stairs from the lift level, but was too late. The doors clicked closed in front of him as he arrived puffing. *Merde.* Sooner the garage fixed his bloody car, the better.

As the train pulled out, he glanced across at the other side then looked down at his paper. Then his head shot back up again and his bowels trembled violently.

Paul Richer was standing on the opposite platform.

Quickly, Gerard stepped back into the cover of the stairway. Richer had not seen him, he was certain.

There was a light breeze, then a low rumble. *There was a train coming on Richer's side.*

Gerard turned on his heels and ran back up the steps. There were only ten of them, but he was out of breath when he reached the top.

As fast as he could, he ran across the overhead corridor connecting the platforms. As he turned to take the stairs down, he collided with an old man and dropped his wine. It smashed and blood red liquid began to roll down the steps.

"Monsieur!" gasped the shaken pensioner. "Are you all right?"

"Fuck off!" he snapped courteously over his shoulder.

The doors-closing tone sounded as he reached the platform. He stopped and gave a quick glance to his right. Richer must have got on further down.

The doors came together.

With a movement born of desperation, Gerard wedged his cake between them. The box crushed and chocolate gateau oozed from it and fell like globs of vomit onto the platform. But it had its desired effect. The doors reopened and Gerard nipped on.

There was cake squashed on his shoes, wine splashed up the legs of his *pantalon* as if he was experiencing some perverse male menstruation, and he was bent double trying to regain his breath.

More than one person from the carriage got off at the next stop.

‡

77. Flic et Voleur

The Marché aux Puces is situated on the northern perimeter of Paris, near the Porte de Clignancourt. On Saturdays, Sundays and Mondays it is a hive of bustle and activity, more like an eastern bazaar than part of the most sophisticated city in the world. The legitimate merchants have single-level open-fronted shops or normal open-air stalls. The illegitimate merchants have little tables, or suitcases, or, in the case of the Africans selling their wares, rugs on the ground.

On a Friday there would be some activity in the market as the stallholders prepared for the weekend trade. On Thursday 1 November 1979 it was deserted.

On the metro Richer changed at Marcadet-Poissonniers for Ligne 4 and alighted two stops later at the terminus at the Porte de Clignancourt. He walked north from the station, past the Stade Bertrand Dauvin on the left and under the flyover. The vehicles on the Boulevard Périphérique thundered overhead.

He was unaware of the portly, dishevelled figure who followed him cautiously but with surprising expertise.

The mesh gates to the market were closed but not locked, and Richer slipped inside. He was fifteen minutes early.

He walked, the blank impersonal faces of the shops on either side, blinds down, each identical, anonymous. Many of the walkways led off at right angles from each other, each with the same rows of shuttered establishments. Just to his left, a group of empty stalls were cluttered together. It was like a ghost town.

There was a movement to his right and Richer stopped abruptly, hand going to his right pocket.

A cat shot out from between two shops and ran across his path.

A smile fluttered across his lips. The cat should have been black, like his Chivas. It would have been lucky. But it was ginger.

He was now well into the market, surrounded on all sides by the identical shops. The sound of the vehicles hummed from out on the Boulevard.

A piece of last week's *Ici Paris* blew across the ground and wrapped itself around his right calf. He was removing it when he heard the voice.

"Hi there, big boy."

He span round.

The girl was ten metres away, near an empty stall. Short blonde hair, generously proportioned body, old raincoat over thick woolly, denims and boots, bag over her shoulder.

Richer said, "Hello, Sylvie."

She was surprised.

"Sylvie Jacquot," continued Richer. "Known latest sidekick of the man himself. The Bonnie to his Clyde. Where is he?"

He was answered by the press of cold steel against the back of his neck. "Ah," he said.

"Good afternoon, Captain," said Mesrine's voice from behind. "You will forgive me please, but it has been a long time and some strange things have happened recently."

Sylvie came forward and ran her hands over his body. She had been taught well.

She held up his gun, then, at a nod from the man behind, stepped back five paces, holding the weapon raised but not aimed directly.

"Thank you," said Mesrine.

The steel disappeared from Richer's neck. He turned slowly.

It was not Mesrine.

At least, it did not look like him. The man holding the shotgun was of the same build as Jacques, but he was old, heavy-jowled, hair thin and iron grey; even the eyes contained the lacklustre unenthusiasm of the aged.

Richer frowned. "Jacques?"

The old man laughed and spoke again with Mesrine's voice.

"Yes, Captain. Just one of my little friends. I have to be careful, things are very hot at the moment."

"It's incredible."

"Thank you, it is meant to be. Now, sir. Eighteen months ago you asked me to retrieve something. In the light of recent events, I must ask you if your request is still valid."

"Oh yes," said Richer. "You have the document?"

"On me, no. But it has been obtained. It is safe."

"You have read it?"

"*Oui.*"

"Then you'll know its implications."

Mesrine nodded tightly. "It is dangerous, Captain. Dangerous. The repercussions could be unthinkable. *Alors...*" The heavy jowls wobbled. "What is its value to the Organisation?"

"Jacques! You of all people! It can be used for blackmail, *mon ami*. At the most basic level. The Windsors of England are, to say the least, very rich. On a more quixotic level, if the Organisation possessed that document it could be very influential in any future matters of government it decided to take an interest in. We could *be* the next government."

"I thought we already were."

"Openly I mean. People would do a lot to keep the document hidden. Certain favours could be bestowed..."

The jowls quivered in a smile. "I understand, Captain. And I do not think I want to know. Did the British kill Lensens?"

"Yes."

"Then they're after me."

"I would think so."

"It is nice to be popular."

"When I have the document our contract will be complete, the favour called in and paid. You must then concentrate on your safety and freedom. Where and when do I collect?"

"Tomorrow. Be at the Porte de Clignancourt station. Fifteen hundred. We will contact you."

"We?" Richer turned to look at the girl.

"Sylvie is my lady," explained Mesrine. "My only lady. You can be the first to know, Captain. We are to be married."

Richer's left eyebrow rose.

"Yes. I am forty-three soon. Finally it might be time to hang up the Smith and Wessons." He laughed. "Can you believe it? Jacques Mesrine is going to settle down! It is true! We have bought an apartment somewhere out of town. I shall perform one last job for my pension, give a final interview to *Paris Match* as a farewell to my public, then I shall be heard of no more. No one will ever find me."

Richer kept his thoughts to himself. He said, "You have it all worked out. Amazing."

"She," nodded Mesrine, "is the amazing one." He slid the shotgun under his old raincoat. His voice changed completely to suit his character. He was not impersonating an old man, he *was* one. "*Sylvie ma fille,* let us go. We have taken up too much of this gentleman's time." He held out his right arm. "Help me, my child."

As they passed, Mesrine's voice came back out of the mouth for an instant. "Tomorrow, Captain."

Sylvie gave Richer back his gun, then the couple walked slowly away.

Would they be walking to happiness? Could Mesrine really retire?

Richer actually found himself hoping "Yes" to both

questions.

‡

78. Découverte

Gerard was lost.

Each alley, each passage he turned down looked the same. He had tried so many that he was now completely disorientated, not knowing whether he was facing north, south, east, west or any point in between.

He flicked a piece of hardened cake off his left shoe. He had been no more than a hundred metres - half a minute, time-wise - behind Richer, but he had not picked up his trail since entering the market. Richer was here somewhere to be sure. But where?

He walked on carefully. At one point he thought he heard the sound of muffled voices, but he could not be certain. The hum from the motorway distorted all but the most direct sound.

He stopped at the intersection of four identical alleys. Each was long and narrow and at the end led off at right angles into another alley.

Suddenly there was a high-pitched screech, a wail from hell itself. His heart leapt as a ginger ball with legs on ran out from beneath a stall and disappeared through a broken doorway.

He steadied himself against the whitewashed side of a shuttered shop, chest banging. Fucking cat. He tried to fumble for a cigarette, but his hands were shaking too much.

He stayed there for five minutes.

As he was about to move away, he heard voices again, distinct voices this time, no mistaking. He flattened himself against the wall as much as he could.

He waited.

The voices became louder, though still muffled.

At the far end of the alley, two people passed by, a young woman leading a doddering old veteran. Who the hell...? They did not look his way.

Who were they? Should he follow? Or should he concentrate on finding Richer? They were probably of no consequence, just stallholders having a midweek inspection.

Nevertheless, he would just check the couple out. If he did not move too far from the gates, he would pick Richer up again when he came out.

He crept on swift tiptoe to the end of the alley, peeked around the corner, saw that they were just turning right further on, and followed.

He tried to make it a professional tail, but all he succeeded in doing was to make himself look an idiot as he zigzagged clumsily from doorway to doorway. Had they turned around, they would have seen him.

The couple went out through the gate and turned right.

Still thirty metres behind, Gerard quickened his pace. He half ran, his fat gut bouncing with each pace. He charged through the gateway, turned right and cannoned into Jacques Mesrine.

Gerard only saw the old man, bending down to tie his shoe, at the last moment. He bounced sideways off the old man's rump. He did not actually fall to the ground, but his balance was lost and the impetus carried him onwards, his feet stomping flatly. He flew with unerring accuracy towards the young girl. His face landed with a soft *whump* in the exact centre of her breasts.

The girl called out.

So did the old man.

Gerard regained his balance and continued on quickly, calling over his shoulder *"Pardon!"* without showing his face. He went down the Avenue de la Porte de Clignancourt and out of sight.

"You are all right, my darling?" The old man took the girl's arm.

"I - I think so," she panted.

The old man looked back. "Where did he come from?"

"*Je ne sais pas.*"

"*Alors*, he was probably just a stallholder having a midweek inspection." He turned, the suspicious frown lingering. "He has gone. Clumsy idiot. Come we must not hang around."

They crossed under the motorway and, in character, walked slowly down the Avenue.

Some minutes later, Richer came out of the gates, crossed under the flyover and went down the Avenue. He did not take any notice of the man who came out of the car park on the other side of the road opposite the stadium, head over-exaggeratedly buried in an upside-down newspaper.

Richer and the man continued in tandem on either side of the Avenue across Boulevard Ney.

As soon as Richer had turned into the metro, Gerard flung the paper down and rushed to the top of the road to the left, past the railway line. The couple were a little way down. He looked up at the blue street sign. Rue Belliard.

His heart was thumping wildly. He would not have recognised the old man, of course, not in a million years. He was a master of disguise, after all. But inside Gerard's head the words they had called out to each other as he had crashed into them echoed with sparkling clarity.

The girl had called "Ja - !" Nothing, perhaps, in itself.

The old man had called "Sylvie!"

And that had settled it.

For as every cop in France knew, Mesrine's latest moll was Sylvie Jacquot.

He had them.

By Christ, he had them! Of all the *flics* in France, it was

Claude Gerard who had found them.

But did Richer have the document?

He stopped, looking back at the metro. Twice he started towards it and twice he stopped in a quandary. It was not an easy choice.

Finally, he turned his back on the metro and continued down Rue Belliard.

‡

79. La Fin

Vendredi 2 Novembre

All Souls' Day 1979 was crisp but bright in Paris, the waning autumn sun reflecting off the Seine and dazzling the *clochards* who still occupied the river banks despite the seasonal temperature. Soon these Parisian tramps would move inland into sheltered doorways or the parks or, if they were lucky, over the warm air vents of the metro. Some might even venture as far north as the Clignancourt metro and seek warmth there.

In fact a *clochard* was already seated on the sidewalk near that station, eating a *pain* and swilling back some anonymous liquid from a bottle inside a bag. Paul Richer noticed him as he ascended from the station at 14:50.

At last, thought Richer. At bloody last he was actually going to get his hands on the infernal and, for the Windsors of England, damning document. The secret which he had kept bottled up inside for what seemed like an eternity, would be his in writing.

He looked at the *clochard*, walked a little way on then looked again.

His heart stopped beating.

Jesus, no!

He recognised the man.

His first reaction was that the recognition must be because it was Mesrine. It was another of his disguises. It was Jacques waiting to hand over his prize.

But it was not.

It was somebody else. Somebody he had seen before. Recently. At Printemps. It was one of the sergeants of the BRB.

It was impossible. They could not have known details of his meeting with Mesrine. Absolutely impossible. How had they found him?

There was no time to analyse it. He could not now hang around at the top of the metro steps as he had intended. He would have to move.

Slowly he walked over to a newsstand, carefully watching the *clochard*. He bought the first thing he picked up, the pop magazine *Podium*, opened it and sauntered away, ostensibly reading.

He stopped no more than three metres away from the *clochard*, and it was then that he realised his error. *He* was not being watched at all. The man had not taken the slightest interest in him. Whilst munching and drinking the man was covertly looking to the east, down Rue Belliard.

Holy shit.

Operation Mesrine was obviously coming to a head. Somehow the criminal had been traced. Naturally he must live around here, that was why he had suggested the meets first at the *marché* then at the station. They had found him. There would be more of them around, like a plague of rats they would be more intense where the meal was to be found. Damn them all.

Deliberately, Richer dropped the magazine and, as he picked it up, looked down Boulevard Ornano to the immediate right. As far as he could see, to the Place Albert Khan, things looked normal. In the narrow Passage du Mont Cenis behind him, everything was quiet.

Giving the appearance that he knew where he was going, he walked forward past the *clochard* and to the right into Rue Belliard.

As Richer passed, the *clochard* casually pulled a walkie-talkie from the brown bag.

Separated from the busy Boulevard Ney by the railway line, Rue Belliard gave the impression of life going on as normal. But to Richer's trained and experienced eyes, it was anything but. The place was riddled with them. A man and a woman walking down the street, self-consciously holding hands; another tramp; a girl dressed louder than the biggest tart on St Denis; and, inevitably, further down the street, the van of *Gaz de France* and the men in overalls pretending to work in the road.

They had Mesrine. The trap was set.

Richer forced himself to walk normally, not to run. He felt like screaming. *No! Not now, please!* At least wait until Mesrine hands over the document. *For God's sake!*

He could not help appreciating the irony of the situation. Of all the *flics* in France, he must be the only one who did *not* know Mesrine's exact location. But chances were it was near the gas men.

He looked at his watch. Two minutes to three.

Down the road, just past the gas van, two people came out of an apartment block.

Inside the gas van, Inspector Cordelier of the BRB also looked at his watch.

"Let's go in *now*." He spoke irritably into a walkie-talkie.

"*Non*," instructed the voice on the other end. "We agreed. Sixteen hundred. If he is not out by then, you may attack the building."

"But that's another *hour*."

"Patience, Inspector, patience. You have no further sightings of either of them?"

"Only the girl at thirteen hundred. She posted a letter, picked up some food, then went back."

"You have not seen Mesrine?"

"No. You're sure he's in there?"

"Positive."

Another voice said, "Any sight of Richer?"

Cordelier spoke to someone next to him, then said "Might just have been spotted near the station. Not confirmed though."

"*D'accord.*"

The first voice came back on. "You have all the exits covered?"

"Certainly. He cannot escape."

"*Bon.* Then I suggest - "

"Wait! Something is happening. There's movement. Christ. I think they're coming out! Yes, it's them - !"

"Are you ready, darling?" Jacques Mesrine pulled on the leather jacket and pressed down the edges of the false beard. He surveyed himself in the gilt-edged mirror, smoothing down his hair. "Your first visit to our new home."

"Perhaps you should carry me over the threshold when we get there?" Sylvie came in from the bathroom, tucking the final piece of blonde hair under the brown wig. She was dressed in a grey skirt and blouse. She too looked in the mirror.

There was a sniffing at her feet and she bent down and picked up the present Jacques had given her two days ago: a white poodle. "Fifi darling, Mummy's not going to forget you." She looked up at Mesrine. "Our first baby?"

Mesrine smiled as he checked his pockets. "You have the bag?"

"There." Sylvie nodded in the direction of the bed. "Do we *have* to take it? Nothing's going to happen."

"Insurance, my love, insurance. There will come a day - sometime - when I will no longer need such policies. But until then we had better be safe than sorry." He unzipped the holdall. Inside were six hand grenades and a pistol. In his jacket also he carried a gun.

He rezipped the bag and picked up their overcoats from a chair.

At the door, Sylvie scooped the dog under her arm and took one last look around. "I hate goodbyes."

Gently, Mesrine stroked her cheek. "It is not goodbye. The rent is paid for another month. There are still things to move."

She cuddle Fifi. "*Bien sûr*, but it is a new life."

"You have regrets?"

She shook her head. "*Pas du tout.*"

"Here," he tucked in a dangling curl of her blonde hair. "Soon we will not have to don these damn disguises every time we set foot outside the door. Soon we will live as normal people."

"I have no regrets, my love, it has been fun." She kissed him. "I am pleased. After the life I have had I ask nothing more than to settle down with the man I love."

"*Allons-y*," Mesrine smacked her on the bottom. "We have to meet the Captain down at the station, then it is Marly-le-Roi non-stop."

It was Mesrine without a doubt. He was bearded but there was no other attempt at disguise. Over his left arm he carried some coats, in his right hand was a holdall. Sylvie was at his side, frumped-up and bewigged. In her arms she carried a white bundle.

Mesrine opened a door of a BMW for her to climb in.

Richer thought of breaking into a run, to shout a warning, but instead he stopped and pretended to be surveying the delights in a *patisserie* window. What should he do? Jacques would have to come this way, it was a one-way street, and he would be heading for their tryst at the station. On the other hand, he could be intercepted immediately without time to hand over the document.

Richer could tell that the gas men had seen Mesrine. While

one continued working in the road, the other climbed into the van. There would be other men and a radio transmitter inside.

He couldn't risk it. He moved, breaking into a run, no time for pretence now.

The BMW pulled away from the kerb and moved smoothly down the street. Inside, bag beneath his legs, seat belt on, Mesrine noticed how clear the road was. In fact, except for the gas van there were no other vehicles at all…

A strong hand grabbed Richer's arm as he was about to run into the road.

"Fancy a good time, ducky?" grinned the girl dressed as a whore.

"No." He tried to shake himself free.

"You're in a hurry aren't you, handsome?" The grip was firm, belying the overpowering smell of *Ma Griffe*.

"I'm one of you, you stupid bitch!" Richer pulled his arm up and down. "Richer, Chief Inspector, BCP!"

"What?" She was confused, not knowing what to do.

Still held, Richer looked down the road. The BMW was moving into third gear, picking up speed every second. No intercept yet. He noticed the driver look back at the gas men.

He pulled his arm again. "Will you let go of me, woman! *Jesus!*"

There was no alternative.

Six of her front teeth flew out as he punched her in the mouth. She went down like a cognac on a cold day, instantly and spreadeagled.

Richer stepped off the kerb, waving his arms frantically in the air.

Mesrine saw him and began to decelerate.

Across the road, another of the tramps pulled a gun from within his rags.

"No!" screamed Richer. "Don't fire, don't fire!" He reversed his action and furiously began to wave the stopping vehicle on.

Then he realised. The tramp was not aiming at the car. *He was aiming at him!*

He crouched down, hopelessly exposed in the roadway. "*Surêté!*" he shouted, drawing his own weapon from his jacket pocket. "BCP!"

It confused the tramp sufficiently to stop him firing.

The car screeched to a stop. Mesrine frowned down at him.

Richer stood up, aiming over the top of the BMW with his right hand, holding out his left. "Get out of here, Jacques! Give it to me and go. Go on, go on, go on!"

"It is safe, Captain. Tomorrow!" Back wheels skidding and nearly hitting Richer, Mesrine sped off, the dog yapping on Sylvie's lap.

Richer was again an open target, standing in the middle of the roadway, aiming at the tramp who, in turn, was aiming at him.

What the hell did Mesrine mean, "It is safe"? Today was the final meet, the day of the handover. *Tomorrow?*

Cautiously he began to move backwards, gun still aimed. "I am Chief Inspector Richer," he called. "Where is Broussard?"

The tramp was perplexed, bewildered at why the Chief Inspector had let Mesrine escape. He watched as Richer lowered his gun, and he answered uncertainly "Up - up at the Porte, sir."

Richer glanced to his left. *Mesrine was heading in that direction.*

He began to run.

The tramp kept his eyes on him, fumbling inside his rags for his radio, desperate for instructions.

Officer Jacqueline Dinon, the one disguised as the whore, stirred from her momentary unconsciousness. As she opened her unfocussed eyes, the first thing she became aware of was the blood flowing down the front of her lace blouse. With the astuteness of all government employees, she then wondered who was going to pay for the cleaning or replacement. Only as she wondered where the blood was coming from did she become aware of the pain in her mouth.

It all came back instantly. The man, the man who was trying to warn Mesrine…

Richer ran. He could hardly breathe. His lungs could not get enough air. His legs slowed…

Dinon pulled herself into a sitting position and shook her head. She was aware that her jaws seemed to be locked together, and yet there were gaps where her teeth should be. Her eyes focussed. Further down the road, a man was running. *It was him!* The one who had hit her.

She groped for her handbag, pulling it towards her.

The tramp saw Dinon move as he got to his feet. Still talking into his radio, he headed across to help her.

Dinon withdrew her gun from the handbag and aimed it at the running figure.

"No!" shouted the tramp as he quickened his pace. "He's one of us!"

Richer stopped.

Dinon fired.

Richer bent forward to catch his breath. Something whizzed over his head and then he heard the bang. *Bastards.* He turned round, fired without aiming, and ran on.

His bullet hit the running tramp in the right eye. The top of the tramp's head exploded but the momentum of his run kept him going even though he was dead.

He fell heavily on top of Officer Dinon, spreading her beneath him, his bloodied face coming to rest on hers in a bizarre necrophilial kiss.

For a moment Officer Dinon was nonplussed. Then she gave a guttural scream, smelling the last breath to emit from the dead body. Then she fainted.

Mesrine was convinced they would be expecting him to turn left into Ornano or head straight across the intersection and continue down the main part of Belliard, so he wrenched the wheel to the right, onto the bridge across the railway.

As he turned onto the bridge, a lorry lurched out from Ornano, hooting loudly. It overtook the BMW and pulled across in front of it at the intersection of the Boulevard Ney.

Mesrine slammed on his brakes. "Sylvie! The bag! Quickly!"

"What?"

"A grenade, get me a grenade!" He tried to engage reverse but failed.

Sylvie leant over between his legs, fumbling one-handedly. In her right arm the dog picked up the atmosphere and whimpered loudly.

With a crunching of gears, Mesrine forced the car into reverse.

The tarpaulin on the back of the lorry flew back. Four men stood there, weapons raised.

"I can't undo the zip!" screamed Sylvie.

The BMW lurched backwards. Mesrine looked behind.

Richer ran round the corner.

Mesrine's car went straight into him, knocking his legs back, his face crashing down and splintering the back window.

Mesrine slammed on the brakes as the Chief Inspector bounced off onto the cobblestones.

Sylvie still groped beneath him.

The dog yapped.

Mesrine turned back and stared at the men in the back of the lorry. For an instant he was back in Chateau-Merle, it was 1944, and the men were Germans. Then he shouted, "Sylvie! Remember I love you!"

The men fired.

In all, twenty-one bullets smashed through the windscreen of the BMW, nineteen of them hitting Jacques Mesrine. The bullets were brass coated to get through the glass, and they exploded as they entered his body.

He jerked as the bullets hit, the seat belt holding him as a literally sitting target. Suddenly there was blood everywhere. A piece of bone bounced off the steering wheel.

Mesrine's hand gave a final twitch in the direction of the bag and that was it.

It was over. It had taken less than five seconds.

Thirty seconds later, a car pulled up next to the BMW. An arm stretched out from the window and fired a single shot into Mesrine's head. A *coup-de-grace*.

The car reversed back off the bridge.

All was quiet. Mission accomplished. Affair concluded. The men in the back of the lorry looked around, as if they did not know what to do now.

Suddenly the passenger door of the BMW burst open. Sylvie staggered out. Because she had been bending down trying to open the bag of weapons, all but two of the bullets had missed her. One had hit her right arm and one had carved a deep furrow in the side of her head.

What had once been the white, whimpering Fifi was now a red, dead object in her hands. Sylvie was confused, unsure on her feet, wig hanging half off to show blood-stained blonde hair below. She looked about at the police who were slowly, quietly converging from all directions. She spoke, almost to herself.

"A- animals! Y - you animals!" She looked at the mess in her arms and asked with the wide-eyed innocence of a child, "Why did you shoot my dog?"

Three paces away from the BMW, she collapsed in the middle of the road.

Claude Gerard stepped from the rear of the vehicle that had backed off the bridge. He looked to the right. Paul Richer lay in the damp gutter, one arm bent awkwardly up onto the sidewalk. Gerard walked over.

Richer's face was a mess and his head was at a curious angle. His eyes stared deadly, almost accusingly, at the back wheels of Mesrine's car. His mouth was open as if he was about to speak, words which would never now be heard.

Gerard bent down and quickly went through his pockets. Then, frowning, he went through them again.

Nothing.

Gerard stood up and then bent down again and closed Richer's eyelids. Then he hurried to the BMW and quickly frisked the bloody, lacerated cadaver that had been Jacques Mesrine.

Nothing.

Absolutely sod all.

"*Merde.*" He sighed heavily. He pulled out a grubby handkerchief, blew his nose and then wiped the blood off his hands. He nodded to the man in the front passenger seat of the car he had got out of. The man nodded back and got out, taking charge.

Gerard walked away.

‡

ÉPILOGUE

Thus ended Jacques Mesrine, publicly executed by the French Establishment. There was never any question of his recapture, he had embarrassed The Powers That Be once too often.

Even in death, Mesrine was allowed no dignity. While he lay, naked, bloodied and exposed, on the slab in the police mortuary, a notice on the locked door read 'Until further notice, Mesrine will not be receiving visitors.' *Macabrely humourless, perhaps, but also necessary because there were literally queues of policemen waiting to scoff over the corpse of their enemy.*

One week later, after the official gloating had been sated and as his mother and daughter began proceedings against the police for manslaughter, Mesrine was buried next to his father in the cemetery at Clichy.

Samedi 3 Novembre

Gerard spent his final night in Paul Richer's apartment haunted by the face of his dead colleague, staring at him from wherever he looked.

Come the morning, he was pale and tired. He settled for a breakfast of three cigarettes and a glass of cognac. Chivas the cat was nowhere to be found.

Gerard's things were easily packed into his old holdall, and he left the apartment finally at 10:30.

Downstairs, the concièrge poked his head out of his door as Gerard shuffled by.

"Monsieur?"

"What?"

"Monsieur Richer, he is in?"

"*Non.* He won't be back for some time." Gerard walked on.

"Monsieur."

"*What?*" Gerard turned back, not concealing his irritation.

"If he will not be back for some time, perhaps you would like it?"

"Like what?"

The concièrge held up a long, white envelope. "It is addressed to Monsieur Richer."

"Stuff it up your - " Gerard stopped with his mouth opening and closing like a fish. The holdall slipped involuntarily from his fingers. "G - give it to me." His throat had dried. "I'll take it."

"*Oui, monsieur.*" The concièrge handed it over.

Gerard stuffed it quickly into his inside pocket, like a boy about to be caught with a dirty book. He picked up his holdall and walked out.

Then he came back, wordlessly handed the astonished

concièrge a hundred franc note, and walked out again.

His car was parked on the opposite side of the road. He had watched the mechanics from the garage in Rue Norvins fixing it yesterday afternoon, after he had returned from the carnage at Clignancourt and after his apologetic phone call to the British Embassy to explain that the document was unavailable, presumed lost.

Would *he* have a surprise for the *rosbeefs*!

Inside the car, he carefully unprised the flap of the envelope as if it would bite him. Slowly, with the tops of his fingers, he withdrew the contents.

There was no covering note, simply a letter and an attached sheet. The paper was unheaded. The letter was handwritten in English, with a sharp forward slope. Automatically he looked at the signature first. *'EP'*. It was dated 26 January 1938. It began *'My dear Mrs Warfield'*.

Gerard looked again at the date. That was certainly a strange thing to call her at that time.

'In accordance with our agreement...'

He read on.

Halfway through, when he realised the significance of what he was reading, his hand began to shake and he lit up a cigarette. So, Elizabeth was *his* daughter?

He finished the letter and started on the attachment. It was typewritten in English and another European language, simultaneously line after line. There were five signatures on the bottom. One was 'Edward Prince'. One was de Gaulle. One was Charles Bedaux. One was Roosevelt. The fourth was of another European head of state at that time.

He read it.

Jesus H Christ Almighty in heaven above...

As he was gingerly replacing the papers in the envelope, there came a tap on the window. He looked up. It was Ron Becker of the British Embassy.

Gerard wound down the window.

"Morning Claude, old stick," smiled Becker. "You all right? You're sweating?"

"I'm… okay." He still held the envelope in his hand.

"Well, if you say so. You don't look too well to me. I phoned your office, they said you'd be here. Just wanted to confirm our telecon yesterday. The document is lost?"

"I - I thought so. But…" Gerard held out the envelope.

"You've got it?"

"Came in the post, addressed to Richer. In the fucking post!" He shook his head. "Take it, for Christ's sake."

Becker took it, staring at it in amazement. "Good God, I never actually thought you would get it. You've read it?"

"Yes."

"I see. Well… great." Becker put it in an inside pocket then bent down as if to adjust his shoe. Then he straightened up. "Well… no more to be said. Till the next time. No doubt some other crisis will raise its head soon."

"No doubt."

Becker turned away.

"Can I give you a lift?" Gerard poked his head out of the window. "I'm going into work."

The Englishman looked back. "No. No - thanks. My car's down on Caulaincourt."

"Okay. See you, then."

"Cheers."

Twenty metres away, Becker turned and called, "Claude? Thanks!" He tapped his pocket.

Gerard nodded and raised his hand. "Fuck you," he muttered.

He watched the small Englishman walk to the end of the street and turn left into Caulaincourt. Cigarette between his lips, Gerard settled himself behind the wheel and switched on the ignition.

The vehicle exploded.

Lundi 5 Novembre

The High Command of the OAS sat together in the room above the butcher's shop in Belleville, a near empty bottle of Calvados on the table.

"But of course we have no proof," finished the Colonel. "His apartments have been ransacked, his safety deposit boxes emptied. His family and all his known acquaintances have been turned inside out by Bouvier and company. Plenty has been found but nothing relating to the secret. Mesrine has taken the whereabouts of the document with him to his grave."

"So it was all arranged," mused the chain smoker. "De Gaulle, Roosevelt, Hitler and the Windsors. And brokered by that sadist Bedaux. Incredible."

The cap man tossed back his fifth brandy. "So the person now on the English throne - "

"Yes indeed," said the Colonel. "I don't believe the children know. Only the grandmother."

"*Why* didn't Richer tell us before? Goddamn it, he was duty bound."

"He was duty bound to protect us. All of us, including our other member."

"Will you tell the President?"

"I don't know. The knowledge is dangerous."

"Hell's teeth," the chain smoker flung his glass across the room. It smashed loudly against the wall. "We were within this much - *this much!* - of getting it."

"Do Bouvier, Devos or Broussard know?"

"No," said the Colonel. "I just told them I was interested in budget papers stolen from the British Embassy."

The cap man stood up. "That's it then."

The Colonel nodded. "It would appear so."

"He was a good man, Richer." The cap man pulled a scarf from his pocket. "Despite our differences." He undid the top button of his overcoat and wound the scarf round his neck, covering his priest's collar. "I will pray for his soul. And Mesrine's."

"Thank you." The Colonel and the smoker also rose.

The three men shook hands.

The cap man stopped, reaching out for the door knob. "I suppose there's no one else we can activate, just in case it's still around?"

"How many true Frenchmen are left?" The Colonel was slipping on his gloves. "Richer was right. Mesrine was the only one who could even get close to it."

The chain smoker raised a hand. "*Un moment, mes amis,* can you smell something?"

The other two men sniffed.

"Yes, Maurice," laughed the cap man, "that bloody camel shit you smoke!" He turned the door knob and leapt backwards grasping his hand. "Christ! That's hot!"

The Colonel jumped across and tugged the door open with his gloved hand. He fell back into the other men.

Flame crackled around the doorway and black smoke tumbled in.

The stairway, their one way out, was an inferno.

The three men turned towards the window, long ago boarded up. They looked at each other.

Mercredi 7 Novembre

On the day that Paul Richer was buried in Dannemois, a small village forty kilometres to the south of Paris in Essonne, the tall thin man from the British Embassy in Paris visited Clarence House in London.

The old lady, the 79 year old matriarch of the British Royal Family, had been forewarned of his visit. She had only one question when the envelope was handed to her. "Does anyone else know of the contents?"

The man coughed deferentially. "Er, no, marm. No one... alive. Your instructions have been complied with."

"Good."

"Except, of course, the Duchess of Windsor herself."

"*That* woman!"

Without opening the envelope, the lady tore it into small pieces and let it fall into a glass ashtray. She then took a cigarette lighter and ignited the pile in three places.

As the paper charred and curled in on itself, she said "Now. No one, except that person of no significance, knows. And she'll have no proof."

"No, marm."

"But she knows. There is nothing we can do about *her*, I suppose?" The lady did not look up from the cinders.

"I await your instructions, Your Majesty," said the man.

‡

In memory of
Jacques René Mesrine
28 December 1936 – 2 November 1979

THE WINDSOR SECRET

by

DAVID CULLEN

Ω

Friday August 1 1997

Montmartre, Paris, France

The woman stood by the window of the apartment and watched the lights of Paris twinkle on beneath her. To her right the view from the *salle de jour* was obscured by the huge whitestone magnificence of Sacré Coeur on the crest of the *butte de Montmartre*. But just to the east, where the Basilica did not extend, she could see at an angle over the ridge with a view sweeping across to the towers of Notre Dame and beyond.

She sipped her Pernod and smiled silkily as the tabby cat wound itself in a figure of eight between her legs. This apartment had always belonged to a cat. Many years ago it had been Chivas, the long-haired black and white. But in the late eighties Chivas had missed her footing on one of her nightly sojourns across the rooftops of Montmartre, and she had plunged to her death onto Rue Lamarck below.

As if the cat world knew that a vacancy had arisen, a few months later Will, the female tabby, had appeared from nowhere and had stayed. She was called Will because when the woman had first noticed the cat perched perilously on the tiles outside, she had invited her in and asked her her name.

"Weeow," the cat had replied – and so Will it was.

The woman had been eighteen when her father had died, murdered not too far away from here. Two other men had also been killed at that time. One of them, a Chief Inspector of Police called Paul Richer, had been working with her father. Richer had owned this apartment. By a perversity that had never been explained, Richer had left this apartment to her father in his will. Richer had been killed just before her father, therefore the bequest was legal – even if her father never knew about his inheritance. The apartment had gone to her mother, who – after much family discussion on what to do with the place and whether to sell it – had agreed to let her daughter move in. That had been seventeen years ago, and she had lived there ever since.

Mother had died three years ago, and she had inherited in her own right.

She lived in the apartment alone – well, just her and Will. Just like any modern woman, men had come and gone in her life. Perhaps, she reflected ruefully, there had been too much coming and not enough going!

There had been one brief marriage, when she was young, impetuous and foolish. But she had soon got rid of him. None of her men (and she blanched inwardly when she thought of the quantity) had been the sort she would want to spend the rest of her life with. None of them matched up to The One – her father. Daddy. The man who had been her idol. The man who had been killed seventeen years ago. The man who was murdered, executed because he was who he was and he knew what he knew. The man who had never been avenged.

Until now.

She had waited all these years She knew she would know when the time was right. And it was now. She could feel it in her very being. Now, her father was calling out to her. It was time the world knew the truth. Time the world knew why her father had been murdered. Time the secret he had discovered and been killed for was revealed.

The quietness of the *salle de jour* was broken by a sharp, singular *crack*. The cat jumped but did not run away. It looked up and watched as the blood dripped down onto the fur on its back.

The woman looked at the broken glass in her hand. She felt no pain from the deep, bleeding laceration in her palm. Her only thought was that thank God she had finished her Pernod – it would have been a shame to waste good booze.

She raised her hand in the air and watched as the blood ran down her arm.

Yes, it had been long enough. It was time.

Time once again that the world heard the name Mesrine.

DAVID CULLEN

THE EYE OF MAKARIOS

IN A WORLD OF TERROR THE ONLY TRUTH IS BETRAYAL

THE EYE OF MAKARIOS

David Cullen

1974. A world in turmoil. Terrorism is rife.

In the Middle East, *El Fateh* plan their first nuclear strike. The Irshman, their hardware supplier, wants a very special item in payment.

In the Mediterranean, Cyprus is an island about to be divided. Resistance leader Grivas is dying. He wants to hit his enemy from beyond the grave.

In Israel, the security services want to finish off their enemies once and for all.

In Europe, Sally wants to find her missing lover.

In a world about to implode, they all have one common link:

THE EYE OF MAKARIOS

ISBN: 978-0-9559911-0-3

Available from *amazon, Lulu* and other online booksellers and thru all good bookshops.

DAVID CULLEN

THE WINDSOR
SECRET

ANYONE WHO KNOWS THE SECRET, DIES - ANYONE

THE WINDSOR SECRET

David Cullen

1997. Three women are out for revenge.

In Greece, a lover discovers that justice has not been done.
In England, a princess seeks to humiliate her ex-husband.
In France, a daughter vows retribution after eighteen years.

A secret which they thought was buried forever comes back to haunt the British Royal House of Windsor. And the deaths must start again.

And this time to preserve the secret they will even kill the mother of the future King of England…

Exactly what happened in Paris on August 30 1997?
Who really killed Princess Diana?
And what is

THE WINDSOR SECRET

Available from *amazon, Lulu* and other online booksellers and thru all good bookshops.

www.ingramcontent.com/pod-product-compliance
Lightning Source LLC
Chambersburg PA
CBHW030401030726
47497CB00002B/426